# FAMILY COMMITMENTS

David Wishart



www.david-wishart.co.uk

# DRAMATIS PERSONAE

(Only the names of characters who appear or are referred to in more than one part of the book are given. The names of historical characters are in upper case).

## Corvinus's family and household

Alexis: the gardener

Bathyllus: the major-domo

Clarus: Marilla's husband

Marilla: Corvinus's adopted daughter, now living in Castrimoenium in the Alban Hills

Meton: the chef

Perilla, Rufia: Corvinus's wife

Phormio: Priscus and Vipsania's chef

Priscus, Titus Helvius: Corvinus's stepfather

Vipsania: Corvinus's mother

## Imperials, senators, civil servants and the military

CLAUDIUS, Tiberius: the current emperor

Crispus, Caelius: an expert in scandal, currently employed in the Foreign Judges' office

GRAECINA, Pomponia: Julia Livia's closest friend

Helena (Sentia): Secundus's wife

JUSTUS, Catonius: co-commander of praetorians. Condemned and executed.

LIVIA, Julia: daughter of the Emperor Tiberius's son Drusus. Condemned and executed.

LIVILLA, Julia: the Emperor Gaius's sister, and Vinicius's late wife. Executed in exile.

MESSALINA, Valeria: Claudius's wife. Their infant son is BRITANNICUS

NARCISSUS, Claudius: the emperor's freedman secretary and one of his chief advisors

RUFUS, Publius Suillius: Perilla's ex-husband

SCRIBONIANUS, Lucius Arruntius: Dalmatian governor who instigated an abortive revolt against Claudius. Committed suicide

Secundus, Gaius Vibullius: a friend of Corvinus's, currently in military admin

Sentius, Gaius: Scribonianus's aide, and Helena's younger brother

SILANUS, Junius: ex-consul and senator, executed for attempted assassination

VINICIANUS, Lucius Annius: Marcus Vinicius's nephew

VINICIUS, Marcus: an imperial; a poetry friend of Perilla's, once married to Julia Livilla

## Other characters

Caprius: a wineshop owner

Damon: Bathyllus's brother, and Oplonius's slave

Eutacticus, Sempronius: a five-star crook

Ligurinus: a thug

Lydia: a waitress/prostitute in the Aventine wineshop

Meleager, Rullius: the owner's agent for the Rullius tenement

Oplonius, Gaius: the murdered man

Polyxene: the proprietrix of a curio shop

Pudentius, Lucius: the Aventine district Watch commander

Satrius: one of Eutacticus's heavies

# 1.

Murders, mayhem, political intrigue, and general skulduggery I can take in my stride, more or less; domestic problems involving the bought help, now, they're another thing entirely. And to be faced with the Mysterious Case of the Disappearing Comestibles, especially when I'd just got back from a relaxing afternoon in town and was looking forward to a quiet cup of wine before dinner, was something I could *really* do without.

'Meton came and told me about it just after you left,' Perilla said after she'd broken the glad news. 'He was quite upset.'

I shifted my weight on the atrium couch, reached for my wine cup and took a morose swallow. When the lady understates things she doesn't do it by halves; reading between the lines and knowing our surly, foul-mouthed, egotistical bastard of a chef as I did, I'd bet good money that *quite upset* would've involved turning the air a deep shade of blue over the course of several minutes and without either hesitation or repetition. The discovery that someone had clandestinely helped themselves from his larder, in his myopic, Cyclopean view, would equate with Parthia invading Syria. *Trouble* didn't cover it, nowhere near; a seriously-unchuffed Meton meant that until the perp was nailed our domestic routine was really up the spout.

Bugger. Double bugger. Mind you, still, and to be fair, he would've had some justification: in the Corvinus household the food and provisions side of things is Meton's province, and he guards it as jealously as Bathyllus does his major-domo'ing. You trespass at your peril.

'He's absolutely, hundred-per-cent, cast-iron certain?' I said.

'Yes, dear,' Perilla said. 'Certain of the items were quite substantial. A whole roast chicken and the best part of a cured ham.'

Gods, it didn't make sense! Oh, sure, you turn a blind eye to a few household bits and pieces going walkies; the bought help, with the possible exception of Last of the Titans Meton himself, are only human, after all, and they view them as perks in an otherwise largely thankless job. The occasional jar of pickles or a few sausages taking an unauthorised hike are par for the course, but joints of ham and whole roast chickens are another matter. To a mind like Meton's – and I use the word loosely – we were talking grand larceny here.

The big question, apart of course from whodunnit, was *why*? Meton might have his faults, but starving his co-slaves wasn't one of them, and I wouldn't've backed him for a minute if it was. There was no valid reason for any of the staff to steal food, none at all. And the dangers if they were caught, particularly by Meton, were huge.

'He's no idea who's responsible?' I said.

'No, none at all. The obvious culprit is one of the kitchen skivvies, but they all swear blind it isn't them, and frankly none of them would dare.'

That I'd believe: those lads and lasses weren't the sharpest knives in the drawer by a long chalk, and trying to put one over on Meton on his home ground would've been about as safe as playing tag with a *qef*-stoned gorilla. Which, as an analogy, given Meton's physiognomy and general behaviour patterns, wasn't all that much of an exaggeration; it might even be unfair to the monkey.

I sighed. I didn't often play the pukkah Roman head-of-household, but sometimes you have no option. I yelled for Bathyllus.

There was an appreciable pause, which there never is, and he came in, fast as an arthritic tortoise.

'You wanted me, sir?' he said. Murmured: old Homer could've used his voice as a model for one of his bat-squeaking Underworld ghosts.

'Yeah, Bathyllus,' I said. 'It's about this kitchen crisis. I want you to –' I stopped. 'Ah...you feeling all right, pal?'

'Of course, sir.'

He didn't look it, not by half: I'd seen less grey dish-rags, and the usual zip and zing was completely missing. For a guy who, when he felt the situation warranted it, could dismiss you with a single sniff, he was a mere shadow of himself.

'You're sure?'

'A slight stomach-ache. Nothing of any consequence.'

'Uh-huh.' I felt a twinge of worry: Bathyllus wasn't getting any younger, and I could count the times he'd been ill – even with so much as a head-cold – on the fingers of one hand. 'Fair enough. But if it gets no better I want you to tell me and we'll send for Sarpedon, clear?' Sarpedon was our family doctor, and one of the best in Rome.

'Yes, sir. Thank you. That won't be necessary.'

'Just remember, and do it. And have an early night. Meanwhile I want you to gather the staff together for me. All of them, in here, after dinner.'

A pause. 'Certainly, sir. I'll arrange it. Meton says that dinner will be slightly earlier than usual, if you'd like to go through now.'

Well, at least it'd seem that the bugger hadn't gone into seriously-put-upon mode yet, which was a huge relief. Boiled turnip as a main course I could do without.

'Fine,' I said.

'Will that be all, sir?'

'Yeah, sunshine. That's it for now.'

Bathyllus left. Perilla and I exchanged looks.

'Perhaps we should send for Sarpedon anyway, Marcus,' she said. 'He really doesn't look well, whatever he says. And he hasn't been completely himself for two or three days now.'

‘Yeah.’ I frowned and got up from the couch, taking the wine cup with me. Domestic worries, obviously, weren’t coming singly at present. ‘Give it until tomorrow. If he isn’t any better I’ll get Sarpedon to check him out.

The staff filed in like they were going to an execution, which wasn’t far wrong: there’re no secrets below stairs, the bought help grapevine would leave the imperial spy network standing, and they’d all know damn well already what this was about. One of them, especially, because it had to be an inside job: the chances and likelihood of an outsider sloping into Meton’s kitchen and liberating so much as a radish were zilch. Actually, my bet, given the grapevine, was that barring the guys at the top, Bathyllus and Meton himself, most of them, if not all, already knew who was responsible for perpetrating the dirty deed. The problem was, that was where it would stop. I knew enough about slaves to know that their first rule of survival was not to rat on a colleague. If you did, life could get pretty unpleasant subsequently, and when you’re banged up for life in the one household with the same people around you, nowhere to go, and no one to complain to that matters in spades.

So I reckoned that part of my job was to make sure we didn’t reach that stage. Me, I couldn’t see that the odd chicken or ham going awol mattered a tinker’s curse, but Meton obviously did, and personalities aside he was right: start ignoring the little things and the whole fabric of society would unravel, the empire would collapse from within, and we might as well put up the shutters, douse the lamps and turn the whole business of world government over to the Germans.

So, like I say, this had to be done, whether any of us, me included, liked it or not.

I glanced round the assembled faces. Not a smidgeon of expression in any of them, except in the case of Meton who was glowering as usual and Bathyllus who still looked like death warmed up. It was so quiet you could've heard a mouse fart.

'Okay,' I said. 'No long speeches. You all know what's going on, and it stops now before someone gets hurt. So long as it does, as far as I'm concerned, and Meton too,' – I gave the bastard a glare of my own; if he didn't like it he could go and fricassée himself – 'then there's an end to it. No hassle, no follow-up, absolutely none whatsoever. Understood?' Throats were cleared and feet shuffled. 'Fine. Off you go.'

They trooped out again.

'Well done, dear,' Perilla murmured as the last of them disappeared. 'You're improving. Very diplomatic.'

Yeah, well, we'd have to see, wouldn't we?

# 2.

Bathyllus was looking a bit chirpier when I came down to breakfast the next morning: not exactly his usual sunny self, but at least the grey dish-rag side of things had lifted.

'Hey, pal,' I said. 'Stomach better today?'

'Oh, yes, sir. A great improvement.'

'That's marvellous.' I went through to the courtyard garden where we were breakfasting. Or rather, at that precise moment, I was. Perilla's no early riser; I'd left her, as usual, flat out for the count, and she wouldn't be up and around for an hour yet.

Bathyllus made a great play of straightening the bibs and bobs on the table into their exact pattern. 'Would you like an omelette, sir?' he said.

I pulled up one of the wicker chairs that the lady had insisted on bringing back with us, together with the small round table, from the previous year's Gallic jaunt.

'No, just the usual.' I sat. 'A couple of rolls and the oil dip will be fine.' He was still hovering. Or maybe 'dithering' would be a better word, because the little guy looked nervous as hell. 'Was there anything else, Bathyllus?'

'Nothing important, sir. But I was wondering if either you or the mistress would be needing me for anything this morning.'

'I don't think so. I'll be going out shortly, and Perilla's got one of her poetry klatches arranged over at Cloelia Faustina's. She probably won't be back before dinner time. Why? You got any particular plans?'

'We have some loose plasterwork in the slaves' quarters, sir. I thought I'd arrange to have it redone before it gets any worse. That would mean a trip to the plasterer's near the Rauduscülan Gate.'

The Rauduscular Gate was right on the far edge of town near the river, south of the Aventine. A fair hike, in other words, there and back, and Bathyllus wasn't much of a walker as a rule, as well as being very much the stay-at-home-type. Besides, if the little guy wasn't feeling quite his best at present...'Can't you send one of the skivvies?' I said. 'I mean, if it's just a matter of getting a workman to come round then –'

'I'd really rather not, sir. From the look of it it's quite a tricky job, and I'd like to make sure they send their best man.'

I shrugged. 'Fair enough, sunshine. You know best. Take your time, though, and don't hurry back.'

'Thank you, sir.'

He left, and I reached for a roll, broke it and dipped one half into the olive oil. I was frowning.

Odd.

I'd finished breakfast and was communing with nature when Perilla came out.

'Good morning, Marcus,' she said. 'I thought you'd be off and away by this time.'

I shrugged. 'I'm in no hurry.'

Bathyllus buttled in. 'Good morning, madam.'

'How are you this morning, Bathyllus?' Perilla pulled up the chair facing me and sat.

'Quite recovered, madam, thank you. The usual?'

'Yes, please.' Meaning a three-egg omelette, some cheese, olives, dried fruit and honey for the rolls. Rolls plural, and very much so. Gods, the lady could shift it! Particularly at breakfast. Not that she seemed to put on any weight, mind. If it'd been me they'd've had to wheel me around in a barrow.

Bathyllus left, and she poured herself some fruit juice. 'So what are your plans for today?' she said.

'Nothing much. It's a good day for walking. I thought I'd go over to Renatius's for a cup or two of wine.' I caught her expression. Bugger! 'Okay; make that just the one cup, then. Fair enough?'

She sniffed. 'What you need, Marcus, is a hobby.'

'I've got one. Only nothing seems to be happening in that direction at present.'

'Personally, I'd be quite pleased about that. There's something ghoulish about waiting around for someone to be murdered.'

'Yeah, well.'

'Actually, if you're going across town you can drop in at Polydamas's bookshop and pick up that copy of Timaeus I ordered. It should be ready by now.'

'No problem. Where's Polydamas's?'

'In the Subura, on Safety Incline.' Not exactly an up-market address, but then knowing the establishments that Perilla patronised it'd probably have been there before the Subura as such existed. Was loosely thrown together. Grew, organically. Whatever. 'I left a deposit, but there'll still be something to pay.'

'You'll be out all day at Cloelia Faustina's place, yes?'

'Unfortunately yes. Faustina's a lovely lady, but she does have this deep-seated belief that she can write sixteen-syllable Sapphics. Which she can't. It really does get quite embarrassing at times.'

'Yeah. I can imagine. I mean, who wants to listen to a run of dud sixteen-syllable Sapphics?'

She gave me a considering look. 'Some day, Corvinus,' she said, 'you are going to wake up with your head beaten in and me standing above you holding a hammer and a copy of Hephaestion's *On Metre*. You know that, don't you?'

'Uh-huh.' I grinned, stood up and kissed her; at which point Bathyllus reappeared, *sans* omelette and wearing his Courier of Doom expression. 'Yes, little guy. What is it?'

'A message from your mother, sir. She needs to see you immediately.'

I groaned. Courier of Doom expression was right: so much for the pleasant morning propping up the bar at Renatius's.

'She say what it was about?' I said.

'No, sir. Only that it was vitally important, and you were to come at once.'

'Bugger.'

'Quite, sir.'

Perilla was looking at me anxiously. 'It does sound serious, dear,' she said. 'And most unlike Vipsania. Do you think she's ill? Or Priscus is?'

'Unlikely.' They were both fit as fleas, and always had been: Mother looked and behaved like someone half her age, and although my stepfather was a dead ringer for old Tithonus on a bad day he was a wiry old devil. Mind you, there was always the chance that their avant-garde chef Phormio had finally come up trumps and poisoned the pair of them. 'I'll go round there now.'

'Don't worry about the book, if you get caught up. I can collect it another day.'

'Fair enough.' I kissed her again, and left.

Mother's place wasn't far away, just up the road on Head of Africa. The door-slave led me straight through to the garden where Mother was pacing between the flower beds like an arena cat with the squitters. She rushed over to me.

'Marcus!' she said. 'Thank goodness you've come! It's Titus!'

Shit, Perilla had been right. This sounded Serious with a capital S.

'Uh...he's not dead, is he?' I said. Oh, sure, if Priscus had dropped off his perch I'd've expected yew branches outside the door, at least, and a lot more funereal pomp and less frontal hair from the door-slave, but still...

Mother frowned. 'Don't be silly, dear,' she said. 'Of course he isn't dead. He's perfectly fine, health-wise, as am I. What on earth made you think otherwise?'

I grinned, only partly with relief; well, that was me told. 'Fair enough,' I said. 'So why haul me over here at a moment's notice? What's the problem?'

'I don't know.' Then, when I looked at her, 'Oh, I know *what* the problem is, dear, I just don't know *why* it is. Or indeed if it is at all, for that matter, and if it is then what I'm to do about it. That's what I need you to tell me.'

Gods! Mother at her most mind-bendingly cryptic I could do without at this time of the morning!

'Look,' I said, steering her towards the grape arbour with its reclining couches. 'Just lie down, make yourself comfortable, take a deep breath, and start from the beginning. Any time you're ready. Okay?'

'Very well.' She took herself through the first three; I waited. Finally she said, 'I think – and I stress *think,* Marcus, because I have no solid proof whatsoever of this – that Titus might have a mistress.'

I had to stop myself from laughing: not only could Priscus have doubled for the contents of a thousand-year-old Egyptian coffin but the guy's field of interest began and ended with ancient Italian relics and the use of the optative in early Oscan. Plus, however bored and jaded she might be, I couldn't see any woman in her right senses considering him as her inamorato of choice for two consecutive seconds.

'Come on, Mother!' I said. 'That's nonsense!'

That got me a very sharp look, and a definite sniff. 'Your stepfather,' she said, 'has hidden depths. I will not go into details, but nonsense it most certainly is not. I may be wrong, and I hope I am, but that is for you to find out.'

Oh, hell. 'And how am I supposed to do that, then?' I said.

'Follow him when he goes out. See where he goes, who he meets. You're good at that.' Another sniff. 'Or at least so you keep telling me.'

'I do nothing of the kind!'

'Yes, well, you are. In any case, that's what I need you to do, please. Off you go. Spit spot.'

'Hang on, Mother, we haven't finished with this. You say you've got no proof that Priscus is having an affair, right? So what makes you think that he is?'

'Little things that only a wife would notice. He's taken to going out regularly immediately after breakfast and sometimes not coming home until dinner time, when he's very evasive about where he's been. He's become more interested in the cleanliness of his laundry –'

'Underwear?'

That got me a withering look. 'Don't be crude, Marcus. Overthings is what I mean. Cloak. Tunic. And he brings me small presents practically every day.'

'Yeah? What kind of presents?'

'Small, as I say, but all antiques. Curios. Yesterday it was a faience hairpin, which is fairly typical.'

'Mother, be sensible! That's what the guy *does*: he haunts antique and curio shops to see what's on offer. If anything was made yesterday he's not interested.'

'I know that, dear, of course I do. But generally he's a looker, not a buyer. And when he does buy he generally goes for something rare and expensive.'

Yeah, well, that was certainly true, at least: bibs and bobs like hairpins just weren't Priscus's style. As little guilt-offerings, though...

'How long has this been going on?' I said.

'Half a month. And yesterday I caught him whistling.'

Whistling? *Priscus?* Gods! I was beginning to be convinced. Oh, no, not that the guy was having some unimaginable form of senile fling with a baker's wife in the Public Pond district, but still; for all her wooliness, Mother was no fool, and there was something odd going on, that was certain.

The whistling clinched it. Priscus had never whistled in all the years I'd known him. And where carrying a tune was concerned *tin ear* didn't cover half of it.

'Okay,' I said. 'So how do I go about this?'

'It's easy enough. As I said, he generally goes out immediately after breakfast, as he did this morning. We're very early risers, so if you're outside the front gate and in position half way through the first hour that should be about right. Whatever you do, though, don't be late.' She frowned. 'In fact, just to be safe, perhaps immediately after dawn would be more sensible. Or even before that, if you can manage it.'

Jupiter! 'You don't think maybe I should just bring a blanket and bunk down in the street for the night?' I said.

'If you think that would be a good idea, then yes, certainly, Marcus. I leave the details completely up to you.' Not a flicker. Yeah, well, I'd known the woman for forty-odd years and sarcasm had never worked yet; it just bounced off her, like dried peas off a rhino. 'Further I'm afraid I can't help you; you're on your own.'

Oh, thank you, gods. Thank you *so* much. 'Fair enough,' I said. 'Leave it with me.' I turned to go.

'Oh, and you *will* make sure he doesn't see you following him, won't you? That is terribly important.'

'Yeah, I think I've taken the principle of the thing firmly on board, Mother,' I said. Mind you, given Priscus's razor-sharp powers of observation I could probably have dressed up as a priest of Cybele and followed on his heels chanting and shaking a bloody sistrum and he'd still not have noticed me. Unless it was an antique sistrum, of course.

'Don't forget, then.' She leaned over and kissed me on the cheek. 'Off you go, dear, and good luck. Let me know when you find out something useful, won't you?'

Hell's teeth; dogging Priscus was something I could cheerfully do without. Still, I wasn't otherwise occupied at present, so it was no big deal. And I'd be interested myself to see what the old bugger was getting up to.

At least Mother hadn't asked us round for dinner.

Well, that little visit hadn't taken as long as I'd thought it would, fortunately, and I'd plenty of time in hand for the promised cup of wine at Renatius's. Besides, after even a short interview with Mother I needed one badly.

I like Renatius's; in fact, taken by and large, it's my favourite city wineshop. Nothing special on the inside, just bare walls, the bar counter with its stools, and a few tables for the less socially-minded drinkers, but for me that's part of its charm. Since it's on Iugarius, which runs round the foot of the Capitol and connects with Market Square, if it'd gone a bit more up-market it would've been popular with the Eighth District's Great and Good, but as things are they tend to patronise the more chi-chi watering holes around Augustus Square and the foot of the Palatine, with their themed decor, overpriced wines and off-the-wall recherché gourmet snacks. Which is absolutely fine with me: you get a far better and more intelligent standard of conversation when your wineshop punters are tunics.

So I spent a very pleasant couple of hours propping up Renatius's bar and shooting the breeze with the regulars. I may've underplayed things a little for Perilla with the 'one cup' business, but not by much, and I spun things out with a plateful of cheese, olives and sliced sausage. I was stone-cold sober when I left just shy of noon and made my way across town to the Subura and Polydamas's bookshop.

Safety Incline was packed, which was par for the course late morning. Streets in Rome are narrow and winding at the best of times, but the Subura, one of the oldest and poorest districts in the city, does narrow and winding in spades. Plus the fact that there're more tenements in rickety condition than you can shake a stick at, not that you'd risk it, which means that in addition to fighting your way through the crowd, watching where you're putting your feet, and keeping one hand on your belt-purse, you have to keep a leery eye out above for inconsiderate slop-tippers and falling roof-tiles.

Yeah, well. It's all part of Rome's rich – and rich-smelling – tapestry. At least walking there you're never bored.

I found Polydamas's shop, collected Perilla's Timaeus, and carried on down the Incline in the direction of the Caelian. I'd almost reached the junction at the end when I spotted Bathyllus about a dozen yards ahead of me, disappearing into the entrance passageway of one of the tenements.

There was no mistake: I'd've recognised the little bald-head anywhere. I stopped dead, and the guy behind me barged into my back. Words were exchanged, mostly on his side, before he pushed on past, still cursing, leaving me standing.

I was seriously puzzled; the Rauduscula Gate was a good mile off, and Safety Incline wouldn't be anywhere near his way home. As far as making any sort of sense went, it was a complete bummer.

Besides, what the hell business would a stay-at-home arch-snob like Bathyllus have in a Suburan tenement?

Yeah, well, at least I could find that out. I pushed through the last of the crowd, between two vociferous bag-ladies on their way home with their net bags of vegetables, and slipped into the tenement entrance. Now I was off the street, I paused and listened. I could hear the slap of his sandals as he climbed the stairs above me.

'Salubrious' isn't exactly the word you'd use in relation to any city-centre tenement, but this one didn't even come up to undemanding Suburan standards. The walls were so thick with graffiti you couldn't see the plaster, the stairs were filthy, and from the smell it would appear the residents were chronic incontinents who didn't have much use for chamber-pots and preferred to do their business beyond their own front doors, albeit close at hand. I held my breath, watched where I was stepping, and carried on up, being careful to keep it quiet and not to move too quickly.

He was obviously going all the way to the top, all six floors, and I had to stop a couple of times while he gasped his lungs out on the landing ahead of me: fit was something our major-domo definitely wasn't, which was fair enough since the only exercise he normally got was buffing up the bronzes. I took the last flight of steps at a snail's pace and waited until I heard a knock, the rattle of a door being opened, and the sound of voices. As the door closed again I shoved my head round the corner in time to see which of the two possibles it had been.

The flat on the left. Okay. Here we went.

Luckily, the door was still unlocked from the inside. I pushed it open.

You don't get much for your money when you rent a top-floor tenement flat, even in areas more upmarket than the Subura. There was just the one room, of course, and that was small and cramped, scarcely big enough for the truckle bed, table, stool, and clothing-chest. What light there was filtered in through a hole in the roof where the tiles hadn't quite managed to cover the rafters. Bathyllus was standing with his back to me, and sitting on the bed was a seriously-unshaven late-middle-aged man in a grubby threadbare tunic.

Bathyllus turned round, the guy got up, and they both stared at me, jaws dropping, like actors at the end of a play where the god is lowered from a crane to sort out a too-convoluted plot.

'Hi, sunshine,' I said to Bathyllus. 'So who's your friend?'

I'd never, ever seen Bathyllus lost for words before, but I saw it now. He swallowed a couple of times, coughed, and then said:

'This is Damon, sir. He's my brother.'

# 3.

'He is *what?*' Jupiter, whatever I was expecting, it wasn't that: before it I'd even have accepted the revelation of a clandestine sexual relationship, and considering this was Bathyllus that takes some admitting. 'Since when have you had a brother?'

Silly question, sure, but you have to remember I was in shock. More so even than they were, which again is saying something. To give Bathyllus his due, he ignored it.

'We haven't seen each other since we were children, sir,' he said. 'Until a few days ago for all I knew he was dead.'

I glanced down at the table. On it there was a wine jug, a cup, half a loaf of bread and a piece of cold ham. Yeah, well, that cleared up that little mystery. He must've finished the chicken.

'Maybe you'd better explain,' I said.

'Yes, of course, sir.' Bathyllus cleared his throat. 'If you'd like to sit down. It may take some time.'

I pulled up the stool and sat. Brother Damon – Jupiter, I still couldn't get my head round this! – sat back down on the bed. Now that I knew who he was, I could see the resemblance. He was younger, sure, by a few years, and he still had some of his hair, where if you'd polished Bathyllus's scalp you could've used it as a mirror for shaving. The nose was the same, and the set of the ears. There was something, though, that didn't sit right about the expression: if push came to shove, I reckoned I wouldn't altogether trust Brother Damon. But then maybe I was being unfair. After all, I hadn't so much as heard the guy speak for himself yet.

'You know your grandfather bought me at the slave market in Pergamum, sir?' Bathyllus said.

'Yeah. When he was out there on a job for the Emperor Augustus.'

'Indeed. I was twelve at the time, Damon was seven. Our father was a stonemason, quite a good one from what I can remember. Originally, anyway. Unfortunately he was also a drunk and a gambler, which was why he got into debt and was forced to sell us. It was that or we'd all have starved.'

Gods! Well, you know that's the way the world works – selling off unwanted kids to clear a debt is standard practice among the poorer classes throughout the empire – but when it's your own major-domo that you've known for years who's telling you that, and in Bathyllus's matter-of-fact tones, it stops you in your tracks. Sure, I knew that old Grandpa Marcus had bought him fifty-odd years back in Pergamum and taken him to Rome, but that was as far as it went.

'What about your mother?' I said.

'She was dead, sir. In childbirth, two years previously.'

'Ah.' There wasn't much more I could say, really. And even I knew that under the circumstances adding an 'I'm sorry' would've been crass.

'Anyway, I was bought first, by your grandfather, and brought straight to Rome. I didn't know what had happened to Damon until years after, and then only the barest details.'

Damon cleared his throat.

'Me, sir,' he said, 'well, they sold me a couple of hours later. First master was a Gnaeus Sentius Saturninus, not that he bought me personal, mind, that was his agent, a real bastard by the name of Lucrio. Pardon my Greek. Saturninus, he was the provincial governor at the time, but he'd a big estate near Padua. I got took back there with most of the rest of his slaves when his stint was finished and I grew up as part of the household.'

Much rougher-spoken than Bathyllus, sure, but that was to be expected given the background life had handed him. More important – and vitally so – I'd noticed that wasn't wearing a freedman's cap. Which meant...

Hell; this could get seriously complicated. Still, I shelved thinking about that particular problem for the time being. Let's get the facts straight first.

'I knew – but not until much later – that Damon had been sold into the Sentius household,' Bathyllus said. 'But nothing further. As I say, not even that he was still alive. I didn't know about the Paduan estate until a few days ago, or I would've tried to get in touch somehow. And Damon only discovered where I was when he came to Rome.'

Uh-huh. So now we got to the real nitty-gritty. *Came to Rome*, right? If everything was above board – which from what I'd seen so far I'd bet a gold piece to a wooden sesterce it wasn't – then what the hell was he doing holed up in a Suburan tenement?

Mind you, I could probably answer that question myself. Unfortunately..

'So you, uh, still belong to the Sentius family, Damon,' I said, trying to keep my voice neutral. Gods alive! Didn't Bathyllus *know* what would happen to him if he was caught aiding and abetting an escaped slave? I'd be in serious schtook with the authorities myself, and I was a purple-striper.

Damon looked at me. 'Here, now, sir,' he said mildly. 'You just hold your horses. I said Sentius Saturninus was my *first* master. He wasn't my only one. When he died his son sold me to a Gaius Oplonius. Oplonius, he was a Paduan merchant.'

'"Was"?' I said.

'Died himself five years back and left me to his son, also Gaius.' Jupiter! This was getting complicated! 'I'm his slave now.' He took a deep breath. 'Or I was until a few days ago.'

Well, Bathyllus's brother or not I couldn't mess about here. It had to be said.

'It makes no odds whose slave you were or are, sunshine,' I said gently. 'The fact is, if you're still one and you've run away, then –'

'*No*, sir,' Bathyllus said. 'You still don't understand. Five days ago Damon's master was murdered.'

I stared. 'He was *what?*'

'Stabbed to death. In a tenement flat on the Aventine.'

Gods! Could we please, *please* have a bit of normality for a change?

'O – kay,' I said. 'I think I'm going to need just a few more details here. Maybe you'd better start at the beginning.'

'Fair enough,' Damon said. 'It's like I told you. My master's name was Gaius Oplonius. That's the son, of course. From Padua. He was in the wool business like his father, nothing fancy, but he got along. We'd come to Rome three days previous looking for new markets. The idea was, we'd be here for about a month, so the master, instead of bunking down at an inn, he takes a short let on a room in a tenement. North side of the Aventine, opposite the Racetrack. You with me?'

'Yeah,' I said. 'Yeah, I think I'm just about coping.'

He shot me a look. Well, at least this Damon was more up on satire than Mother was.

'Anyways,' he said, 'five days ago we'd finished up for the day and gone back home, and the master sends me down to the local cookshop for a takeaway. When I come back he's on the floor dead with a hole in his chest and blood all over him. So I scarper.' He paused. ''S it. 'S all I know.'

‘Why didn’t you call the Watch?’ I said.

He looked at me as if I was being stupid. Which, maybe, I was.

‘Yeah, right,’ he said. ‘And get nailed straight off for being the perp. “Nailed” being the operative word, Oplonius being a citizen and my master into the bargain; nailed by my hands and feet to a couple of sodding planks and left for the crows to pick at. So no Watch, not bloody likely. I scarpered, and lucky to have the option.’

‘He came to me, sir,’ Bathyllus said. ‘He knew I’d been bought by your grandfather – another Marcus Valerius Corvinus, of course – so he asked around in the hopes that I was still with the family.’

‘Din’t take me long,’ Damon said smugly. ‘Had it done and dusted the next day. I just kept asking until I found someone who knew the address of a nob family by the name of Valerius Corvinus. After I’d got the right place and made sure Bathyllus was still part of the household I hung about outside until I’d the chance of a word.’

‘Very enterprising,’ I said.

He grinned. ‘Yeah, well, I try.’

‘I got him set up here, sir,’ Bathyllus said. ‘He had a little money – all his master had on him at the time – but it wasn’t much, because when Oplonius arrived in Rome he’d left most of it with a banker.’ Uh-huh: standard practice for a visitor to the city if you weren’t staying with reliable friends. Unless you were a complete idiot you didn’t carry around more than you needed for everyday expenses, and if you were dossing down anywhere else you sure as hell didn’t stash it away under the mattress. And the banker wasn’t going to cough up to a mere slave without written authorisation, just for the asking. ‘I paid most of the quarter-month’s rent myself, out of my savings. The landlord didn’t ask any questions.’

No, he wouldn't, not in the Subura. Suburan landlords aren't exactly conscientious citizens, and cash in hand is cash in hand. They're cautious, too: short-let Suburan tenants have a habit of sloping off unannounced, but they aren't, as a class, sufficiently flush enough with money to cough up a whole month's rent in advance. Hence the usual practice of gearing payment to the old country-district nine-day system.

Still, it did raise certain questions of its own. Or rather, it added to the same one.

'Fine,' I said. 'So now give me the why.'

Damon frowned. 'Why what, squire?'

'Come on, pal! Why the hell your master was murdered in the first place. I mean, this is Rome, yes, we've got guys with knives who'll slit a punter's throat for the price of a bowl of bean stew, granted, but they do it out in the open, in a dark alleyway somewhere after sundown. A scenario like that I could've believed. But what the bastards don't do, no way, nohow, never, is walk into a tenement on the off-chance of hitting on a likely target, commit murder, and then leave without even bothering to take the victim's purse with them. That makes no sense at all. So come clean, right?'

He was quiet for a long time. Then he said, 'Simple truth is, sir, that I don't know. Okay?'

'Right. Right. Got you. And my maternal grandmother was Cleopatra.'

His fist slammed down on the mattress. 'Gods almighty, I swear so help me I don't ...bloody...*know!* That's how it happened, I swear it, first to last, chapter and verse. You think I'd make something like that up?'

Yeah, well, the jury was out on that one. Or at least if not in regard to the broader circumstances – I reckoned those had the ring of truth, however improbable – where the background details were concerned. Still, he was

Bathyllus's brother, and I owed Bathyllus a bit of slack. Enough, certainly, to give his brother the benefit of the doubt. For the present, at least.

'Fair enough,' I said. 'We'll leave it there for now. Tell us about this Oplonius.'

He shrugged. 'Not much to tell. Like I say, the master was a wool merchant from Padua, down here on business,'

'He know anyone in Rome?'

'Not a soul. He'd never been here before.'

'You're sure about that?'

'Look, I knew the master from when he was in leading strings. He'd never been south of Pisa.'

'So no enemies?'

'Why should he have had enemies?'

I sighed. 'Yeah, well, whoever stuck a knife into him couldn't exactly have been a bosom buddy, could he? He must've had some good reason for doing it.'

'Granted. But whatever it was, it's a mystery to me.'

Uh-huh. Still, we weren't going to get any further in that direction. Not without the help of thumbscrews. I changed tack.

'Where did you say this tenement was?'

'On the edge of the Aventine, near the Racetrack. About half way along. What's that got to do with anything?'

'I thought I might just take a look at it, that's all.'

Damon frowned. 'What would the point of that be?' he said. 'The master was killed five days ago and his body'll be long gone. The room might even have been re-let.'

True. Rented accommodation is at a premium in Rome, and no self-respecting landlord is going to let a little thing like a murder stand in the way of profit. Oplonius had been damned lucky to get anywhere at all at such short notice, particularly somewhere so close to the centre. Get rid of the corpse, clean any inconvenient blood stains off the floor as well as you could, and you're ready for the next punter.

Even so...

'Valerius Corvinus knows what he's doing, Damon,' Bathyllus said. 'He's had a lot of experience in this area.'

'Has he, now?' Damon flashed me a look that was difficult to assess. 'Fair do's, then. I'm much obliged, sir, I'm sure.'

I stood up. 'Okay,' I said. 'I'll leave you both to it for the present. Bathyllus.' I pointed to the remains of the ham. 'This stops here, right, like I said at the staff meeting. Agreed?'

He swallowed. 'Agreed, sir.'

'I don't want Meton on my back, and nor do you. You need anything, you buy it.' I reached into my belt-purse and took out what coins there were. Not bad; even after Perilla's Timaeus there was change for the best part of a gold piece. 'Pay yourself back for the rent. And when you need more, come to me and we'll arrange things.'

'You won't give him away?'

'Uh-uh. Not at present, anyway. But no promises, right, because as far as the authorities are concerned we're aiding and abetting an escaped slave, and they're not exactly sympathetic to that sort of thing. I'm going right out on a limb for you here, sunshine.'

'I know that. Thank you, sir.'

'Don't mention it. I mean, *really* don't mention it. To anyone. And you' – I turned to Damon – 'stick close, right? You don't move from this room, got it?'

Damon grinned and winked. 'Don't you worry on that score, squire,' he said. 'Me, I'm not going nowhere.'

'Fair enough.' I gave Bathyllus the coins, and left.

Shit.

So where did we start? I'd go and have a look at the tenement, sure, for what it was worth, just to see the scene of the crime, but I could do a whole lot better than that, starting with a visit to my Watch Commander pal Decimus Lippillus. He was in charge of the Palatine district now, but with any luck he'd be able to give me an intro to whoever had the Aventine beat. That was a guy I really had to talk to, because from what I'd seen of Brother Damon I wouldn't've trusted him to give me the right time of day. It was odd how he and Bathyllus could be brothers and yet be so unlike.

Not that I wasn't grateful to him, mind, all things considered and if truth be told. Things had been getting pretty boring recently.

And Perilla would be delighted.

# 4.

'So.' Lucius Pudentius set the note Lippillus had given me for him down on his desk. 'Valerius Corvinus, right?'

'As ever is.' I gave him my best sycophantic smile.

He sucked on a tooth. 'Care to tell me how you knew about this man Oplonius's death and what your interest in it might be?'

Ouch; straight for the jugular. Yeah, well, I had thought the question might be asked pretty early on; not that I had an answer ready prepared, mind. And according to Lippillus, although Pudentius had his limits he was far from being stupid, so maybe I should've had.

'He's not the smartest cookie in the jar where thinking's concerned, Marcus,' Lippillus had said as he was writing the note of introduction. 'But he isn't stupid. He's honest, he's efficient, he's dogged, and he's conscientious to a fault. A good Watchman, in other words. Give him this and you should be all right.'

Me, now I'd met him, I had my doubts about that part. The guy didn't exactly look the accommodating type.

'Ah...' I said.

Pudentius grunted. 'I assume that means no.' I said nothing. 'Well, we'll let it pass. I've a lot of time for Decimus Lippillus, and I trust his judgment. If he vouches for you, and he does, then that'll do me.' I breathed a mental sigh of relief. 'One thing, though. If you do happen to know the whereabouts of a certain slave belonging to the deceased who seems to have gone missing I'd strongly advise you to make damn sure you continue to do so. Am I clear?'

Uh-huh. *Definitely* not stupid. 'Yeah,' I said. 'Clear.'

'Fine. Not that you do know where he is, of course. Perish the thought. If I thought that for one minute you'd be in real trouble. Now. What do you want from me?'

I swallowed; Lippillus's recommendation or not, I was walking on eggshells here. 'Anything you can give me, really,' I said. 'All I know at present is the guy's name, that he was a wool merchant from Padua just arrived in the city, and that he was stabbed to death in the tenement room he was renting five days ago.'

'Wool merchant, eh? Then you're a bit ahead of us after all. All our informants could tell us was that he was a Paduan businessman.' There was the barest smidgeon of emphasis on the word 'our', but otherwise his voice was expressionless. 'On the other hand...stabbed. Yes. He died from a stab wound to the chest, certainly, but he'd been in a serious fight beforehand as well.'

'What?'

'You didn't know that? We're all square again, then. From the bruises on the body and the general state of the place he must've put up a hell of a struggle before he died. We checked with the neighbours, but you know the Aventine.' He put on an accent thick with nasal Aventine vowels. '"No one heard nothing, officer. Besides, we was out at the time."'

'"The state of the place"?'

'The room looked like a herd of bulls had been through it. Bed overturned, mattress ripped, clothes chest on its side and emptied. Stuff scattered all over the floor.'

Shit; Damon hadn't mentioned any of this. And the obvious question was, why hadn't he?

'What sort of stuff?' I said.

'Just what you'd expect. Nothing out of the ordinary. Clothes, personal effects, that sort of thing.' He frowned. 'In fact, if you hang on a minute...' He got up, went to the door of his office, and yelled, 'Publius!'

The young squaddie who'd been manning the desk when I arrived came in.

'Yeah, boss?' he said.

'The stuff from the Rullius tenement case. Bring it in here, will you?' The squaddie disappeared. 'My lads bagged it the same time as they took the body away, in the hopes that there'd be a next of kin we could hand it over to.'

Brilliant! Score one for the efficiency of the Aventine Watch. Lippillus had said he was conscientious; not many Watch commanders would go to that amount of trouble.

'Is there, by the way?' I said. 'A next of kin?'

'Bound to be. But Padua's a long way off, and he was a complete stranger here. No one to ask, no one to tell. The chances are it was a waste of time. Some of it'll vanish eventually, no doubt – my lads are honest enough, but there's nothing of any great value and if it's going begging there's no harm done – and what doesn't will just get thrown out.' The squaddie reappeared with a couple of bags. 'Empty them on the floor, Publius. That's right.'

He watched as I sorted through the result. Like Pudentius had said, it was nothing special: in the clothing line, a couple of spare tunics, underclothes and a cloak with a simple iron pin; otherwise a dozen other bibs and bobs you'd expect a single man on his own to carry with him when he travelled, including a sewing kit and a packet of corn plasters, all of which were of the cheap and cheerful variety you could pick up for a few coppers at any cut-price market stall. *Small-time* was right: Damon had taken any money there had been, sure, he'd told me that, but what was left was more appropriate to a man almost on his uppers than a respectable businessman.

The really interesting thing, though, was what *wasn't* there. I checked and re-checked carefully, but there was no sign.

'That's everything?' I said.

'All that there was,' Pudentius said. 'The owner's agent – he lives on the premises, by the way, and his name's Meleager, if you're interested – insisted we clear the room in case he got a quick let.'

'You know if that's happened?'

'I'm afraid not. You can check with him yourself, if you want to take the trouble to call at the property. Ask for the Rullius place, one in from Racetrack Road about half way along.' He started piling Oplonius's effects back into one of the bags, and I did the same with the other. 'Oh, one more thing. I said the man didn't know anyone here, and that's so, to my knowledge. But my lads called in at the nearest wineshop in the hopes that he'd spent some free time there. Standard practice; you never know what you might pick up in the way of extra information. Seemingly he had, once or twice, and although the barman wasn't much help otherwise it did transpire that he'd been friendly with one of the girls. If you know what I mean.' Yeah; some wineshops double as brothels, of a pretty basic kind, and they'd keep two or three girls on the staff for waitressing and other duties. 'Her name's Lydia. I doubt if she'll be able to tell you anything more than I have, or than she told the lads at the time, because it was purely a business arrangement, but it's best you know.'

'Yeah.' I filed the name for later consideration. 'Thanks a lot, pal. You've been a great help.'

'Don't mention it.'

'Two last things from my side. There's, er, a good chance that Oplonius lodged some money with a local banker. You know anything about that?'

'No. Not so far, anyway. But the chances are that if he did the man will report it when it's not claimed. Bankers are honest enough by their lights, and it's not in their interests to keep that sort of thing hidden. It'll go to the next-of-kin, naturally, if and when we find out who that is.'

'Right. Right.'

'And the second?'

'Hmm? Oh. Yes. A question. You mentioned that the guy had serious bruises. Did any of your lads think of looking at his hands?'

'His *hands*?' Pudentius frowned. 'No. Why would they do that?'

'Just a thought. It doesn't matter.' Like hell it didn't, but I didn't want to complicate things at this stage. In any case, I might be completely wrong. 'Thanks again.'

'You're very welcome. Give my regards to Decimus.'

'Will do.' I handed him the bag I was holding and turned to go.

There was still a slice of the afternoon left before I had to head back home for dinner; time enough to check out the tenement. Not, I knew, that there'd be anything to see any more; Damon had been right about that. Still, I might as well tick all the boxes; the agent – what was his name? Meleager, right, so probably a freedman – might remember something useful that he hadn't passed on to the Watch. At the least, he'd had personal contact with Oplonius when he was alive, and given that my only other informant on that score was Damon – enough said – anything at all that I could get from him would be useful.

Of course there was the wineshop girl, Lydia. But her I'd probably have to leave until another day.

I had a passer-by point out the Rullius tenement and went inside. We'd gone upmarket from the Subura, but not by much – this was the Aventine, after all – and the best you could say of the stairs was that they were reasonably clean and the graffiti were better spelled. I climbed to the first floor and knocked on one of the doors. There was no answer, so I tried another. There was the sound of shuffling feet and eventually the door opened.

'Yes?'

'I'm sorry to bother you, Gramps,' I said to the guy behind it. 'Are you the agent? Meleager?'

'Rullius Meleager. That's right.' Gnome-like, eighty if he was a day, with a freedman's cap perched on top of only marginally more hair than Bathyllus could manage. 'How can I help you, sir? If you're looking for a flat to rent then I'm afraid –'

'No. No, that's okay.' Bugger; by the sound of it he'd re-let after all. 'I've come from the local Watch headquarters. Lucius Pudentius.' The smudging was intentional: the guy might prove naturally helpful, but implying that I had Watch connections without actually saying so would get me there faster. 'He said you might have some information for me on the murder.'

'*Ssshh!*' He pulled me inside the flat and shut the door. 'Goodness me! Keep your voice down, *please!*'

'You mean it's not common knowledge?'

'Yes, Yes, I suppose it is. But that's no reason to go shouting it out all over the building.' He shuffled off down the short entrance corridor. 'Through here.'

Bathyllus would've loved it. The living room was neat to the point of fussiness, with everything polished to within an inch of its life. There was even a bowl of flowers on the table.

'Now,' he said. 'You'll find that stool perfectly comfortable. If you'll forgive me' – he stretched out slowly and painfully on the day-bed next to the wall – 'I'll lie here.' I sat down. 'Mark you, there's nothing more I can tell you than I told your colleague. I hardly knew the man. I certainly didn't see him except for when he moved in. And as for the' – he paused – 'the *unpleasantness* five days ago, I can't tell you anything about that either. The flat was on the third floor, you know. Two above this one. There must have been a...well, from what the Watch officer said, there was no doubt a great deal of noise, but I never heard it. And all the tenants are out during the day barring Lollia Alexandra on the fourth, and she's deaf as a post.'

'He have any visitors at all? I mean, before the, ah, unpleasantness.'

'He might have done, for all I know. There are people in and out of here all the time, but that's the tenants' business; so long as they pay their rent on the dot who comes visiting is none of my concern.'

Fair point. It'd been worth a try, mind. 'You say you met him?'

'Of course I met him. I'd have to, wouldn't I, if he was one of the tenants. Only the once, though, as I told you.'

'He, uh, strike you in any way in particular?' He frowned. 'I mean, job like yours, you must be pretty good at sizing up a prospective tenant right off. Particularly where a short let's involved.'

Smarm, smarm. But it worked. He leaned a little closer and lowered his voice, like a gossipy housewife passing on a bit of scandal over the honey wine and biscuits.

‘To tell you the truth, sir,’ he said, ‘and now you come to ask, I wasn’t altogether taken with Master Oplonius. Nor with that slave of his. Cast from the same mould, the pair of them, and a dodgy mould, at that.’

‘Is that so, now?’

He sat up again.

‘I don’t trust the ones who look you straight in the eye,’ he said. ‘Not deliberately making a point of it, like he did. Most people say the opposite, that it’s the shifty-eyed ones that are the bad apples, but in my view that’s nonsense. Oh, I could be wrong; perhaps I’m doing the poor man an injustice. But I don’t think so. I ran my ex-master’s business affairs for over forty years, and I flatter myself I can tell when someone can be trusted and when they can’t. He said he was a businessman, and perhaps he was; but if so he wasn’t the sort that in my younger days I’d’ve chosen to have any dealings with. When he paid me the rent I made sure that I counted the money and checked the coins one by one for fakes into the bargain. Too right I did.’

Interesting. ‘The flat’s been re-let, yes?’

‘Yes, it has. Only this morning, to a nice young couple with a baby.’

‘Damn! I was, ah, hoping I could take a quick look at it.’

‘Oh, I don’t think that would be a problem, sir. Not that there’s anything to see now, of course. I had the Watch empty the room completely. Barring the furnishings, naturally, such as they are; they’re part of the let.’ He eased himself slowly and painfully off the couch. ‘The new tenants won’t be moving in until tomorrow, so they told me. I’ll just get you the spare key.’

The place looked – understandably – bare and cheerless, particularly after Meleager’s cosy hideaway. Still, that was fair enough; he was a permanent fixture, it was his home, he'd probably been there for years, and besides the flats on the first floor of a tenement are always more upmarket than the ones above. We weren't under the tiles yet, like at Damon's place, but there was only the one room with bed and clothes-chest. No doubt the young couple would be bringing in a few sticks of furniture of their own to make it more homely, plus a cradle for the baby, but at present the only touch of luxury, if you can call it that, was a thin rug covering the floorboards next to the bed .

A rug...

I lifted the corner and looked. Right: Meleager's underlings had done their best with the stain, but blood on wood never comes out completely with scrubbing. I just wondered what he'd told the youngsters.

Well, there was nothing to see here, not that I'd expected that there would be. All the same, I was glad I'd made the effort. Call it ticking a necessary box.

The window was open for light, and it being May there was a nice breeze blowing in. Give it time: come December, I'd bet the place would be freezing, and charcoal braziers are never a good idea in a tenement. I looked outside and down into the street below...

Meleager had said he was good at assessing a prospective tenant's character; it went with the job. Me, for the same reason, I can spot when I'm being tailed or watched. Or, as in this case, when there's a bastard on stake-out.

In actual fact there were two bastards, directly across the street from the tenement's entrance. Not that I could feel too smug, because they were being pretty obvious about it; all they really needed to put the lid on it was a placard saying 'I'm watching you'.

So the facts weren't in question. What was, yet again, was the 'why?' And that would take a lot of careful thinking about.

Meanwhile, under the circumstances, I reckoned that the best course of action was the direct, in-your-face approach. I went back out, locked the door behind me, clattered down to the first floor, returned the key to Meleager with my thanks, and set out to confront the buggers.

When they saw me coming they stopped propping up the wall and turned to face me: two heavies straight out of the standard mould, such as you'd get working as bouncers in the rowdier clubs or at the blunt end of a local protection racket.

'Afternoon, gents,' I said. 'Anything I can –?'

But I was talking to myself; they were off like scalded cats, in different directions. I thought of giving chase to one of them for all of two seconds before deciding the game wasn't worth the candle. In any case, I needed to be getting back home for dinner: the sun was well into its last quarter, and Meton in his present mood wasn't a force to be trifled with.

Interesting. Very interesting.

# 5.

Luckily as a result of my declaration of amnesty to the staff that morning Meton had a sulk on and was in go-slow mode, so it turned out that I'd plenty of time before dinner to break the glad tidings about developments to Perilla. Both sets of glad tidings, including the Curious Case of the Wayward Husband.

'So what did Vipsania want with you, dear?' she said when I'd got settled on the couch and Bathyllus was handing me my pre-dinner cup of wine. 'She isn't ill, is she?'

'No, Mother's fine. So's Priscus, as far as health goes, at least.' Bathyllus was edging out. 'Stay right where you are, little guy,' I said to him. 'I'll get round to you in a moment.' He froze. 'Mother thinks he has a fancy woman squirrelled away somewhere, that's all.'

'*Priscus?*' She burst out laughing. 'Oh, no! Not really?'

I shrugged. 'I don't believe it more than half myself, lady. But you know Mother. She gets these bees in her bonnet from time to time, and they're pretty hard to shake loose. Mind you, there's definitely something odd going on. I've told her I'll hang around and tail the guy, see what he's up to.'

'It's really none of your business. Even if it is true.'

'You want to try telling Mother that? And as far as being true goes, I'll suspend judgment. Remember the last time he went off the rails? In Baiae? We couldn't believe it then, either.'

'Marcus, that was *ages* ago! And it was only a small, temporary aberration.'

'Even so. Little urges like that can lie doggo for years and then break out when you least expect them.'

'So what exactly does she want you to do?'

'I told you: follow him, just that. Catch him *in flagrante*. Seemingly if he is an adulterer he's a pretty consistent one. Does his tomcatting first thing every morning, prompt, once he's got a good breakfast inside him. If you can call the muck that Phormio dishes up breakfast, or even food. I'll get it done tomorrow, for what it'll be worth. There's bound to be an innocent explanation, and at least it'll put Mother's mind at rest.'

'How was your day otherwise? Did you manage to collect my book?'

'Yeah, I did. And actually, the day was pretty eventful; that's the real news. I caught the chicken-napper, for a start.'

She frowned. 'The what?'

'The callous criminal who's been making free with our larder.'

She sat up straight. 'Marcus, that is amazing! Who was it?'

'Our light-fingered major-domo here.' Beside me, Bathyllus gave a small whimper.

'*Bathyllus?*' She was staring like a hooked guppy. Then she laughed. 'I'm sorry, dear, for a moment you had me believing you. Who was it, really?'

'Bathyllus. I told you. Cross my heart and hope to die. Oh, he had his reasons. He was taking the stuff to his brother who's presently on the run and holed up in a Suburan tenement.'

The hooked guppy look was back, in spades, with added goggle. 'Bathyllus has a *brother?*'

'Yeah, that was my reaction when I walked in on them. Name of Damon. He's hiding out from whoever stiffed his master five days ago. Oh, and from the Aventine Watch as well, of course.'

'Marcus, please. I have spent the day at Cloelia Faustina's making polite noises while she recited the most appalling drivel, and as a result both my reserves and my patience are at a very low ebb. So just tell me simply and in due order what is going on or I will strangle you where you lie. Fair enough?'

I grinned. 'Fair. Bathyllus, you can go. And to warn you, I've counted the spoons.'

He sniffed and left. I told Perilla about the day. The whole boiling.

'So you don't believe him?' she said when I'd finished. 'Damon, I mean.'

'Perilla, his story is so full of holes you could use it for a colander. For a start, Oplonius was no businessman. Not in the usual sense, that is. The tenement agent Meleager spotted that, and I'd agree with him.'

'Why are you so sure? Surely –'

'Damon said he was a wool merchant, here to suss out new markets. I went through the stuff Pudentius's boys brought back from the flat – which was all that was there at the time – and there were no samples. None. Nor was there anything else you'd expect him to have if he was who Damon claimed he was, like a list of potential customers. Whatever his business might have been, it sure as hell didn't involve wool.'

'Hmm.' She was twisting a lock of hair. 'So why *was* he here?'

'Your guess is as good as mine. But I'd bet a year's income it involved something shady. I never saw him, of course, but Meleager did, and that old bird is no one's fool. He had him sussed straight off for a wrong -'un.' I took a swallow of wine. 'And I have met Damon. Him I wouldn't trust as far as I could throw him, Bathyllus's brother or not.'

'Bathyllus genuinely didn't know he existed?'

'Uh-uh. They haven't been in touch since they were kids, and for all Bathyllus knew Damon was dead long ago.'

'Strange that they turned out so differently.'

'Yeah. Well, nurture versus nature, I suppose. Who's to say if it had been the other way round we wouldn't've had a sarky, sniffy, order-fixated major-domo called Damon?' I frowned. 'One thing, though. I'd bet another year's-worth of income that whoever killed the guy was looking for something, and Damon knows what it was.'

'How so?'

'According to Pudentius, the flat was a mess. Which, incidentally, Damon didn't mention. Pudentius thinks that was because the dead man put up a struggle before he was stabbed, but I don't think that'll wash. Oh, sure, he was badly bruised like he'd been in a fight, but he wasn't armed, and you'd expect, in that case, that his fists would show some damage.'

'And didn't they?'

'They could've done, and if so Pudentius's theory might be right. But in that case the Watch boys didn't spot it, or at least didn't mention it to Pudentius; I know, because I asked.' Shit; if we'd still had the body, and my smart-as-paint doctor son-in-law Clarus had been around, he could've given me chapter and verse on that one in two minutes flat and we'd be able to log it as a nem. con. However, there was no point in grieving, or blaming the squaddies for not checking; pre-Clarus I wouldn't have thought of it either. 'Me, I'd work on the assumption that he'd been systematically beaten up to get him to talk, and either before or after that the killers – plural, probably – tore the place apart.'

'You think they found it? Whatever "it" was?'

'Uh-uh.' I shook my head. 'And that's the interesting thing. They had everything going for them; just the one room to search, hardly any furniture, virtually all the time in the world with no interruptions. And if "it" was valuable – which it had to be – then Oplonius would've kept it by him to be sure it was safe. Even if he didn't give it up of his own accord finding it would be easy-peasie. Only for some reason they didn't. The fact that they, or their reps, were hanging around outside the place five days later proves that.'

'Perhaps he gave it to Damon to look after. He wasn't there, remember. And it would explain why he's in hiding now.'

'Yeah. I thought of that. But that won't wash either.'

'Really?' There was a touch of acid in her voice. 'And why not?'

I sighed. 'Come on, Perilla, use your head! If we're reading this right then they were both crooks. Damon certainly is. You think they'd trust each other to that extent? Chances are, if Oplonius had handed over anything of real value to that shifty bastard he would've been off and heading for the tall timber before you could say knife, and Oplonius couldn't've done a blind thing about it. He wouldn't've come back, either. Which he unquestionably did.'

She sniffed; not a lady to take contradiction in good part, Perilla. 'Very well, Marcus. Another suggestion. He'd made himself some sort of hiding place that wasn't obvious. Somewhere the killers were unlikely to look unless they knew it was there. Under the floorboards, for instance.'

'Yeah. Better. Oddly enough, I did think of that, and sure, it's possible. But I don't think it's likely.'

'Is that so, now?' You could've used the tone for pickling mummies. I ignored it.

'That is so. Look. Granted that Oplonius did have the guts to hold out on them to the end, which I'm not ready to do, and they knew whatever they were looking for was still on the premises, the fucking place was empty for five days. Right?'

'Yes. And don't swear. It isn't necessary.'

'Okay. So if they – and I use the plural just for the sake of argument – didn't want to risk another clandestine search, in depth this time, what's to stop them doing things legitimately? Go to Meleager and take out a short lease of the place themselves? Then they'd have all the time in the world. They could take the room apart right down to the bricks and mortar and no one would be any the wiser.'

'Perhaps they didn't think of that, dear. They probably don't have the advantage of your heated and tortuous imagination.'

That had come out sarky as hell; I'd got her, and she knew it. 'Come off it!' I said. 'It's the obvious solution. But as it was the flat was only re-let this morning, to a young couple with a baby. Or do you think they might be our perps heavily disguised, with the kid as the mastermind?'

'So why *are* the killers still keeping an eye on the place?'

Yeah; right. That was the question I'd been asking myself ever since I'd spotted the stake-out, and it was one that had me beat for an answer six ways from nothing. It couldn't be in the hopes that Damon would come back; no one would be that stupid, and Damon certainly wasn't, particularly if against all the odds he had the thing already. While if that was their hope, because the whatever-it-was was still hidden and Damon knew it, and they knew he knew it, then why the hell faff around? Why not just get inside, one way or another, like I said, and do the searching themselves?

We were floundering here. The bottom line was, nothing made sense, however you sliced it. And it had to, somehow or other, because like it or not that was the way things were.

'I don't know, lady,' I said. 'I just don't know.'

Bathyllus buttled in. Now the terrible truth was out and he no longer had to live a lie, as it were, he was almost back to normal. That sniff, when he'd left, had been music to my ears: Bathyllus without the aura of disapproval he exuded when he thought his dignity was being threatened just wasn't the happy bunny we'd come to know and love.

'That is dinner, sir,' he said.

'Great!' I got up; I hadn't had anything since breakfast barring the plate of nibbles at Renatius's, and I was starving. 'Incidentally, Bathyllus, I'll want to talk to your brother tomorrow as a matter of some urgency.' Too right I bloody would; the duplicitous bugger had been lying through his teeth, and the sooner I shook the truth out of him the better. 'That be okay?'

'Certainly, sir. You'll always find him at the tenement. He was most disinclined to go out, even before you gave him that instruction.' Yeah; and I didn't blame him. If I had a very pissed-off killer looking for me, not to mention the Aventine division of Rome's finest, I wouldn't be taking any morning strolls in Maecenas Gardens either.

Bathyllus had turned to go. Hell; I couldn't leave it there, it wouldn't be right. Certain things had to be said up-front, before this went any further.

'Hang on a moment, sunshine,' I said.

He turned back. 'Yes, sir?'

I hesitated; this was going to be tricky, but making sure it was understood might be important later. 'Uh, you do realise that that brother of yours isn't exactly, well –' I stopped.

'Not exactly honest. Or trustworthy. Yes, sir, I am completely aware of that.' Bathyllus cleared his throat. 'Still, he is my brother. Not the one I would have chosen, but all the same the only one I have. And that in itself has come about totally beyond my belief and expectations. Thank you for helping us, sir. Whatever the final outcome may be.'

'Fine. Fine,' I said. 'No problem. Just make sure he doesn't show his nose above the parapet, right, or we're all screwed.'

'Yes, sir. I'll do my best.'

As would we all. I only hoped it'd be good enough. Well, we'd just have to see what the future brought.

# 6.

For a start, perforce, at least where the next day was concerned, it brought the fulfilment of my promise to Mother re the erring Priscus. Not a job I was looking forward to, particularly at that early hour.

To make matters worse, Homer's Rosy-Fingered Dawn had taken the morning off and handed the weather side of things over to whatever god or goddess specialised in having it piss down hard from first light onwards. So there I was, breakfastless barring the roll I'd chewed on coming over, huddling under the shelter of my hooded cloak, and cached behind the wayside shrine opposite Mother's gate waiting for our lad to sally forth on his nefarious errand. Feeling a right fool about doing it, what was more. You don't normally get many passers-by in Mother's cul-de-sac off the main Head of Africa drag, especially at that time of the morning and in that kind of weather, but in the half hour or so that I'd been hanging around I'd been eyeballed suspiciously by two door-slaves, an itinerant knife-grinder, a home-going Lady of the Night, and a wall-eyed dog of indeterminate breed who evidently viewed the shrine as his own personal toilet and was clearly miffed to find it otherwise occupied. As a result, I was feeling distinctly jaundiced.

Given the weather conditions, I'd been doubtful whether Priscus would shove his nose outside his own front door at all that day; but sure enough the sun couldn't have moved by all that much above the lowering clouds when his caped and hooded figure came through the gate. I let him get three-quarters the way up the cul-de-sac, then fell in behind. At the junction with Head of Africa proper he turned left towards the centre of town, and I closed the gap slightly: now we were into the morning as such the streets were busying up, and I couldn't afford to lose him at this stage.

I needn't have worried. Priscus wasn't a fast mover at the best of times, and the wind blowing rain into our faces slowed him down even more. All the same, I almost missed it when he took a sudden right onto the Sacred Way and ducked into one of the little shops just past the crossing.

I didn't follow him in, of course, but it would be simple enough to hang about on the other side of the narrow street and watch events through the opening above the stone sill. *Antique shop* would've probably dignified the place – for pricey establishments like that you generally have to go to chi-chi shopping areas like the Saepta – but it looked pretty much typical of a lot of the businesses on the Sacred Way, particularly the ones on the Subura side of Head of Africa junction: a slightly seedy concern that stocked items that just made it out of the junk category into the curio bracket. Not Priscus's style at all, in other words, because the old guy was an antiquities snob. Maybe Mother was right to be suspicious...

Which was when I caught sight of the proprietor. Or propriet*rix*, rather, because she was definitely female: an olive-skinned, dark haired little stunner, maybe late twenties or early thirties. As I watched, she moved towards Priscus, enveloped him in a hug, and kissed him.

I moved quickly back into the shelter of a doorway, my mind spinning. Gods, this I just did not believe! No *way* did I believe it!

I looked again. They'd broken from the clinch, and the woman had stepped back and was holding both of Priscus's hands in hers, not letting go, pulling him towards the back of the shop, the part that I couldn't see. She laughed and said something, and Priscus nodded...

Jupiter!

To say that I was shocked wouldn't be the half of it, and deciding what to do next really, *really* needed thinking about. Reporting straight back to Mother as promised wasn't a viable option, for a start, because Mother would kill him out of hand. That was sure as tomorrow's sunrise. Also out was marching in there with all the righteous indignation of a stepson who's just caught his seriously-age-challenged stepfather intertwined with a woman who could've been his daughter; or rather – scrub that – with a woman who could've been his sodding *granddaughter.* And daughter-stroke-granddaughter the lady most emphatically was not, of that I was cast-iron certain. Priscus had been a widower when he and Mother had got hitched, sure, but the marriage had been childless, and it had been Priscus's only one; while given the man's observed character, interests and ingrained habit of total domesticity all the time I'd known him the chances that she was the product of a clandestine extramarital affair were so remote as to be practically non-existent. So bugger that theory for a game of soldiers.

All the same, the absolute bottom line, as Perilla had said, was that it was none of my business. Although I might stand back and goggle at the thought of Priscus engaging in an illicit sexual liaison what he got up to outside the confines of his own home was no concern of mine. And for the same reason getting him alone for a man-to-man, heart-to-heart talk in the hope of squaring things before Mother found out what was happening and reached for the disembowelling knife was out as well...

On the other hand, when Mother *did* find out, as she certainly would eventually, she'd assume, correctly, that I'd been covering up for the two-timing old bugger and add my guts to his. Accordingly, much as I would've liked just to turn a blind eye and let the pair of lovers get on with things wasn't a viable option either.

All of which left me, as far as I could see at present, with absolutely zilch where a possible future course of action was concerned. What we had here was definitely a no-win situation.

Fuck.

Well, whatever the answer might be there was nothing to be gained by hanging around here any longer. We'd just have to hope that, in the course of time, inspiration might strike. And that there would be a flock of flying pigs.

The rain was getting worse. I pulled the hood of my cloak further down over my face and headed for the Subura and Damon's tenement.

Sure enough, as Bathyllus had told me he would be, Damon was in residence, although when he opened the door at my third knock I had the distinct impression he wasn't exactly over the moon about seeing me. Which, under the circumstances, was completely understandable: if I'd told my long-lost brother's master, who was the only person standing between me and an extremely painful and unpleasant death as a runaway slave and murderer, a load of absolute porkies and he turned up unexpectedly on the doorstep practically first thing the day after then I'd feel a bit jittery myself.

Not that he showed it, the jitteriness, that is. I was beginning to have a healthy – and wary – respect for Brother Damon's ability to keep the head.

'Valerius Corvinus, sir,' he said. 'What a pleasure.'

'Yeah, right.' I pushed past him, went inside and sat down on the bed while he closed the door behind me. 'So tell me what the situation here really is.'

He looked blank. 'Come again?'

I sighed. 'Look, pal, I may be willing to break a few rules to help the brother of a much-valued major-domo out of a jam, but I'm neither especially gullible nor a complete brain-dead moron. First, I've talked to the Aventine Watch, who tell me that prior to being stabbed your master was given a serious going-over and the place torn apart stick by stick.

Obviously you didn't actually notice those little details when you got back from the cookshop, because if you had, being the truthful little bunny that you are, you'd've mentioned them, right?' He said nothing. 'Second, when I'm up having a look at the place I notice a pair of very doubtful characters hanging about outside obviously taking a keen personal interest in things, and who cut and run when I try to have a word with them.' Still no reaction. 'So my guess, based on this and other evidence, is that your simple-wool-merchant story is a load of fucking hogwash; that your Oplonius – and by extension you – had something valuable you wanted to hide and a certain party or parties unknown took serious exception to the fact. Now, shall we start again with the truth or should I just hand you over to the Watch and let them sort it out? Go ahead; your decision.'

He sat down on the stool. 'Fair enough, squire,' he said. 'Maybe I didn't tell you the whole truth after all.' Hah! Our master of the understatement here could've given Perilla lessons on that score. 'I'd my reasons, believe me.'

'Is that so, now?' Damn right he did; that much I *would* believe. 'The floor's yours, sunshine. Convince me.'

'There's a –' He stopped, took another deep breath, and started again. 'Look, Master was from Padua, and he was a wool merchant, okay? That's straight up, I told you no lies there, gods' truth, right?'

'Go on.'

'Yeah, well, that's just the problem right there, you see. It's the going on bit that's tricky. There's someone else involved, someone besides me and the master who can be hurt bad if things go wrong. And that's the last thing he'd've wanted.'

'You're breaking my heart, pal,' I said. 'Get on with it.'

'You mind if I have a drink first?' He reached for the wine jug on the table, poured and drank. I waited until he'd put the cup down and wiped his mouth with the back of his hand.

'Okay,' he said. 'Here's how it is. There's this young girl. In Padua. Name of Postumia Matronilla.'

'Is that so, now?'

'Corvinus, this is all above board, I swear to you by every god there is, right?' I said nothing. 'Only it wasn't my secret to tell, see. Not just for the asking. This girl and the master, they were planning to marry, only her family weren't having none of it. The father – well, he's one of the local magistrates and rich as Croesus. He wanted better.'

'Uh-huh.' I kept my face expressionless.

'She's a lovely girl, Mistress Postumia, and she loved the master. So they were going to run away together, secret, like. Only the father, he finds out and stops them.'

Yeah, well, that was understandable, I suppose: no rich daddy with political and social ambitions wants his daughter hitched to a low-grade no-account merchant, and Paduans as a rule have a reputation for being pretty strait-laced.

'So how come Oplonius ended up in Rome?' I said.

'Him and the mistress made the plan together. He was to go ahead, she'd get away as soon as she could give her parents the slip and come and join him. They'd arranged a place to meet up – the Temple of Saturn on Market Square, she'd heard of that – and he'd be sure to be there at mid-day every day to check. Which he was. She gave him a necklace to sell so they'd have something to live on while they waited for her father to come round.'

Right. Now we were getting to the nitty-gritty. 'A necklace,' I said.

'I told you, old man Postumius is rolling. She had it from him for her fourteenth birthday. How much he paid for it I don't know exactly, but it must've been fifty thousand at least.'

I whistled: fifty thousand sesterces was serious, serious gravy. Even if Oplonius got only half of that – which he probably would've done, at most, because without evidence of provenance no reputable jeweller would touch the deal, even in Rome – the two of them could get along pretty well until Daddy could be suitably worked on. Despite myself – and I really, really mean that, here, considering that I knew the slippery bastard, even on short acquaintance, as well as I did – I was beginning to be convinced. At any rate, so far, it all hung together.

'And then Pappa Postumius tracked Oplonius down, right?' I said.

'That's it. How exactly I don't know. The mistress wouldn't've told him, that's for sure, but somebody did. Probably one of her maids. Anyways, all he needed to know was that the master had gone to Rome and that he'd be at Saturn's temple every day at noon, and that was that. He sent a couple of his people here, they hung around the temple until they spotted him, then followed him back to the flat and killed him.'

'So who were those people, exactly?'

Damon shrugged. 'Dunno. Could've been her brothers. She has two, both older than her. But that doesn't really matter, does it?'

Maybe not; still, he wasn't off the hook quite yet. 'So tell me about this necklace,' I said. 'I'm assuming they didn't find it.'

'No. No, they didn't.'

'So you've still got it?'

'Uh-uh.' He shook his head. 'The master sold it a couple of days before he died.'

'Who to?'

Another shrug. 'Search me. I wasn't there at the time, and he didn't tell me nothing. Me, I'm just a slave, after all. Maybe to a jeweller, maybe he did a private deal with someone he met.'

'Okay. So what happened to the money?'

'Can't help you there either. He didn't bring it back with him, 's all I know.' Yeah, well, at least that made sense: you don't hide twenty-odd thousand sesterces under your mattress, not if you're putting up in an Aventine tenement and want to hang on to it. As events had proved. 'He most like lodged it with the banker that was holding his travel money.'

'Which was who?'

His fist came down on the table, hard enough to make the empty wine-cup topple.

'The hell with this!' he said. 'You're just not listening to me, are you? Look, I *don't fucking know*, right? If I did I'd tell you, and at the least we could get it back to the mistress. But I don't, because like I say the master kept that side of things to himself. He'd a business near Market Square, that much I do know, but that's as far as I go.'

Not exactly helpful: the streets around the centre have been the main stamping-ground for bankers ever since the first one set up his table in the Square itself centuries back. Well, we'd just have to hope that what Watch commander Pudentius had said about the honesty of bankers was true, and the guy would come forward of his own free will.

Meanwhile...

'Something I still don't understand, though,' I said, 'is the circumstantial stuff.'

'Sorry.' He frowned. 'I'm not with you there.'

'You claim you got back after your master was dead, right? And that the guys who'd done it were gone.'

'That's right.' He was definitely wary now.

'Okay. But that doesn't make sense, does it? I mean, if that was the case then we have three possible scenarios.' I counted them off on my fingers. 'First, they'd got what they came for, one way or another, and left. Only that can't be right, because you say Oplonius had already sold the necklace and the money – presumably – was with his banker and out of their reach. Plus the fact that, six days down the line, they're out there watching the place. Why should they bother?' He said nothing. 'That gives us scenario two.' I held down the second finger. 'Oplonius holds out to the end, tells them nothing, and despite the fact that they've searched the place thoroughly and not found a bean they still think it's hidden on the premises. That'd explain the stake-out, sure, to some degree at least, but not the fact that the flat's been empty for five days and they haven't had the gumption to come back and do a thorough job. Not to mention that if they knew about him then they sure as hell knew about you. Which leads us to scenario three.' I bent the third finger. 'They're waiting for you to come back in your turn because they think you've either got the necklace yourself or that you know where it is.'

'Why in hell would I come back? If I had the thing already there'd be no –'

'No point in coming back at all. Right; agreed. And the same goes for if you knew the hiding place all along, because you'd already have picked the thing up and be heading for the tall timber. With, no doubt, the most honourable of intentions re returning it to sweet little what's-her-name, granted, but still. Staking the place out would be a complete waste of time and effort. So that scenario's a bummer as well. You see the problem? So what we need is a fourth scenario. One that actually works.'

His face shut. 'Yeah, well, maybe so,' he said. 'But I can't help you there, sir, because that's how it happened.'

Hell's bells; I was flogging a dead horse here, and no mistake. 'Okay, pal,' I said. 'Have it your own way. But something is screwy, I'm certain of that much, at least. Somewhere along the line for some reason you're still lying through your fucking teeth, and we both know it.' He shot me a nasty look, but said nothing. 'We'll get there eventually, don't you worry.' I stood up. 'I'll see you around. Have a nice day.'

There wasn't anything I could constructively do at present, so I went home. Bathyllus met me at the door.

'There are two...men...to see you, sir,' he said. 'In the garden. They arrived just after you left, but they insisted on waiting.'

'Is that so, now?' I handed him my cloak. '*Men*, eh?' In Bathyllus-speak, particularly when the word was sandwiched between distinct pauses, that meant plain-tunic tradesmen at best. And this time not even that: the fact that they were twiddling their thumbs out in the garden rather than inside the house implied that he thought that as soon as his back was turned the buggers would have it away with whatever they could lift.

I went through to see what new joys fate had in store for me. Well, at least he'd gone the length of taking them out a couple of wicker chairs to sit on. Ever the conscientious major-domo, Bathyllus, even when the visitors didn't fit within his parameters of social acceptability.

I knew who they were the moment I'd cleared the portico. My two incompetent watchers from the Aventine tenement.

My feet slowed, and the two guys stood up. Yeah, just as I remembered them; we had a pair of prime heavies here, and no mistake. No wonder Bathyllus had put the bastards in virtual quarantine.

So not, I would think, candidates for well-born young Postumia Matronilla's brothers. Still, as Damon had said, their precise identity wasn't important.

'Uh...you're from Postumius in Padua, right?' I said. 'You can start by explaining–'

'Who the fuck's Postumius?' the guy on the left said. 'Come on, Corvinus, don't play games. You know perfectly well who we are.'

I stared at him. Sure, now I came to look more closely his face was familiar, but I couldn't place it at all. Even so, the very fact that he'd –

'The boss wants to see you,' the other guy said. 'Right away. And he is not a happy bunny.'

'Is that so, now?' I said. 'And what boss would that be, then?'

Heavy Number One – the half-familiar one – chuckled. 'Always the joker,' he said. 'The boss. Sempronius Eutacticus. Remember him? 'Course you do. And like my friend here says: you, pal, are in serious schtook.'

I swallowed. Uh-oh. Sempronius Eutacticus, eh? Right. Right. Now *there* was a name I'd never wanted to hear again, far less renew acquaintance with the crooked bastard it belonged to. And now that I had a context to fit him in, I recognised Laughing Boy here from the last time our paths had crossed six years back.

Oh, shit.

# 7.

So we set out for the Pincian, where Eutacticus had his not-so-humble little mansion, with me carefully flanked and watched every step of the way.

I was seriously worried. This did not look good, because Sempronius Eutacticus was bad, bad news. To say the guy was a crook was like saying that Hannibal had shown pretty fair promise as a military man, and as far as range and complexity were concerned his organisation had the imperial civil service beaten into a cocked hat. Added to which, or rather as a corollary of it, he'd probably sent more poor bastards to swim the Tiber in concrete sandals or buried them where no one would find them for a couple of thousand years than I'd had hot dinners. The last time we'd met he'd twisted my arm to find out what had happened to his missing stepson, and although I'd solved the case as a result he'd ended up minus one favourite daughter. Not my fault, as it happened, but when you're dealing with an evil-minded homicidal control-freak like Eutacticus reason, logic and the correct allocation of blame tend to get lost along the way. I didn't know what connection he had with the business of Oplonius's murder, but obviously judging by events his finger was very deeply in the pie somewhere or other. And just the thought of that sent shivers down my spine.

We'd done the trip in silence: neither of my flanking heavies, evidently, was a sparkling or eager conversationalist, and I'd matters of my own to think about, largely concerning concrete sandals and unmarked graves. Finally the familiar gateposts of Eutacticus's place with their dinky tritons perched atop – seriously OTT even by generous *nouveaux-riches* Pincian standards – hove into view. Then we were past the doorkeeper-gorilla, up the gravelled drive, and through the bronze-studded front door. I'd expected, like last time, to be taken up to the great man's study, but we kept to the ground floor, all the way to the colonnaded private garden at the back.

Eutacticus was standing on the lip of the ornamental fish-pond, with a slave beside him holding a tray of meatballs. Raw meatballs. He took one of them and threw it into the pond.

Beneath the surface, dark shapes converged on the splash and the water boiled, briefly.

He turned.

'You took your time getting here, Corvinus,' he said.

Heavy Number Two's assessment of him not being a happy bunny was evidently smack on the button. If anyone ever looked seriously unchuffed then Sempronius Eutacticus was it.

Fuck. Double fuck.

'Ah...yeah,' I said. 'Yeah. Possibly.'

He indicated the pond. 'Know what those are?'

'Uh-huh.' I tried to keep my voice steady. 'I've, ah, met up with them before. Moray eels, right?'

'Correct. Want to feed them?' My blood ran cold. He chuckled. Not a very reassuring sound, the way it came out; me, if I were giving a prize for the one with the better sense of humour, I'd go for the eel. 'With one of these.' He picked up a ball from the tray and handed it to me. 'Go on. Throw it.'

Bastard; he'd done that deliberately. I tossed the meatball towards the circling shapes, and the water boiled again.

Eutacticus took the napkin that was draped over the slave's shoulder and wiped his hands clean.

'You two,' he said to my pair of minders. 'Get lost. But not too far away. You' – that was to me – 'over here. We need to talk.'

There were a couple of chairs in the shade of an arbour formed by a trellised vine. We sat.

'Okay,' Eutacticus said. 'So what's your connection with Oplonius?'

'Ah...strangely enough, that's the question I was going to ask you, pal,' I said.

'That so, now?' His top lip lifted slightly to one side. Maybe he intended it as a smile, but the fact that all it did was to reveal one of his incisors did a lot to spoil the effect. Basking crocodiles came to mind. 'Interesting. Let's just say I asked first so I have priority, right?'

'His slave Damon is my major-domo's long-lost brother,' I said. 'Bathyllus – that's the major-domo – had him squirrelled away in –' I stopped myself just in time; maybe, under the circumstances, handing Eutacticus the information concerning Damon's present whereabouts wasn't such a clever idea. 'In wherever he was hidden. Seemingly, the guy's master had been stabbed to death a few days before, cause unknown, perp or perps unknown.' I gave him a quick sideways glance, but his face was expressionless. If you didn't count the crocodile expression, that was. 'He ran, Bathyllus hid him, I got interested, that's all. And that's about it, really.'

'You got interested.' You didn't get any deader-pan than that.

'Yeah, well, you know me,' I said. 'Can't keep my nose out of things that aren't really my business.'

'Quite,' he said. 'So you'd no dealings with him while he was alive?'

'Oplonius? Uh-uh. Never even saw the guy, alive or dead.'

'This slave of his. You know where to find him?'

Bugger; well, I couldn't say the question was unexpected. 'That might be tricky. According to Bathyllus, he moves around a lot.'

'Pity.' He let the word hang just long enough to show me he knew I was telling porkies. 'Fair enough, we'll leave it. For the present, anyway. He happen to mention a necklace?'

'Uh... Yeah.' Oh, bugger: so *that* was what all this was about! I started to sweat. 'Yeah, he did, in fact.'

'That's good.' The top lip lifted again. 'Then maybe we're getting somewhere after all. He knows where it is?'

'Oplonius sold it the day before he died. At least, that's what Damon claims.'

'You don't believe him?'

I shrugged. 'Me, I'd take whatever the slippery bugger told me with a very large pinch of salt. But it's certainly possible. Maybe even likely.'

'Now that would be a *real* pity.' He frowned. 'So you're sure whoever killed that bastard Oplonius doesn't have it?'

Everything went very still. Something went *gloop* in the pond. Possibly one of the eels varying its diet courtesy of a passing frog.

'Hang on a minute, pal,' I said. 'Let's go back a bit here. Are you saying your lads *didn't*? Kill Oplonius, that is.'

Eutacticus grunted. 'They might've done, sure,' he said. 'That's if they'd tracked the fucker down in time and got my necklace before someone else did the job for them. But no, as a matter of fact they didn't. That what you thought?'

'Uh...yeah. Yeah, it is. More or less.' Jupiter! 'I'd good reason to, hadn't I? When I went to the tenement the buggers were hanging around outside mugging it like bad extras in a tragedy, then when I tried to talk to them they took off like they'd been greased.'

‘Put that down to surprise, Corvinus. They’d been told to keep an eye on the place, nail Oplonius when he went in or came out, whichever, and bring him back here relatively undamaged. That’s about as much detail as those boys can hold in their heads at one time.’ Despite myself, I grinned. ‘Only what happens is five minutes after they turn up this mad purple-striper comes straight at them out of nowhere and blows their cover six ways from nothing. What the hell would you expect them to do? They didn’t even know at the time that Oplonius was dead; he could’ve been upstairs and seen the whole thing from his window. It was just lucky Satrius recognised you.’

Satrius? Oh. Right. Heavy Number One, Laughing Boy; I remembered the name now. And ‘lucky’ wasn’t exactly the word I’d use, not from my side of the fence. Witness my being hauled up to the Pincian and threatened with playing dinner to Bastard Eutacticus’s piscine menagerie. More important, though, and back-tracking again...

‘Uh...you said “*my* necklace,’ I said.

Eutacticus frowned. ‘That’s right. So?’

‘It’s, like, yours then.’ I had to quash the sudden inward vision of Eutacticus sporting a snazzy ruby-and-emerald necklace plus matching tiara, earrings and carefully-coiffeured wig. ‘Your property. It belongs to you.’

He was staring at me.

‘Naturally it does,’ he said. ‘Who the hell else would it belong to?’

Good question. So much for the star-crossed lovers saga. I felt my teeth gritting; next time I saw Damon, I would kill the lying bastard myself. He wouldn’t die quickly, either.

'Ah...so you haven't heard of a guy in Padua by the name of Postumius with a marriageable daughter called Matronilla?' I said. 'Just checking, you understand.'

'No, I fucking haven't. Why should I?'

'No reason. None at all.' I told him. The whole story. Or at least the Alexandrian tunic-ripper fable that Damon had foisted off on me. When you actually came to put it into your own words it sounded thin as hell. Evidently Eutacticus thought so too, because he laughed; genuinely laughed, and that's something I never expected from that humourless bugger.

It wasn't a pleasant sound or sight, mind.

'You've been had, Corvinus, right, left and centre,' he said. 'Me, I'd be ashamed.'

'Yeah.' Well, he hadn't met Damon, had he? Evidently where the rogue brother was concerned all the energy and brain-power that in Bathyllus's case made him the administrative genius that he was had gone into forming the archetypal con-man. 'Never mind that now. So. You going to tell me just how Oplonius *did* get his hands on this necklace of yours?'

'It was an anniversary present for Occusia.' His wife: I'd met her the time of the missing stepson incident, a small, dumpy, ultra-respectable, old-style Roman matron, and about as unlikely a mate for Rome's top criminal mastermind as you could ever imagine. 'I bought it through a colleague of mine in Brundisium.' *Colleague*. Right. Right. Well, whoever the guy was, I'd bet a gold piece to a handful of beans he wouldn't've been a member of the Brundisium Jewellers' Guild. 'Over two hundred years old, used to belong to Philistis, Hiero of Syracuse's wife.' He shot me a sideways look. 'The necklace, not the colleague.'

'Uh-huh. Got you.' Jupiter! First the laugh, now a joke. Or what passed for one. Eutacticus was certainly lightening up. Maybe it had been the fun of throwing meat to the eels. 'And Oplonius stole it, yes?'

'It was pure bad luck. The courier who was bringing it to me stopped at an inn and got himself robbed.' I winced; in so few words are whole tragedies writ. I'd bet the unfortunate courier was now very much an ex-employee, wherever Eutacticus's lads had stashed him. 'Turned out later that this Oplonius bastard and his pal – that'd be your major-domo's brother – worked a nice little scam in that direction. They pick a likely mark, tag along with him for part of the way to get acquainted and overnight wherever he puts up. Then that evening they sucker him into sharing a flask of wine, slip him a go-to-sleep googly and rob him blind. After which the pair of them vanish into the night with the loot.' He sucked appreciatively on a tooth. 'Not bad, as amateur scams go. As long as you target low-grade punters and move around a lot, if you're careful there'll be no come-back. Only this time the bastards overreached themselves.'

Yeah, right: that I *would* believe. When they'd found out what they'd got – and I'd bet Damon's estimate of fifty thousand for a two hundred-year-old antique which had belonged to a reigning queen was well on the low side – plus, and far, far worse, who the courier had been taking it to, they'd've had conniptions.

Bad luck was right – and not just for Eutacticus and the courier, either. Oplonius and Damon would've known with horrible certainty that they were dead men walking. No wonder they'd been keeping their heads down.

Still, it left us with the great unanswered question: if our pair of watchers – aka Eutacticus's Satrius and his mate – weren't the killers, then who was? And how the hell did they fit in with this necklace business?

'So I want to talk to this slave,' Eutacticus said.

Shit.

'Ah...I told you,' I said. 'I don't know where he is. He moves around.'

'Corvinus, you're not listening, are you? Read my fucking lips. I want. To talk. To the slave. Okay, Oplonius might've sold the necklace already, but I can work round that.' Yeah, I'd bet he could: should the unfortunate buyer be offered the choice of either giving up Eutacticus's wife's birthday prezzie of his own free will or spending the happy occasion on crutches drinking the toast through a straw the poor bugger wouldn't be able to agree fast enough. 'And if by any chance he didn't before he was stiffed then I'm sure his erstwhile colleague will know of its whereabouts.'

'Not if whoever killed him has it, he won't,' I said. 'Now your pair of stooges are off the list of possible perps that scenario is back on the table again.'

He looked at me pityingly. 'Come on, Corvinus! You're supposed to be the great brain. If that'd been the case your Damon would've told you so straight off, or better still not have mentioned the thing at all. Why faff around?' That stopped me. True, and certainly something to think about: why *had* Damon brought the necklace into the story? 'Anyway, I'm going to work on the reasonable assumption that he knows damn well where it is until he convinces me different.'

By which time, no doubt, the poor bastard would be lucky to have a single intact bone in his body, sight in both eyes, all his bodily parts attached, and the ability, should he ever have the opportunity in future, to reproduce himself. And much as I was beginning to feel seriously pissed off with Damon I wouldn't've wished all that on him.

Well, not quite *all* that, anyway.

'Hold on, pal,' I said. 'I hate to bring this up' – absolute truth; you didn't cross Sempronius Eutacticus on his home ground if you'd a single ounce of sanity in your makeup – 'but you owe me. In fact, you owe me twice now, once for that racehorse business and again for the business of your missing stepson. Simple old-fashioned Roman *do ut des*, and now I'm calling in the payback.'

He was staring at me like I'd crawled out from under a rock and he was wondering how best to rise up and smite me dead.

'You *what?*' he said.

'Listen. Here's the pitch. We do a deal; I talk to Damon, see if I can get the truth out of him about this necklace of yours.' Touch wood, it shouldn't be all that difficult, given that I'd tell him in no uncertain terms what the alternative was. 'If by any chance he does have it, or knows where it is, and hands it over, then that's the end of it. No comeback, no recriminations, above all no concrete sandals. Agreed?'

'And if he doesn't?'

'Yeah, well, we'll just have to hope you're right about him knowing, won't we?' If that happened I could always turn my back on him for a second, give him the chance to split and run. He wouldn't get very far, sure, but at least I'd've done my best. 'We'll cross that particular bridge when we come to it.' I held out my hand. 'Deal?'

'On one condition. You go now, and my lads tag along.'

'That's two conditions.'

'All right, so it's two. I'm not having you tip that crooked bastard the wink and let him slip away this time around.'

'Would I do that?'

He gave me his crocodile-fang smile. 'Too fucking right you would, and we both know it. So I'm going to make sure it doesn't happen.'

Bugger. 'Fine,' I said. Well, I'd tried my best for the little rat. He was on his own now, and serve him right. Mind you, it might not be altogether a bad arrangement: having two of Eutacticus's brightest and best glowering at him in the background as a reminder of what happened to duplicitious slaves who continued to play fast and loose with the truth might make all the difference.

'Fair enough.' My hand was still stretched out. He shook it. 'Deal.' He turned his head in the direction of the house and shouted: 'Satrius! Largus!'

My two heavies must've been kicking their heels just inside. They came through the portico and lumbered over.

'He giving you trouble, boss?' Satrius glared at me under brows like a couple of mating earwigs.

'No. I've a job for you. I want you to go with Corvinus here and watch him have a talk with Oplonius's slave. Just watch him, okay? Don't interfere, and no rough stuff.'

'Got you, boss,' Heavy Number Two – Largus – flexed his fingers. 'You're sure, though? Bastard might need a little encouragement.'

'I'm sure. If he hands over the necklace then and there, fine, you take it and leave like lambs. If not, whatever he says, you bring him back here.'

'What about Corvinus? You want him back as well?'

Eutacticus gave me a long, considering look, and I held my breath. Finally –

'No,' he said. 'No, I don't think we'll be needing Valerius Corvinus any further. He can go where he likes.' I exhaled. Thank the gods for that, at least. 'All that clear?'

'As crystal, boss.' Satrius turned to me. 'Let's go, pal.'

. . .

We got to the tenement without incident, and again with a total lack of conversation. I led the way up to the flat, knocked and waited. No answer. I tried a second time, then a third...

'Bugger this,' Satrius grunted. He pushed me aside, raised his industrial-grade-sandalled foot to the level of the lock, and drove it at the door like a pile-driver.

The lock burst with the sound of splintering wood and tortured metal and the door sprang open. We went inside.

The flat was empty. All that was there, resting on the table, was the illicitly-purloined ham-bone, picked clean.

Fuck.

# 8.

Bathyllus was waiting at the door for me, as usual.

'Okay,' I said, handing him my cloak. 'Where is he?'

The little guy looked blank. 'I'm sorry, sir?'

'Where the bloody hell is your brother?'

'Ah...at the tenement, sir. You saw him yourself this morning.'

'The first time I called round, yeah.' I picked up the full cup of wine from the tray he'd set down on the hall table and drank half of it in a oner. 'The second time, which was about an hour ago, he'd gone, and the flat was empty.'

'*What?*'

I didn't answer, just took the cup and accompanying wine jug through to the living room, Bathyllus trailing me like a lost sheep.

'He probably just decided he needed a breath of fresh air, sir,' he said. Bleated. 'It's very hard for him, being cooped up there all day. I really wouldn't be too–'

'Look, sunshine,' I said. 'The bugger has gone. Gone as in disappeared, decamped, done a split, scarpered, headed for the tall timber, any fucking synonym you like. The flat's empty; he didn't leave so much as an old sock. And the really embarrassing thing was, I'd brought company. Two of Sempronius Eutacticus's lads. You remember Eutacticus?' Bathyllus blenched; clearly, he did. 'They were not happy bunnies, and when they get back to their boss and tell him the glad news, which they'll no doubt already have done, that evil-minded bastard will be spitting nails.'

'Er...where exactly does Eutacticus come into this, sir?'

'Long story.' I sank the other half of the wine and refilled the cup. 'Just take it from me that he has a vested interest in finding your brother, and if he manages it before I do you, pal, are going to be short one sibling. So where has he gone? Do you have any idea at all?'

'Of course I don't!'

'Fair enough. Well, at least he can't stay holed up for long, not without ready cash, and he can't have much of–' I stopped; Bathyllus had gone even paler. 'Come on, little guy! You're not going to tell me you were stupid enough to give him that money I gave you for the rent and so on.'

'Ah...'

Gods. Sweet, bloody, immortal gods. Relatively speaking, it hadn't been a lot, true, but in the sort of places he'd be frequenting it'd be enough to tide him over for quite some time. And I'd bet that where urban survival skills went Damon would be up there with the best of them. So what the hell did I do now?

'Is the mistress in?' I said.

'Upstairs in her study, sir. Oh, before I forget. A message came for you via Commander Lippillus from a Lucius Pudentius of the Aventine Watch.' He took a sealed flimsy from his belt and handed it over. 'The messenger said there was no reply.'

I took the flimsy, broke the seal, and read.

Shit.

'Is it to do with Damon, sir?' Bathyllus said anxiously.

'Ah...no, little guy. No, it isn't. Or not directly.'

I picked up the full cup and took it upstairs to the lady's study. This needed talking over.

Perilla was sitting at her desk doing something complicated involving several open book-rolls and a note tablet.

'Hello, dear,' she said when I came in. 'You're back early. What did those two men want? Bathyllus said you'd gone off with them, and that you didn't seem too happy.'

'Yeah.' I set the wine cup and jug down on the table and stretched out on the reading-couch. I felt drained; drained and sick 'They were Sempronius Eutacticus's boys.'

She put the pen down and stared at me with wide-open eyes.

'Oh, Marcus!' she said.

'Right. Turns out that Bathyllus's brother and his late master took something belonging to him, and he wants it back.' I told her the whole story, including Damon's little foray into the realm of romantic fiction. 'Problem is,' I finished, 'Damon must've realised things were about to get too hot for comfort and done another runner; not that that'll help him, because when Eutacticus tracks him down – which he will – however things pan out, at the end of the day he'll peg the bugger out for the crows.' I hesitated; this was where things got sticky. 'Only that's not the worst of it. I've just had a message from the Aventine Watch commander. Seemingly, the banker Oplonius used has come forward and the guy's total deposited sum was two hundred and eighty-three sesterces. That's all there was; no valuables, no sealed packages left for safe keeping. Nothing. Zilch.'

'So?'

'Perilla, Damon said Oplonius had sold the necklace, right? Even if he'd only got a quarter of what it was worth we're talking well into six figures. And if he hadn't sold it, and didn't keep it by him, the probability was he'd left it for safety as an anonymous package in the banker's strongbox. Now we know for sure that he didn't do that either; which means that it's still out there somewhere, and the chances are that, unless his killers took it, Damon either knows the location or he has it himself.'

'Marcus, I'm afraid I don't quite see what's worrying you here. If Damon can produce the necklace after all, then surely that's good, isn't it? You say you have an agreement with Eutacticus that he'll let bygones be bygones if it's returned.' I had my mouth open to speak. 'Yes, I know the situation's changed slightly, but Eutacticus isn't an unreasonable man and–'

'Jupiter, Perilla! Listen to yourself!'

'Yes, well, not completely unreasonable. And as you say he does owe you two considerable favours. I'm sure you can talk him round.'

'Maybe I can,' I said. 'I'll definitely try; I'll go up to the Pincian first thing tomorrow and give it a go. But whether or not Damon has the necklace isn't the point any more. Or not the whole point.'

'So what is?'

Okay, so here we went. I took a fortifying swig from the wine cup. This wasn't going to be pleasant.

'Leaving the inconsistencies aside,' I said, 'when we thought what turned out to be Eutacticus's men were the killers things were pretty straightforward, right? They were still after whatever they'd been looking for – we know now it was the necklace – and the likelihood was that Damon was the key to finding it.'

'Yes. So?'

'Lady, think! Because they weren't the killers after all, they were irrelevant. *Are* irrelevant. Take them out of the picture and all we have left is the murder itself and Damon's own version of it; that he came up and found the killers gone and his master lying dead on the floor. Oh, sure, he changed his story to fit what I found out from Pudentius and spun me a new tale involving the necklace, but at root it was the same one: he wasn't there when the murder happened.'

'Marcus, dear–'

'Only now it turns out that, despite Damon's claim to the contrary, Oplonius didn't sell the necklace after all; he couldn't have done, or he'd've had the money from the sale. And if he didn't deposit the thing with the banker, which again now we know for a fact, then presumably he kept it with him and hid it somewhere in the flat. Somewhere pretty damned effective, because his killers searched the place from top to bottom and still didn't find it. Which is odd, right?'

'Odd, certainly. But not impossible.'

'Granted. Except that it assumes three things: that Oplonius had the guts to hold out to the end under intensive questioning, that his killers were seriously lacking in imagination, and most of all – because they must've known about Damon – that they were pretty damn stupid not to wait around until he got back from wherever he'd gone and grill him like they'd grilled his boss. Oh, sure, like you say, none of that's impossible. But the more oddities there are as a possible scenario the less likely it gets. And now, when we start getting contrary information from elsewhere and his story begins seriously to come apart at the edges, Damon suddenly decides to cut and run. All that suggest anything?'

She was looking at me in horror. 'Oh, Marcus, no!'

'Right. That there weren't any murderers as such at all; Damon killed Oplonius for the necklace himself. It's the simplest explanation, it fits the known facts, and it clears up all the oddities problems at a stroke. If we hadn't been blinkered by the fact that he was Bathyllus's brother we'd've thought of that straight off, at least as a viable possibility. As it was, untrustworthy bugger though he quickly turned out to be, we gave him the benefit of the doubt.'

Perilla was quiet for a long time. Then she said: 'How are we going to tell Bathyllus?'

I shook my head. 'I don't know. That's what's worrying me, too. Oh, sure, he's under no illusions about Damon's character, so that part'll come as no surprise. But after all they are brothers. And whether Eutacticus takes a hand in things or not, as a thief, murderer and runaway slave the guy is for the chop three times over. There's absolutely nothing we can do about that.'

'I suppose not.' Perilla was twisting a lock of her hair, always a sign that there was something cerebral going on underneath it. 'Marcus, don't you find it strange that Damon mentioned the necklace at all? I mean, *as* a necklace. He didn't have to. Oh, yes, I know, after you faced him with the business of the search he'd obviously have to admit that Oplonius was hiding something of value. But why what it really was? In fact, why not a large sum of money? Surely that would've been just as plausible.'

'Yeah, I've thought about that.' I frowned. 'Eutacticus made the same point, more or less. Thing is, right from the start Damon's kept as near to the truth as possible. Which is probably why the bastard is such a good liar, because the fake story isn't cut from whole cloth. Sure, his master died from a stab wound, but that's all he says initially, because to have mentioned the beating and the search would've led to unwelcome questions. Then, when I get that part of it from Pudentius and add the business of the watchers on my own account, he changes the story to fit – but again, just far enough. I mean, given you've got a wealthy young girl involved then why not a valuable piece of female jewellery? And if that, why not a necklace? It's all logical, so it works, it's convincing. And he wasn't to know I had any connection at all with Eutacticus, was he? So the chances of the necklace per se becoming significant were pretty slim.'

'What will he do now, do you think?'

I shook my head. 'Jupiter knows. He's up the creek without a paddle. Without even a boat. For a start, he can't sell the necklace: it's a two-hundred-year-old antique, it was made for royalty so it'll be Valuable with a capital V, and I'd bet there isn't a fence in Rome, let alone a reputable jeweller, who'd touch it with a long stick and gloves. Particularly with him as the seller. Oplonius was a hick provincial, or that's the impression I get, but at least he was free-born middle class. Damon's a slave, obviously a slave, brand, nicked ear, the lot, and he hasn't got a hope in hell. Any legit dealer he approached would hand him over to the authorities straight off without even stopping to think, and if he tried to fence the thing on the black market chances are with his contacts Eutacticus would know within the hour and Damon would be dead in two.'

'He could leave Rome. Try somewhere else.'

'Uh-uh. Same applies. And in a smaller place he'd just stick out all the more. Plus the fact – a slave on his own? Without manumission papers? How long do you think he'd last before some honest citizen turned him in?'

'Mm.' She was still twisting the lock of hair. 'So what can we do for him? For Bathyllus's sake?'

I shrugged. 'Not a lot,' I said. 'I told you, I'll go and have another talk with Eutacticus tomorrow.' Gods! Now that was something I *definitely* wasn't looking forward to! 'He'll have put the word out that Damon's to be found and brought back, naturally, that goes without saying, and the bugger's got as much hope of staying lost as whistling Pindar's Second Pythian through his ears. So it's what happens when Eutactus does get his hands on him that's important. My hope is that things won't reach that stage; that once he's sat down and had a good think he'll realise his safest course of action is to get back in touch with Bathyllus.'

'Even though we know – and Bathyllus will know – that he's very probably a murderer?'

'Come on, Perilla! He's a con-man to his fingertips. A professional. Even if he's guessed that he's under suspicion now I'll bet he firmly believes he can talk his way out of it.'

'What about the necklace?'

'That's non-negotiable, absolutely; unless he's a complete fool, which he isn't, he'll know that now. If he's got it, as I hope he has – and I agree with Eutacticus, to my mind, that's practically a cert – then it'll have to go back straight off, no deals, no faffing around. And if he comes out the other end alive and with everything attached he can count himself bloody lucky.'

'But if he hasn't? Got it, I mean, or know where it is.'

'Then I'm afraid he's toast; Eutacticus will see to that. Unfortunate, but sadly true.' I stood up. 'Well, there's no point in putting things off, is there? We may as well get it over with.'

Perilla looked worried. 'You're going to tell Bathyllus now?'

'He has to know sooner or later, and this time he's involved in the case. Keeping him in the dark wouldn't be fair.' I opened the door, went outside, leaned over the banister and yelled: '*Bathyllus!*'

He'd been waiting at the stair's foot, and from the way he sidled into the room, eyes averted, it was pretty clear he'd a fair suspicion at least why I'd called him up.

Fuck; I hated this.

'Yes, sir,' he said.

I lay back down on the reading couch and took a deep breath. Here we went.

'Ah...the mistress and I have been talking things over, little guy,' I said. 'Apropos developments. Regarding, uh, your brother's disappearance and so on. Now don't take this the wrong way, because I'm sure there's another explanation for it that's completely innocent, but all the same under the circumstances you have to realise there is the outside possibility that –'

'Damon isn't a murderer, sir.'

Oh, shit.

'I'm sorry, Bathyllus,' Perilla said gently, 'but you can't know that for certain, now, can you? After all, you've only known him for–'

'That doesn't matter, madam. He may be a thief, he's certainly dishonest, untrustworthy and a persistent liar, but he is *not* capable of murder. Whatever the indications to the contrary are, I'm convinced of that.'

'Look, pal,' I said. 'You have to face the facts here, as far as we know them. Thief he certainly is; we know from Eutacticus that he and his master stole a valuable necklace which has now gone missing. Oplonius didn't sell it and according to that note you gave me from the Aventine Watch commander he didn't leave it with his banker for safe keeping either, which means it was still in his possession when he was killed. Agreed?'

'Yes, sir, if you say so. But–'

'Okay. Now it turns out that our only suspects for the murder – the two guys staking out the tenement – weren't responsible after all. They couldn't've been, because they were Eutacticus's men, and he only found out where Oplonius was staying after the event. So I'm afraid that leaves Damon himself. Or at least he's the most likely possibility.'

'Not necessarily, sir,' Bathyllus said stubbornly. 'The actual killer could have been someone else entirely, someone you don't know of yet.'

Gods! This was difficult!

'Look, Bathyllus.' I kept my voice level. 'I only said Damon was the most likely possibility, which he is at present. I can't be sure he killed Oplonius, of course I can't. For all I know we've a long way to go yet. All I can do is work from what facts I have, and if other facts emerge that point in a different direction then well and good, we take it from there. If you want to help your brother then the best thing you can do is to play it my way. Okay?' No answer, but he gave a brief nod. 'Fine. Now.' I took another deep breath: crisis over, or at least in abeyance. 'You sure you're up to this, or would you prefer to go downstairs again? No worries, whichever.'

'No, that's all right, sir. I'll stay here.'

'Fair enough. Well done, pal.' I cleared my throat. 'Okay. Case against. First and most important, motive, means and opportunity. Damon had all of them in spades. He knew the necklace existed and that Oplonius had it, they were sharing a room and there was no reason, as far as we know, for his master to think he was in any danger. Plus the fact – I'm sorry, Bathyllus – the guy was an out-and-out crook to begin with. Second, the simple fact that he's done a runner. Third–' I stopped, and frowned. 'There isn't a third, is there?'

'No, dear, there isn't,' Perilla said. 'And to tell you the truth, I'm not totally convinced that your second point is particularly valid, either.'

'Yeah? And why would that be, now?'

'You said yourself: when you last talked to him Damon wasn't to know you had any connection at all with Eutacticus, and you didn't have your' – she paused – 'your *interview* with the man until later. So there really was no reason for him to abscond, was there? Not a specific reason, anyway.'

'It didn't have to be specific. We covered that: he'd know that the story he was spinning us was coming apart at the seams. He couldn't take the risk.'

'Hmm.' She frowned. 'Very well. It's possible, Marcus. But the comment still stands.'

'Actually, madam,' Bathyllus said, 'I think the master is probably correct.'

Uh-oh. Things went very quiet, and I glanced sideways at the lady. Me, after all those years of marriage, I can generally risk a head-on contradiction like that and get away with no more than superficial sarcasm burns, but this was Bathyllus: the little guy was courting certain death here. However, to give Perilla her due not an eyelid did she bat.

'Indeed, Bathyllus?' she said mildly. 'And what makes you think that?'

'Damon isn't–' Bathyllus hesitated. 'I'm sorry if I'm speaking out of turn, madam, but even from what little I've seen of him I would say that to run for cover at the first hint of danger, immediate or envisaged, is built into his nature; that it can't be taken automatically as a sign of guilt.'

Hey! Character analysis now! The little guy was really getting into this. Mind you, Bathyllus was a smart, smart cookie at base, I'd always known that: anyone capable of running a household with the ruthless efficiency of a Caesar planning a military campaign was a brain worthy of respect.

'Besides,' he went on, 'Damon's a slave. What else could he do in the last resort if he felt threatened but run?'

I winced. Brutally put, sure, but smack on the button. Slaves aren't people where the law's concerned, they're property, with no more rights than a pair of sandals would have. We tend to forget that, or rather we take it for granted, most of us. Maybe the reminder wasn't altogether out of place.

'Very well,' Perilla said. 'Point taken. So all we really have on the debit side, Marcus, are the circumstantial details. Motive, means and opportunity, yes?'

'Yeah.' Which, to be fair, would've been plenty and enough in my book to put the guy at the top of the list, particularly since there were no other candidates, but I wasn't going to say that with Bathyllus standing there. Besides, despite that 'really' Perilla knew damn well the way things were shaping up. 'Okay. Arguments for.'

'The fact he mentioned the necklace at all,' Perilla said promptly. 'Yes, I know you dealt with that before, dear, and you may be right, but still if Damon did kill his master for it it cuts too close to the bone. Particularly since he couldn't possibly have known you'd find out about it from another source.'

'Fair enough.' I shifted my weight on the couch. 'While we're about it you can add the beating-up aspect of things.' I glanced at Bathyllus: the little guy wouldn't know about that, of course, because I'd got it from Pudentius. 'Chances are, if he'd had a double-cross in mind, Damon would've made damn sure before he made his move that he knew where the necklace was and that he could get it without any trouble. He's a pretty weedy specimen to begin with, and although Pudentius didn't say in so many words that Oplonius was a big enough guy to handle himself in a fight the implication was there. A quick stab while his master was off his guard, asleep or whatever, would've been all he could've risked. All that was necessary, in fact. Also' – I looked at Bathyllus again – 'I'd agree with Bathyllus: crook or not, short acquaintance or not, he didn't seem the murdering type.'

'Thank you, sir,' Bathyllus said quietly.

'There's also the matter of getting rid of the necklace once he had it,' Perilla said. 'We talked about that. And if Oplonius had already sold it then for Damon to hang around with a fortune in his possession would make even less sense.' She frowned. 'Marcus, I really am beginning to believe that despite appearances Bathyllus is right. His brother can't be the killer, or at least it's very unlikely. There are too many inconsistencies.'

'Yeah. Agreed.' Out of the corner of my eye, I saw Bathyllus sag with relief.

'So what happens now?'

Fair question. I shrugged. 'We have to find Damon. Or have him contact us. What he's covering up and why he's doing it I haven't the faintest idea, but although he may not be a murderer he has serious and relevant beans to spill.'

'Would Eutacticus help? I mean, with the resources he has available he could–'

Gods! 'Once and for all, Perilla, listen to me, okay?' I said. 'Of course he could, no argument. That bastard will have people combing the city right now. He'll find him eventually, sure he will, and when he does Damon is crow's meat.' Bathyllus winced. 'I'm sorry, little guy, but that's a definite fact. As far as Eutacticus is concerned, who killed Oplonius is irrelevant; what he wants is his necklace, probably, now, together with Damon's head on a plate. Our only chance is that Damon sees sense and turns himself in to us before Eutacticus gets to him. Then if he's still got the thing maybe I can do a deal as per the original agreement.'

'And in the meantime?'

'Search me, lady. Oh, I'll take a trip up to the Pincian tomorrow morning, see if Eutacticus is still prepared to play ball, at least in theory, but I don't hold out much hope. We'll just have to keep our fingers crossed that friend Damon has a crisis of conscience.'

Yeah; and pigs might fly. Even so, I was sorry for Bathyllus, bitterly sorry: whichever way things went, I doubted if the poor guy would have his new-found brother for all that much longer.

'Incidentally, dear, and to change the subject,' Perilla said as Bathyllus moped his way out. 'How did things go regarding Priscus? You did follow him this morning, didn't you?'

Oh, shit; with all this happening I'd completely forgotten about the Priscus side of things. Coping with my stepfather's uncharacteristic venture over the matrimonial wall was yet another example of our current unbounded joys.

'Uh...yeah,' I said reluctantly. 'Yes, I did.'

'And?'

'Brace yourself, lady. The guy's having an affair, all right. With a woman in a curio shop on the Sacred Way.'

She stared at me wide-eyed. 'Oh, Marcus, *no!* For heaven's sake! You're absolutely certain?'

'As certain as I can be.' I told her what I'd seen. 'So what do we do?'

'Absolutely nothing. It's none of our business.'

'Agreed. You want to come and explain that to Mother when she hauls me round and asks me for a report? Which she will, and pretty damn soon. I can't fudge things, either, because that woman can see through a brick wall when it suits her.'

'Talk to Priscus himself, then. Persuade him to see sense.'

'And admit that I've been spying on him? Besides, he's old enough to know what he's doing without me telling him.' I frowned. 'Well, actually, scrub that. The guy never has been up to speed in the seeing-sense department as long as we've known him, so age doesn't come into it. Even so, it just isn't on.'

'You could always talk to the woman. If it's a question of money, bribery–'

'Come on, Perilla! If I offered to buy her off Priscus would never forgive me, whichever way she jumped. In any case, we don't know enough in detail about the situation for that to be an immediate option.'

'Very well, then. Go to the shop, talk to the woman in any case. Get some background, weigh things up. You don't need to be too blatant. Lead into it gradually.'

'Yeah, right. So I call round to buy a knick-knack or a gewgaw or whatever, then while she's wrapping it I drop in the intimation that I'm her sugar-daddy's stepson and I'd be really, really grateful if she didn't liaise with him any more. That the sort of thing you mean?'

'Of course not, dear. Don't be silly. But that *is* the general idea, taken over time. You're sure to think of something when the occasion arises.'

Hell; why was it always me who drew the short straw? Still, Perilla was right; having a word with the woman, finding out exactly how things stood, was the best move we could make. Frankly, it was the only one.

That didn't mean to say I had to like it, mind. And, *pace* Mother's diktat, it wasn't something I was going to rush into, either. I'd give it a few days, let things settle; you never knew, something might come up. Priscus might get himself run over by a delivery wagon, or he might have a crisis of conscience and confess the whole shoddy affair to Mother off his own bat. Mother might decide to give the whole thing up as a bad job and take him off to the fleshpots of Baiae for a month. Pigs might fly.

In any case, with the Damon business I'd got enough on my plate to be going on with already. The Priscus affair could wait its turn.

# 9.

The sun was just moving into its second quarter next day when I got to Eutacticus's place. I was on a hiding to nothing here, that I was practically sure of, but the motions had to be gone through if only so's I could look Bathyllus in the eye and say I'd tried. Besides, chances were that after the debacle at the tenement if I didn't make the first move it wouldn't be too long before Laughing Boy Satrius and his mate were banging on my front door with an invitation to talk to their boss re the absconding Damon at my earliest inconvenience, and that I didn't want: with touchy bastards like Eutacticus the less trouble you cause the better.

So I gave my name and business to the muscle-bound hulk on the gate and twiddled my thumbs while he shambled up the drive to check if the master was At Home. That, it transpired, didn't take long, which considering that Corvinus wouldn't be flavour of the month in the Eutactus ménage was probably a bad sign.

The lad himself was working out in his private gym. Yeah, I'd forgotten that Eutacticus was a fitness freak, or the next thing to it: he was a big guy and well-rounded, sure, but unlike most of his comfortably-padded co-millionaires his extra poundage was muscle, not flab. When the slave who'd come to collect me at the gate showed me in he was stripped to his loin-cloth, swinging a pair of dumb-bells, and grunting away like a hairy rhino with a bad case of croup.

I waited until he'd given a final grunt, set the dumb-bells down, reached for the towel that the slave in attendance was holding, and wiped the sweat from his torso.

'You've got a nerve coming here, Corvinus,' he said. 'After that cock-up yesterday I'd've thought you'd be steering clear of me and thanking your stars you aren't hobbling around on crutches. Which' – he fixed me with his eye – 'you may be yet, depending on how things go.'

Ouch. He wasn't kidding, either. 'Yeah, well.' I tried a grin. 'Maybe it was a bit unfortunate the way things turned out.'

Eutacticus dropped the towel, picked up one of the dumb-bells, and levelled it at me.

'Look, you overbred purple-striper bastard,' he said. 'This is no laughing matter. That necklace cost me a cool half million, and unless I get it back pretty damn quick other people besides that light-fingered fucker of a slave are going to suffer. Particularly if they include a smartass purple striper who was stupid enough to let the bugger slip through his fingers when he had him. You get me?'

I swallowed. 'Yeah, I get you. But–'

'There aren't any buts. The only reason you still have all your faculties attached is that as you so carefully pointed out I owe you a favour. There isn't much of the debt left to repay now, so you be damned careful how you go.'

Uh-huh. Well, this looked even less promising than I'd thought it would be, but I had to try, at least. 'You've put the word out already, then?' I said. 'That you're looking for Damon.'

'I told you, Corvinus, lose the jokes. Of course I fucking have. That bastard is dead meat, whether he has the necklace or not. The only difference is that if he doesn't, or if he's been fool enough to get rid of it, he's going to die very, very slowly.'

Gods. 'So what about our original bargain? Safe conduct for Damon if he delivered the necklace to you of his own free will?'

'The hell with that. That deal was null and void the minute the bastard did a runner. What else could you expect?'

‘Come on, pal!’ I said. ‘Be reasonable! When we struck the deal Damon was already gone. I didn’t know that at the time, but even so. The point is, he never knew a deal existed in the first place, so how can he be guilty of welshing on it?’

Eutacticus frowned and laid the dumb-bell down carefully beside its partner, taking his time over it. I held my breath. Then he straightened.

‘Okay,’ he said. ‘I’ll tell you what I’ll do. Here’s how it works. No arguments, no bargaining, you take it or you leave it, understand?’

Well, whatever he’d decided I knew it was going to be the most I could expect. And anything was better than nothing.

‘Yeah,’ I said. ‘Go ahead.’

‘I’m not calling off the search. That’s flat. And if and when I find the bastard he’s dead, whether he has the necklace or not. Clear?’

‘But–’

‘I said: no arguments. This is the way it is, the only way, and if you don’t like it then tough. On the other hand, if between then and now he gets back in touch and turns the necklace over to you the original bargain stands.’

‘And if he doesn’t have it, or know where it is?’

‘Then he’d better run far and fast. Not that it’ll do the little fucker any good because by that time I’ll know where he is.’

Hell. None the less, I had to admit that Eutacticus was playing fair by his lights: if Damon turned himself in off his own bat then we’d be back to the status quo of the original deal, while if he decided to chance his luck after all when the shit hit the fan he had only himself to blame. Either way, I reckoned my conscience was clear: I’d done my best for the slippery bugger, and at least going cap-in-hand to Eutacticus had done some good.

‘Fair enough.’ I held out my hand. ‘Agreed.’

Eutacticus shook. 'Now piss off, Corvinus,' he said. 'I've got things to do. And don't even think about welshing on the bargain yourself, or I will be seriously upset.'

Yeah. Right.

I pissed off.

. . .

So; what now? Until Damon showed up again – if he ever did, which I'd put in the flying pigs category – I was effectively stymied: I'd no other leads to follow up, none, and without them I might as well go home and take up basket-weaving.

Except–

One person connected with the case I hadn't talked to. Oh, sure, it probably wouldn't do any good – when he'd given me her name Watch Commander Pudentius had said as much – but beggars couldn't be choosers, and there was always that outside chance: the girl in the Aventine wineshop that Oplonius had been friendly with, what was her name, Lydia. I'd no exact location for the place, but there couldn't be many wineshops close by the Rullius tenement, so finding it shouldn't be a problem.

I set out for the Aventine.

In actual fact, I'd no problems at all: the wineshop was the only one on offer, on the corner a few dozen yards from the tenement's entrance. I went in.

Not a very prepossessing place, but this was the Aventine after all, where the local punters aren't too demanding. Even so, it was a step up from the spit-and-sawdust joints that constitute the Aventine average, with a couple of trestle tables opposite the bar counter at each of which three or four workman-type tunics were sitting shooting the breeze over their wine cups. The conversation died briefly as I came through the door and they clocked the purple stripe. Which, I supposed, was fair enough: south of the Racetrack isn't exactly purple-striper territory.

I went up to the bar, and the loungers propping it up moved aside. The barman detached himself from his conversation with a punter at the far end and came over.

'What can I get you, sir?' he said.

I glanced up at the board. 'Care to recommend?'

'The Nomentan's not bad.'

'Nomentan it is, then. Just a cup.' I reached into my belt-pouch, took out a few coins and laid them on the counter. 'You have a girl here by the name of Lydia?'

He'd been reaching for the wine jar in its rack. He paused, turned and gave me a look. None too friendly a one, either.

'Might have,' he said. 'What's it about?'

I shrugged. 'I just wanted a word with her, that's all.'

He hefted the jar, filled a cup, set it down in front of me with a bang, and scooped up the coins.

'Your pals've already had that,' he said. 'She can't tell you nothing more than she did then, so you can drink up and get out.'

I frowned. Okay, fine, the civil authorities aren't too popular with Aventine residents in general, but this was pushing things a bit too far. 'Uh...look, friend,' I said. 'If you mean the Watch then–'

'Fuck that. Those bastards weren't Watchmen. Besides, the Watch had already talked to her.'

There was something screwy here, and whatever it was it had rated pretty low in the popularity stakes: conversation in the room had gone down to nothing, and I was getting glares from more than one of the lads at the counter.

'Look,' I said again, 'I've no idea what's going on here, but it has no connection with me. I got Lydia's name a couple of days ago from Commander Pudentius of the local Watch.' His eyes shifted; that obviously weighed. 'My name's Valerius Corvinus; you ask him about me if you like, he'll vouch for me. According to Pudentius, your girl Lydia was friendly with a man by the name of Gaius Oplonius who was murdered eight or nine days back. Me, I'm trying to find out who did it and why. That's it; that's all there is. Now do I get to talk to the girl or not?'

He gave me a long, hard look. Then he grunted and gave a nod towards the curtained alcove between the two trestle tables.

'She's upstairs,' he said. 'She's got a customer with her at present, but she shouldn't be all that long.'

'Fine.' I took a sip of the wine: not great, but better than I would've expected in a place like this. 'While we're waiting. These guys who weren't the Watch. Care to tell me about them?'

'Nothing much to tell. There were two of them, came in asking for Lydia just after the Watchmen had left. They wanted to take her upstairs, but I wasn't having that, not the both of them at once: she's a good girl, Lydia, and I didn't like the look of that pair of beauties above half. Anyway, it turned out they just wanted to talk.'

'What about?'

'Your friend Oplonius. Seemingly he'd had something valuable belonging to them and they wanted it back. They thought he might've left it with Lydia for safe keeping.'

'That so, now? And had he?'

'Nah. Chance'd be a fine thing. She's a good girl, Lydia, like I said, but this Oplonius was just a customer and he'd hardly known her five minutes. You think he'd be that stupid?'

'They say what the thing was?'

He shook his head. 'No. Just that it was something valuable, that it wasn't his in the first place, and that the proper owner was looking for it. Anyway, when Lydia told them to fuck off they got pushy and me and a few of the regulars had to persuade them to leave. Things got a bit bent, but they saw sense in the end. And before you ask, I'm not stupid either. It can't've been no coincidence the poor bugger gets himself murdered and a day or so later there's a couple of no-goods looking for something of his that's gone missing.'

'You didn't tell the Watch about this?'

That got me a long, considering look. 'What did you say your name was?'

'Corvinus. Valerius Corvinus.'

'Well, Corvinus-Valerius-Corvinus, thinking something and doing something about it are two different things. The Watch can take care of themselves, I don't get involved. It's no business of mine, nor of Lydia's, neither. Clear?'

'Yeah. Yeah, clear.' I took another sip of the wine. 'At least you can tell me–'

The alcove curtain parted and a guy with the looks and build of a stevedore came out, closely followed by a plump, hard-faced girl in her late teens. She gave me an appraising glance as she picked up a cloth from the counter and began drying cups.

'You're Lydia?' I said to her.

‘That’s right.’ The glance became a direct look which shifted to the purple stripe, and she brushed a stray curl of hair from her forehead. ‘What can I do for you, sir?’

‘He’s asking about Oplonius,’ the barman said.

‘Oh.’ The appraising look vanished.

‘Can we talk in private?’ I said.

Her eyes went to the barman, who nodded briefly. ‘Sure, if you like,’ she said. ‘It’ll cost you, though. The usual price is two silver pieces, but in your case I’ll make it three.’

‘Fair enough.’

She put the dishcloth down, pulled back the curtain and stood aside. I took the coins out of my belt-pouch, laid them on the counter, and went past her up the stairs.

The room at the top was tiny, scarcely big enough for the bed that constituted all the furniture apart from a wooden clothes chest. It smelled strongly of sweat and the cheap perfume the girl was wearing, and there was a pile of dirty underwear with a greasy plate and spoon perched on top of it in one corner. Very homely.

‘Sit on the bed if you like,’ she said, following me in and closing the door. ‘Make yourself comfortable. Me, I’ll stand. It’ll make a change.’

I shoved the crumpled blanket to one side and sat. ‘This Oplonius,’ I said. ‘He, uh, visit you often?’

‘A couple of times. Three, exactly, if you’re counting. He hadn’t been in Rome for long.’

‘So what was he like?’

She gave a small, sideways smile ten years older than her years. ‘How do you mean?’

‘Come on, sister! Physical build to start with. Tall? Short? Skinny? Well-built?’

‘You didn’t know him?’

‘No, I never met the guy. Didn’t know he existed until after he was dead.’

‘Average height, stocky. Muscular, even. Very dark curly hair.’ She ducked her head to hide another smile. ‘All over, front and back, if you’re that curious. Quite a looker, and he knew it, too. Fancied himself.’

‘Uh-huh.’ So much for the idea that Damon could’ve taken him in a fight. Not that I’d ever really entertained that possibility. ‘As a person, then. Anything you particularly noticed? Apart from the fancying himself aspect of things.’

‘He was just another customer. What’s to notice?’

I took two more silver pieces from my pouch and laid them on top of the bunched blanket. ‘Try,’ I said.

‘Okay.’ She closed her eyes briefly. ‘He wasn’t well off. Drank the cheapest wine on the board and made two or three cups last the evening. Me, I’d say I was his bit of extravagance. Some punters are like that, they’ll skimp on their drinking money to pay for the girl. It’s just how they’re made, I suppose. Mind you, that did surprise me a bit. That he was so short of cash, I mean.’

‘Yeah? How so?’

It was the way he spoke, like. Whatever he was now he’d been brought up proper. A touch of the lah-de-dah, you know?’ The little smile was back, and the quick challenging look with the lowered head. ‘A bit like you, really. It was quite nice. You’re sure you just want to talk?’

‘I’m sure. Thanks anyway.’

She shrugged. 'Suit yourself. You're paying. Anyway, there were touches of the real gent about Gaius. You don't get that round here very often, and it made a change.'

'He was from Padua. A wool merchant. Or at least that's what I was told.' I put the barest hint of a question in my voice.

'Yeah. That's what he told me too, except for the wool bit.' She frowned. 'Still–'

'Still what?'

'It's nothing. Only the first time he was with me he had this fancy signet ring on. Gold, it was, or at least it looked it, with a carved ivory bezel. Real gent's property, must've cost a packet originally. Second time it wasn't there. I asked him about it and he got a bit embarrassed; turned out he'd pawned it with a money-lender. Me, I wondered if it hadn't been a – what do you call them things get passed down in families?'

'An heirloom,' I said. I'd serious doubts on that score myself. The chances were, from what Eutacticus had told me about Oplonius and how he operated, that if it was then the passing down had happened in some other family and he'd lifted it from the current scion.

'That's right. An heirloom.' She was still frowning. 'The poor bugger. It might've been all he had left. I gave him that day for free.'

'That was good of you.'

Her shoulders lifted. 'Yeah, well. What goes around comes around. And when he was found dead a couple of days later I was glad I done it.'

'Okay. Let's talk about that,' I said. 'The two guys who came into the wineshop after the Watch had been said that Oplonius had had something valuable of theirs that they wanted back, right?'

'Not of theirs. They said the original owner wanted it.'

'Fair enough. And they didn't say what the something was?'

‘No. They just asked me if Gaius had left anything with me for safe keeping. Said they’d make it worth my while if he had and if I handed it over. I just laughed in their faces. I mean, look at me, look at this place. You think it’s likely?’ I said nothing. ‘And as for *valuable* the poor bastard can’t hardly’ve had a pot to piss in.’

‘So what did they say to that?’

‘They didn’t like it, that was for sure. The big one, the guy who’d done most of the talking, he makes to grab me, so I spit in his eye and tell him straight to fuck off. Things could’ve got nasty then if I’d been up here on my own, but this was downstairs, remember, and there were plenty of regulars around. They slung the bastards out on their ear.’

‘So what did they look like, those two? You recognise either of them?’

‘No. They weren’t from round here, that’s all I know. Hired muscle types, real hard cases. Like I said, there was a big one and a smaller one, and it was the big one did most of the talking.’

She could’ve been describing Satrius and his sidekick, but unless Eutacticus for reasons of his own that I couldn’t begin to fathom was playing a far deeper game than I thought then that just wasn’t on. Even so, if they were after the necklace this business of an ‘original owner’ was a real puzzler. Something, in an ideal world, to take up with Eutacticus himself, maybe, but then our relationship at present wasn’t exactly all sweetness and light, to say the least of it, and the bare thought of raising the subject with him gave me goose-bumps.

One thing was sure, though: I’d bet a year’s income to a bust sandal strap that whoever the bastards were and whoever they were working for they’d been responsible for the actual killing. I stood up.

‘Thanks, Lydia,’ I said. ‘You’ve been a real help.’

She smiled – a genuine, straightforward smile this time, that took some of the hardness from her face and made her look much younger.

'Well, maybe, but I doubt it,' she said. 'Anyway, you're welcome. And if you do change your mind and feel like' – she gestured at the bed – 'any time, you just let me know, okay?'

'I'll do that,' I said, moving past her and opening the door. 'Look after yourself.'

I'd got my foot on the first step when she said: 'Wait a minute.'

I turned. 'Yeah?'

'I've just remembered. Maybe it's important, maybe it isn't, but you might as well know anyway.'

'Tell me.'

'The last time Gaius was with me. The day before he died. He was...I saw he was excited about something. A bit high, you know?'

The back of my neck prickled. 'Excited about what?'

She shook her head. 'I don't know for sure. I asked him and he said he'd done a deal with a local merchant, that it could mean a lot of business for him. A breakthrough, he called it.'

Oh, shit. 'Did he say anything else? Give you any details?'

'No. That's all there was, he wouldn't tell me any more. After we'd finished, though, and he went back downstairs he ordered half a jug of the best wine we have.'

'Uh-huh.' Jupiter!

'You think it's important? I mean–'

'Yeah. Yeah, I think it well might be. Thanks again, sister.'

I carried on downstairs.

‘Enjoy yourself?’ the barman said when I came through the curtain, but I didn’t answer, just pushed past him and went back outside. My brain was buzzing.

*Breakthrough*, eh?

Interesting.

# 10

It was late afternoon when I got back to the Caelian. As usual, Bathyllus was hovering with the welcome-home cup of wine.

'The mistress around, sunshine?' I said, giving him my cloak.

'Yes, sir. In the atrium.' He was looking anxious. 'Did you talk to Eutacticus?'

'Yeah. No sign of the missing Damon, I suppose? He hasn't got in touch?'

'No, sir.'

Ah, well, I hadn't really expected that he would have: that bird was well and truly flown, probably permanently. 'Tag along, Bathyllus. He's your brother, you've a vested interest, so you're conscripted onto the team for the duration, okay?'

'Thank you, sir.'

I took the cup and led the way inside. Perilla was on the couch, reading as usual. She set the book-roll down.

'What did he say, Marcus?' she said.

'It's not good.' I told her about the deal, such as it was, with one eye on Bathyllus. 'Chances are, barring some sort of miracle, Eutacticus will nail him before the month is out. I'm sorry, little guy. I did my best.'

'Yes, sir, I know.' Bathyllus looked grey and old. 'It's not your fault.'

True; even so, it didn't help much.

'Isn't there anything you can do, dear?' Perilla said. 'I mean–'

'Not unless Damon turns himself in. That aspect of things is completely up to him now.' I settled down on the other couch and took a morose swig of the wine. 'Mind you, I did make some progress in another direction.' I told her about the talk with Lydia. 'Reading between the lines, it looks like just before he was killed Oplonius had a deal set up with someone; that he was on the point of selling the necklace on. Only at the same time its original owner – whatever that means – was trying to get it back and had tracked him down.'

'But, Marcus, that doesn't make sense. Eutacticus said he'd had the necklace from a colleague in Brundisium, yes? That it was legitimately bought and paid for.' She paused, frowning. 'Well, at least that it was bought and paid for, anyway.'

'Right. And I'm not claiming it makes sense, far from it; there's something seriously screwy here, no argument. On the one hand, sure, Eutacticus is no angel, and I very much doubt that any so-called colleague of his would be, either, which gives you the possible scenario that the necklace was hot in the first place; that the 'colleague' had no more right to it than Oplonius had, and that the genuine owner was out to get his property back. There again, crook five ways from nothing though he is, Eutacticus is honest enough by his lights: if he tells me straight, off his own bat and with no prompting, that the sale was on the square then I'd be inclined to believe him.'

'Unless he didn't know himself that the necklace was stolen.'

I frowned. 'Yeah, that's possible,' I said. 'Even so, Sempronius Eutacticus is a smart, smart cookie; more, he wouldn't take kindly to being played for a sucker, not kindly at all. Me, I'd think a lot more than twice before trying it, and I'd bet you that unless that colleague of his was a head-banging idiot he'd do the same.'

'All right. If you discount that theory – although personally I wouldn't dismiss it altogether, far from it – then where does that leave us?'

'Perilla, I don't *know!* I told you, you're right, it doesn't make any kind of sense. Even so, Lydia was clear: the guys who came round to the wineshop – and they must've been the ones responsible for Oplonius's murder – said they were repping for the original owner. Chapter and verse. If you can get past that then I can't.'

'They might have been lying.'

'Come again?'

'Marcus, what else would they say in the circumstances? They approach the girl, tell her that her boyfriend, or whatever you like to call him, had something that didn't belong to him, that they want it, and that they'll make it worth her while to hand it over. All above board, ostensibly at least. Of course they have to say they've a right to the thing, to establish a legitimate claim, however spurious, if only to save face. What would you expect?'

Uh-huh; put like that it did add up, to a certain degree, anyway. And given the sweetener of a reward, considering the kind of girl they were dealing with it was a reasonable way of going about things.

'Okay,' I said. 'Fair enough. Only if they weren't who they claimed to be then who were they?'

'What about the...whoever Oplonius was arranging to sell the necklace to? Could they have been working for him?'

Hell! Now *there* was an angle I should've thought of but hadn't! I kept my face straight. It's never a good idea to let Perilla know she's ahead on the theorising, at least not too far ahead. She only gets smug.

'Uh...yeah,' I said carefully. 'Yeah, that's a possibility.'

'I mean, if the necklace is as valuable as Eutacticus says it is then that would be quite a temptation for a double-cross, wouldn't it?'

True. And as a scenario it made the best sense yet: Oplonius finds his buyer and cuts a deal, whereupon the guy decides to save himself a bundle by sending his heavies round to pre-empt the exchange. Of course they'd have to know about the Aventine tenement, but that, assuming a certain amount of amateur laxness on Oplonius's part and some clandestine shadowing on theirs, would've been easy-peasie. The only real question was why our theoretical buyer – call him X – hadn't ended up with the necklace in his hot-and-sticky after all. Plus, naturally, where the hell it had got to in the meantime. And to answer that, unfortunately, we needed friend Damon.

'One thing that does puzzle me, though,' Perilla went on, 'is the ring. The one your friend Lydia said Oplonius had pawned with the money-lender.'

'Yeah?' I said. I was feeling distinctly...well, 'chagrined' is a pretty good word, but I'd prefer 'jaundiced' myself. 'And why would that be, now?'

'I mean, where would a second-rate provincial wool merchant – yes, I know he probably wasn't one really, dear, but even so that's his proper level – get something like that? If the girl was right in her description then it must've been valuable in itself.'

'Perilla, the guy was a professional con-man and a practising crook. Where do you think he got it?'

'Granted, but again from what she told you it was the only thing of value that he did have. If he was that short of cash then why hadn't he sold it before?'

'Jupiter, lady, I don't know! Maybe he hadn't needed to. He wasn't on his uppers altogether.'

'He wasn't far off it. Two hundred and eighty-three sesterces, which is what you told me he'd lodged with his banker, is a long way from being a fortune, particularly since he had his everyday living expenses to take care of while he was looking for a buyer for the necklace. Also, according to the girl Lydia he was being very careful indeed over his spending. And if he *did* sell or pledge the ring, even for a fraction of its value, then what happened to the money? He was dead two days after it disappeared; he couldn't've had all that much time to spend it. In any case, what would he have spent it on? The only evidence we have that his financial position had improved was that he treated himself to a better grade of wine on his final evening in the wineshop, and from what Lydia said that was because he was pushing the boat out, celebrating an upturn to his prospects. Besides, that must've been two full days after he had sold it, without any change to his habits in the interim.'

Shit; she was right again. This was getting seriously annoying.

'He had some cash on him that Damon took,' I said. 'We know that.'

'Marcus, a ring such as Lydia described would be worth a great deal more than a pouchful of petty cash. If Damon had had funds like that do you think he'd've been so desperate to sponge off Bathyllus?'

I glanced at the little guy. He hadn't spoken since he'd followed me in, but he'd been hanging onto every word. 'Over to you, pal,' I said. 'He's your brother. What do you think?'

Bathyllus hesitated. 'I can't be sure, sir, of course I can't,' he said. 'But I really don't think he was lying about having very little money. Even if he had already decided to get in touch with me following the murder he'd have done it after arranging accommodation himself, which he didn't because he couldn't afford the rent of the room in advance. I had to pay that for him, as you know.'

True. 'So what did happen to the ring?'

'I don't know, dear,' Perilla said. 'It's just another mystery.'

Fuck. I felt tired: there were just too many unanswered questions, and at present it didn't look like I had a hope in hell of finding the matching answers. We'd simply have to wait and see what transpired. Trouble was, I had no idea how that was going to work; without Damon, we were well and truly stymied.

'Okay,' I said. 'Leave it for now. I'll go back round to Eutacticus's tomorrow, check out the possibility of a crooked colleague angle.' That was something I really, really wasn't looking forward to – the odds were that I'd just end up with a flea in my ear at the very least – but it had to be done, if only for completeness' sake. 'You want to go and find out where we stand regarding dinner, Bathyllus?'

'Yes, sir. Of course.' He turned to leave, then hesitated. 'I wonder, though, if I might go round to the tenement tomorrow morning. See if by any chance Damon has decided to come back after all.'

He'd be a fool if he did, in my view; chances were that Eutacticus would've had the place staked out and he'd just be putting his head in a noose. However, I could see how worried the little guy was. It couldn't do any harm, and at least he'd feel he was doing something. 'Yeah, no problem,' I said. 'You do that, sunshine. And if Damon does happen to get back in touch with you somehow you let me know at once, right? No hassle, I promise.'

'Understood, sir.' Bathyllus left.

Ah well. We'd just have to sweat this out.

# 11

So back I went next day to the Pincian. This was getting monotonous, and I'd no illusions about the likelihood of a warm welcome and an amiable hug.

I wasn't disappointed, either. The lad himself was sitting in the garden, obviously in conference with a couple of his minions, and he looked about as pleased to see me as Thyestes was when he found out he'd just eaten his sons.

'What the fuck are you doing here again, Corvinus?' he said. 'It'd better be because that thieving slave has shown up with the necklace, because if not–'

'Uh, no,' I said. 'I'm afraid he's still missing.'

He glared at me for a good soul-searing half-dozen heartbeats, then grunted and jerked his thumb over his shoulder. 'You two push off for the present,' he said to the minions. 'We'll carry on later when this bastard's gone.' Then, when their retreating backs were half way to the house: 'Okay. So what's it about this time?'

I pulled up one of the minion-vacated chairs and sat. Here we went.

'Ah...Perilla and I were talking yesterday about this necklace business,' I said. 'You know Perilla? My wife?' That only got me a stony stare. 'Anyway, I'd just got back from seeing Oplonius's girlfriend, name of Lydia, works in the local wineshop.'

'So?'

Now we got to the hard part. 'Seemingly a day or so after he was murdered Lydia gets a visit from what must've been the guys who did the job. They're asking whether Oplonius left something valuable with her for safe keeping.' I saw his interest sharpen. 'Which he didn't, by the way.'

‘So what has it to do with me? If she didn’t have the necklace then–’

‘They, uh, claimed to represent the original owner. Quote. Fair enough, they were probably spinning a line, but we thought, at least my wife thought, that there was an outside chance that, ah, not to put too fine a point on it, it was just remotely possible that maybe–’

‘Spit it out, Corvinus. You’re babbling.’

Oh, hell. ‘The guy you bought the necklace from. The colleague in Brundisium. I suppose he came by it legitimately in the first place, yeah?’

That got me the long, slow death-stare again. Jupiter! I started to sweat. Well, maybe using the word *legitimately*, given where I was and who I was talking to, had been a step too far.

‘You’re suggesting he stole it.’ Statement, not question. ‘And that whoever he stole it from was making an effort to get it back.’

‘Ah...yeah. At least in principle. Although I wouldn’t’ve put it as strongly as a suggestion myself. Maybe a possibility would be better. A remote possibility. Or simply one theory out of many. And not the most likely one, either.’

Gods!

‘You think I’d give Occusia a piece of hot jewellery for our anniversary?’ His voice was dangerously low. ‘Something I knew had been stolen?’

‘No! *No!* Perish the thought!’ I could feel the sweat beginning to soak through my tunic at the armpits. ‘Certainly not deliberately. But we wondered, at least Perilla wondered, whether you might possibly have been accidentally and unwittingly, ah, sold a pup. As it were.’

‘Really.’ The death-stare still hadn’t let up, and I felt a tic start in my right eye. Then, finally, he turned away. ‘I’d agree with her; as you say, it’s a possibility. A remote one, but still.’ Glory and trumpets! ‘I’ve done business with' – he hesitated – 'with this colleague of mine before, and he's always been trustworthy in the past. All the same, he's a relatively small-timer, and to be honest with you considering the sum and the temptation involved I wouldn't put it past the bastard to try it on. Thanks for telling me, Corvinus, I'm grateful. Leave it with me and I'll look into it.' I breathed again. 'Still, it doesn't change nothing where the necklace itself is concerned. That fucker has it, we both know that. The deal still stands; if I find him he's history. Now bugger off, I'm busy.'

I stood up. Well, that hadn't been so bad after all, and it had opened up a possible avenue. Whether or not it would lead anywhere was a moot point, but at least it was there.

'You'll let me know if there are any developments?' I said. 'On the, ah, colleague front, I mean.'

He turned a liverish eye on me.

'Sure,' he said. 'I pay my debts, you know that. It'll take time, of course, because I'll have to send a man down to Brundisium to nose around and ask a few pertinent questions. In the meantime, though, I'll put the word out that I want to talk to your wineshop friends. If I find them I'll let you know. After I've done with them myself, naturally. Fair enough?'

I swallowed. 'Fair enough.'

'Bugger off, then.'

I did. With both relief and alacrity.

So. We were moving again, or possibly we were. Mind you, it hadn't escaped me that in all likelihood the whole point of this case was scuppered, or at least close as dammit thereto. I'd taken it on originally to help Damon, or Bathyllus, rather, which came to the same thing, but with the distinct possibility – practically a certainty – that that poor bugger's days would shortly be numbered I doubted that would serve as a viable reason for much longer. Still, whatever happened, I was into it now, and I couldn't see myself giving up just because the client, as it were, was likely to be taking a one-way trip to the bottom of the Tiber before the month was out.

Even so, there wasn't much I could do at present, or rather, scratch that, there was absolutely sod all. Not as far as the case was concerned, at least. Oh, sure, with my other hat on there was the visit to Priscus's girlfriend's curio shop to get over with, but – and call me a coward if you like – I couldn't quite bring myself to muster up the bottle for that one yet. Besides, I did feel pretty strongly that whatever Mother's views on the subject were it was shoving my nose into something that was none of my damn business, and laying up serious trouble for the future. I reckoned a compromise was in order: I'd hang fire until Mother started needling, then take things from there.

So. In the absence of gainful employment I might as well cut across town to Iugarius and stop in at Renatius's wineshop for a cup of Spoletan and a natter. Besides, after that visit to Eutacticus I needed to unwind.

So that's what I did.

I got back home close to sundown feeling a bit more cheerful, which had only a little to do with the wine: now that Eutacticus was on the team, albeit for reasons of his own and with his own axe to grind, the chances of finding Lydia's gruesome twosome had taken a definite hike, and with Damon effectively out of the picture they were the only game in town. However things panned out vis-à-vis Eutacticus's Brundisium colleague things were looking a lot more promising.

I climbed our steps, but the door remained closed. Odd; one peculiarity about Bathyllus – one of many, to be fair, but let that pass – is that he has this almost psychic ability to tell when the Master is Home. The front door opens and he's standing behind it with the obligatory cup of wine. That had been the pattern for years, and I could count the number of times he'd broken it on the fingers of one hand.

This was evidently one of them. I knocked, and the guy who opened up for me was one of the run-of-the-mill household skivvies. I gave him my cloak.

'No Bathyllus, pal?' I said.

'No, sir. He's out.' There was something odd about his voice, but I just took it for subdued nervousness at having to talk to the master direct.

I frowned: Bathyllus had said he was going to the Suburan tenement to check if Damon had turned up, sure, but that had been right after breakfast, and even at the snail's pace Bathyllus moved at he should've been back hours ago.

'The mistress in?' I said.

'Yes, sir. She's waiting for you in the atrium.'

*Waiting for you.* That didn't sound good, and the nervousness – if that's what it was – was there in spades. I went on through.

Waiting for me was right: she was on her feet and pacing up and down, looking anxious as hell.

'Marcus, thank goodness you're home,' she said. 'Have you seen Bathyllus?'

'Uh-uh.' The first real prickle of unease stirred in my gut. 'Why should I have?'

'I don't know. No reason. I thought you might've gone to the tenement after you'd spoken to Eutacticus, perhaps met him there. If Damon had reappeared after all he might have stayed on and you might still be talking. Or something.'

Oh, shit. 'He hasn't come back?'

Silly question, I knew he hadn't, of course, but her anxiety was infectious – it just showed how concerned she was that in her normal thinking state she'd've seen the obvious flaws in the scenario she'd offered me straight off – and I was getting seriously worried myself now.

'No. And it's almost dinner time.' That might've sounded pretty inane, sure, under any other circumstances, but this was Bathyllus; he'd as soon have gnawed his own leg off as failed to turn up for one of the most important buttling offices of the day. 'Do you think something's happened to him? An accident?'

'Look, let's just take this calmly,' I said, leading her back to the couch and sitting her down. 'He's just been delayed, that's all. He'll probably be back any minute.'

'Do you believe that? Honestly?'

Yeah, well, she had me there. Of course I didn't. 'Okay,' I said, settling down on the other couch. 'Scrub that for an explanation. But there's still no reason to panic. Let's talk it through. What are the possibilities?'

She took a deep breath. 'Yes, dear, you're quite right. I'm sorry, just give me a moment to collect my thoughts, will you?' I waited. 'Very well. Perhaps Damon has reappeared. Or got in touch somehow.'

'Uh-huh.' That was the one I'd've gone for, personally, first off, despite the obvious objections. They had to be voiced, though. 'Problem is, lady,' I said, 'Bathyllus knows that if that happened he was to tell me straight away. It was the last thing I said to him yesterday when we discussed it, and he agreed it was the most sensible thing to do.'

'He may not have had the opportunity. Eutacticus was almost certainly having the tenement watched; you said that yourself. If Damon was silly enough to go back there then Eutacticus's men would've had him before he crossed the threshold.'

'So?'

'So he may have got a message to him somehow. Damon may have got a message to Bathyllus, I mean. To meet him somewhere else, somewhere safer.'

Yeah, barring the fine operational details, and we didn't have the leisure to think about those at present, that would make sense: Damon was a natural at subterfuge – it was his main survival trait – and he'd keep moving around, not stopping anywhere long enough for his safety to be compromised. And if Damon was moving around Bathyllus wouldn't have risked leaving him.

'Why couldn't they just have arranged to meet here?' I said. 'That'd be safe enough, surely, and it was the object of the exercise, after all.'

She shook her head. 'I don't know, Marcus. But if that is the explanation then Damon would've had his reasons, valid or not.'

Uh-huh; I supposed that was true. Under the circumstances Bathyllus might not have been able to persuade his brother that I was on the level about granting amnesty. Or, indeed, that the bargain with Eutacticus was a genuine offer. We were still, I knew, dealing with the slave mentality: if you're on your own with your back to the wall, never trust anyone but yourself, because it might well kill you.

'So what do we do?' I said.

'Wait and worry. There's nothing else we can do, I'm afraid.'

Dinner came and went, still with no sign or news. So did bedtime.

Neither of us got much sleep that night.

# 12

News came the next morning, in the shape of a sealed flimsy that had been shoved under the door overnight. The stand-in skivvy brought it to me while we were having breakfast – both of us together, and early for a change, because Perilla hadn't been in any mood for her long lie.

I opened and read it.

Oh, gods. Sweet gods almighty.

'Marcus, are you all right?' Perilla set down her honeyed roll. 'What is it?'

'Bathyllus isn't with Damon after all,' I said. 'The bastards who killed Oplonius have got him.'

*'What?'*

I handed the flimsy over. 'Read it for yourself.' I felt sick.

The note was short and to the point: *We have your chief slave. If you want to know where, and you want him back alive, bring his brother to the Grotto of the Nymphs in the Asinian Gardens at the third hour today.*

'What do we do?' Perilla was looking at me, wide-eyed and scared.

'There's nothing we can do,' I said. I was trying to fend off my own panic, and thinking hard. Dear immortal gods! How the hell was I going to handle this? 'Not involving Damon, at least. They think we have him squirrelled away somewhere, that's clear enough.'

'If they have Bathyllus he must have told them we don't.'

'Maybe he had to say that we did to save himself from worse treatment. That would give him a bit of breathing space, at least, plus it would tell us indirectly what had happened to him. And the early handover would suggest he's told them that Damon is here in this house already, which would mean there was no point in beating an address out of him where they could pick Damon up without involving me. He's no fool, Bathyllus.'

'No.' She was looking at the flimsy again, and frowning. 'It isn't a direct exchange, is it? Bathyllus won't be there.'

'Uh-huh. I might be able to use that. Try a couple of delaying tactics of my own.' For what they'd be worth, even if they worked to begin with. But then I needed to keep the lady optimistic to some degree; one of us looking on the black side of things was enough and to spare, and I couldn't shake off the feeling that Bathyllus was already dead. After all, why would they need him once they'd put the pressure to deliver on me?

'Would Eutacticus help?' Perilla said.

'He might have done, in the circumstances – he has his own reasons now for wanting to track those bastards down – but the Asinian Gardens are right at the southern edge of the city near the Latin Gate. Third hour doesn't give me near enough time to go over to the Pincian to arrange things and still make the rendezvous. And even if I had the time to contact the First District Watch I couldn't risk involving the authorities, not when Damon's involved. Fuck!'

'Gently, dear. All this is quite deliberate, of course. On the kidnappers' part this time.'

Yeah, right; the third hour was half way through the morning, the sun was already well clear of the horizon, and the Asinian Gardens were half an hour's brisk walk from here. Plus I'd have to locate the Shrine of the Nymphs when I got there. Never mind recruiting help, I'd have to get my skates on if I was to meet the deadline at all.

What I was going to say when I did, though, I hadn't the faintest idea. No doubt that was deliberate as well: keep your target under the maximum stress, don't allow him any leeway for thought.

Bastards!

Well, there was no point in sitting around mulling things over. Whatever would happen, would happen. But I promised myself that if things did go pear-shaped and Bathyllus died as a result one way or another they'd be dead meat themselves within the month. I got up.

'Okay, lady, wish me luck,' I said.

'At least take someone with you.' Perilla stood up too. 'A few of the household slaves.'

I shook my head. 'These guys are smart. Force won't do this, and however they're playing things they'd've taken that possibility into account. No, we'll keep it simple, no tricks on my side. It'll be just me.'

She leaned over and kissed me. 'Be careful, and good luck.'

Yeah, I'd need it.

I yelled in the direction of the servants' quarters for my cloak and went through to my study where I kept the handy little knife I used to carry on occasions like this in one of the desk drawers. *No tricks* was one thing, but there was no reason for being stupid and going completely unprotected. Ideally, I'd've strapped it to the inside of my wrist, but there wasn't time for that: I sheathed it and slipped it into my belt at the back, where I could reach it easily.

Then I set off for the Asinian Gardens.

I'd no plan, of course, and hardly time to make one, even if that had been possible at such short notice. I reckoned that my best bet was to be absolutely truthful. If I could convince the kidnappers that neither I nor Bathyllus knew where Damon was and persuade them to cut me a bit of slack over the delivery then that was about all I could hope for. If they'd play ball maybe I could talk Eutacticus into taking a more urgent interest, and if he could find the bastards – and consequently Bathyllus – before they lost patience and decided to cut their losses then....

Yeah, right. Far too many ifs and maybes. The long and short of it was, practically speaking, I hadn't a hope in hell.

Fuck.

There was one aspect of all this, though, that did puzzle me, and if I'd been more in the mood for an intellectual challenge I'd've given it a bit of extended thought. How had the kidnappers known I'd had any dealings with Damon at all? Let alone – as they thought – be in a position to hand him over? Oh, sure, they'd known about the Aventine tenement and Damon's existence from the start, no argument, but the guy's subsequent movements and contacts were another thing entirely. And what they *didn't* know on that subject was just as interesting: they didn't know where he'd been hiding out, because if they had they'd obviously have bagged him in the interim and saved themselves a lot of grief. And they clearly didn't know he'd done a runner.

It was odd, to say the least, and I don't do odd. Certainly, when – *if* – I got the chance to think things through it'd be well worth the effort.

It was well into the second hour when I reached the Gardens. I went through the gate. This early in the morning there was no one around. These places don't get busy until much later in the day, and even then only when the weather's good, which that day it wasn't; and besides, unlike the city's other, bigger public gardens – the Sallustian on the Quirinal and Maecenas Gardens to the north – the Asinian ones aren't so popular. Which, obviously, was further evidence, if I needed it, that there'd been a planning brain at work here.

Fine; I'd got to the Gardens on time. But where the hell was the Grotto of the Nymphs? Small or not, they still covered a fair acreage, and I just didn't have time for the luxury of getting lost. I took a path at random and tried to keep my increasing feeling of desperation in check.

I was lucky; when I rounded the first bend there was an old guy hoeing one of the flower beds.

'Morning, Gramps,' I said. 'I'm looking for Nymphs' Grotto. Can you tell me where it is?'

He stopped hoeing and turned to look at me. Peer at me, rather: he was eighty if he was a day, and not a spry eighty, either.

'What?' he said. 'I'm sorry, sir, you'll have to speak up. Ears aren't too good this morning.'

Fuck. 'The Grotto of the Nymphs,' I shouted. 'Where is it?'

'Oh. Now you're asking.' He leaned on his hoe and looked around him like he'd suddenly been transported to a country far away and beyond the ken of mortals. Then he pointed to the left. 'Over there, sir. Near the boundary wall. Carry on for a bit and there's a path leading that way further on. You can't miss it.'

'Thanks,' I said, and moved past him. I'd only got a few yards when he called me back.

'Hold on, sir. *Nymphs'* Grotto, did you say?'

I turned. Jupiter! 'Yeah. Yeah, that's right.'

'Sorry, sir, my mistake. That's the Grotto of Pan. You want to carry on straight. You'll see a big ilex where the path forks. Take the right hand fork and it'll lead you straight to it.'

'Got you.' I started off at a half-run. I didn't trust the old bugger's directions further than he could stagger on a good day with the wind behind him, but there wasn't much time left and they were all I had. I'd just have to keep my fingers crossed.

Well, at least the big ilex was where he'd said it would be, and yes, the path forked just beyond it. So far so good; score one for Tithonus. I took the right hand branch and broke into a proper run.

I could see the grotto ahead of me now, an outcrop of stone at the end of the path with water cascading down it partly hiding the cave opening, and with some serious female statuary showing coyly through the ferns on either side. There was a low wall in front holding the water in to form a pool, and a man sitting on it.

I slowed to a walk, and he glanced up and past me. He didn't look too pleased, which I supposed was understandable under the circumstances.

'Valerius Corvinus?' he said. He was a big guy built like a wrestler, the hired muscle type. Obviously the more loquacious of Lydia's wineshop pals.

'That's me,' I said.

'Where's the slave?'

'We, uh, need to talk about that.'

'What's to talk about?' He stood up slowly. Six feet, easy, and like I say solid muscle. 'You were told to bring him, end of story.'

'Yeah, well, truth of the matter is I didn't have him to bring.'

He turned to one side and spat.

'Is that so, now?' he said.

'That's so. I did have him but he ran off three days back. I haven't seen him since. Sorry, pal, but I can't help you. Not for the present, at least.'

He gave me a long, slow, considering look. Then he grunted. 'That's a pity,' he said. I didn't reply. 'A real pity. Whether you're telling the truth or not.'

'It's the truth. Where's my major-domo?'

'Safe enough.' He grinned; not a pleasant grin. 'For the moment, anyway. Although seeing as you've come alone I doubt if that'll last long.'

'You bastard.' I said it quietly.

'Proud of it.' The grin widened. 'How do you want it done? Throat cut? Stabbed like that fucker Oplonius? Or something a tad more lingering? He might be able to help us more than you claim to be able to, and it'd be stupid not to give him the same chance as we gave Oplonius. Your decision, friend, but make it now and make it quick.'

'Bathyllus doesn't know where Damon is any more than I do,' I said.

'Fine. Then it'll make it all the worse for him, won't it?' I'd begun reaching surreptitiously beneath my cloak for the knife, and he shook his head. 'I really wouldn't do that. Dagger in your belt, is it? Believe me, I'd break your arm before you had a chance to use it, and then I'd use it on you myself. Slowly. Besides, if I'm not back by noon your slave's dead in any case.'

I took my hand away. 'Look,' I said. 'This whole thing's pointless. I'm telling you, neither of us knows where Damon's got to, and we haven't a hope in hell of finding him, either. All this is for nothing; you're killing an innocent man for no reason. If you and your boss, whoever he is, want the fucking necklace then look for it elsewhere, and good luck to you. All I want is my major-domo back in one piece. Understand?'

He was staring at me. 'Necklace?' he said. 'What necklace?'

Things went very quiet, and we were staring at each other in mutual incomprehension when Satrius walked out of the undergrowth to one side of the grotto. Without breaking stride, he pulled the guy towards him and stuck a knife three times in rapid succession into his chest.

The guy slumped, his wide-open eyes still fixed on me; I doubt if he'd even noticed Satrius coming until the last split second. Satrius stepped back, letting him slip to the ground. Then he bent, wiped his knife on the man's tunic, and put it back in his belt.

'You okay, Corvinus?' he said.

I was still in shock. 'Where the hell did you come from?' I said.

'Been here all the time. At least, as long as chummie here has.' He poked at the corpse with his foot. 'Boss's orders.'

'*What?* How did Eutacticus know that–'

'Look, just save it, right? We can't stick around, not with him' – he kicked the corpse again – 'lying there. Somebody might come along and notice, and we'd both be in schtook. Anyway, the boss will want to see you. Any questions, you can ask him personal.'

He was already heading off down the path, and I was on the point of following when the implications of what had just happened hit me.

Bathyllus.

'Wait a minute!' I said. 'You stupid bastard, you were listening, so you must've heard! He told me if he wasn't back by noon my chief slave would be dead. What the fuck did you have to kill him for?'

He stopped and turned. 'Boss's orders again, pal,' he said. 'It's over and done, no problem. Don't let it worry you.'

He carried on walking. I caught him up and pulled him round to face me. 'The hell with that!' I snapped.

He didn't move, just looked down at my hand gripping his arm. I let go, quickly, and he shrugged.

'Don't talk,' he said. 'Just walk. It's a long way to the Pincian, and the boss isn't a patient man.'

I felt sick. Gods! What was I going to do now?

. . .

We got to Eutacticus's place when the sun had barely an hour's worth of distance to go to noon. Satrius took me straight up to the great man's study.

He was sitting at his desk working through a pile of wax tablets and flimsies. Yeah, well, I supposed that even crooks had to keep on top of the paperwork these days.

He looked up as we came in and put down the pen he was holding.

'Corvinus.' He gave me a genial nod. 'Everything go okay, Satrius?'

'Yeah, boss. Easy as pie, all taken care of. No problems.'

'That's good. Give us a few minutes.' Satrius left, closing the door behind him. 'Sit down and relax, Corvinus. You've had an exciting morning.'

There was a stool next to me. I sat. I was shaking, and it wasn't with fear this time. I was angry as hell.

'You bastard!' I said. 'Your tame ape of a hit-man has just cost the life of my major-domo!'

'Is that so, now?' Eutacticus said quietly. He picked up the pen, made a note on the tablet in front of him, and set it down again. 'I'm really sorry to hear that. But call me bastard again and you'll leave this room on a stretcher.' He smiled his hungry-crocodile smile. 'As for your description of Satrius, well, it's not too wide of the mark so I'll let it pass. Although I wouldn't use it to him if I were you.'

I took a deep breath and willed my fists to unclench. 'Fair enough,' I said. 'But the least you can do is answer a few questions. How did you know in advance about the rendezvous in the Asinian Gardens?'

'I didn't.'

‘Come on, pal! Your...Satrius said he’d got to Nymphs’ Grotto ahead of me, ergo he didn’t follow me there, ergo he knew where I was going before I arrived. And he was there on your orders. Add all that up for yourself.’

‘He didn’t follow you. He followed the other man.’

‘Okay. So how was he able to do that? Follow him from where?’

‘From where he and his friend were holding your slave.’

‘*What?*’ I jumped to my feet. ‘You mean you knew where he was all the time and you left him there? You complete and utter–!’

‘Careful.’ Eutacticus hadn’t moved. He hadn’t even reacted. ‘You’ve been warned already. And I don’t give warnings twice. Now sit back down.’

I did, slowly. There wasn’t any point in losing my temper, quite the reverse; in fact, it might well be the biggest mistake of my life. And wherever they were keeping Bathyllus it’d be too late now to do anything about it.

Gods!

‘To finish answering your question, then,’ Eutacticus said mildly, as though nothing had happened. ‘Give me a bit of credit, I’m not an amateur like those bastards were. I told you I’d be looking for them, and when I look for someone I don’t mess around. With that pair I didn’t even have to break sweat. Although to be fair the starting point was a complete accident.’

‘Yeah? And how was that?’

‘Come on yourself, Corvinus! Use your brain! I’ve had men watching your house sunrise to sunrise ever since I knew you were hand-in-glove with that Damon character in case he turned up again. And seeing your major-domo was the fucker’s brother they had particular instructions to watch out for him and stick to him like glue if he set a foot outside.’

Hell! I should've thought of that possibility, sure I should. Maybe it was just as well that Damon hadn't got back in touch, because Eutacticus wouldn't've given him the benefit of the doubt and nailed him before he could reach me.

'So when your Bathyllus goes out on his own yesterday morning,' Eutacticus went on, 'my lads naturally follow. Then they notice that they're not the only ones interested in him, so they hang back to check what's going on. Bathyllus gets lifted at the door of the Suburan tenement and taken inside, and they don't interfere, because that's not their remit, but they watch and wait until the three of them – Bathyllus and our two pals – come back out, then tag along behind and see where they end up. Which, by the way, isn't far from the Gardens: the cellar of a wineshop outside the Latin Gate. They report back to me. In the meantime you've been round here yourself with your story about–'

There was a soft knock on the door. It opened, and Satrius put his head round.

'Ready yet, boss?' he said.

'Just about done. It doesn't matter, send him in anyway.' Eutacticus gave me another of his basking-crocodile smiles.

The door opened fully. I goggled.

'Bathyllus!'

'Ah...yes, sir.' The little guy was looking embarrassed as hell, and far grubbier and more dishevelled than I'd ever seen him, but he didn't seem to be any worse for wear otherwise. At least he was alive with all his bits still attached, which was a miracle in itself. 'I'm sorry if I've caused you any trouble. Please believe me that it was not intentional.'

'Bugger that, sunshine! No trouble at all!' I turned back to Eutacticus, beaming. 'You want a favour from me in future, any time, any thing, you've got it, pal, just ask. That is *brilliant!*'

'Oh, I'll be sure to do that, Corvinus, don't you worry,' he said. 'I pay my debts, but I also collect when they're owed. And now you owe me, never forget that because I won't. Ever. Clear?'

'Sure. No problem.'

'Good. Just so long as that's settled. Mind you, to be fair, it was the other bastard I wanted, the second of the two, the man who was holding him. Your house slave here was just an incidental.'

My interest sharpened. 'You've got him here?' I said.

He gave me a long, cold fish stare. Then, finally, he said, 'What's left of him, yes.'

Oh, shit. 'He's dead?' Bugger! That was both of them. There went the shooting match again; I could've wept. 'Why the hell kill him? You had him safe!'

Eutacticus just looked at me. He definitely wasn't smiling now. 'Corvinus, let's get one thing straight, okay?' he said. 'Your interests and mine are two different things, and frankly I couldn't give a toss for yours. All I'm interested in – all I've ever been interested in, right from the start – is getting my necklace back. Now, when I thought, thanks to you, that those two were after it as well I was happy to play along. Only in the course of the prolonged chat between me and the bastard who was looking after your slave here it turns out that they weren't interested in the necklace at all. That they didn't even know it existed. So what would you expect me to do? Pat him on the back and say, "My mistake, friend"?'

'You could've let him go.'

Eutacticus chuckled; not a nice sound. 'The hell I could! After all the trouble he'd put me to? Besides, believe me, the state he was in by the time we'd finished our talk killing him was a mercy.'

My guts went cold, and I noticed Bathyllus was looking pretty green as well. 'What about the other one?' I said. 'The one Satrius killed. He have to die too?'

'Sure he did, and with even more reason. I'd already got one of the pair under wraps, or at least I would have by the time Satrius was done, so I didn't need his pal. And when I gave Satrius his orders I still thought he was after the necklace, so I couldn't have him running around free, could I? On the other hand, lifting him like he'd lifted your Bathyllus and bringing him back to the Pincian would just have been too damn tricky. The game wasn't worth the candle. Don't complicate things any more than you have to, that's always been my rule, boy, and it's the best there is.'

Yeah, all very logical, but the logic made me sick to my stomach. I wouldn't be shedding any tears for that particular beauty, mind – I'd met him, after all, and if anyone deserved what he'd got it was him – but I was sorry, and felt slightly guilty, about the other one. Him I hadn't met, sure, but from Lydia's description of the conversation in the wineshop, or lack of one on his side, he struck me as a bit of an also-ran.

'So if the pair of them weren't after the necklace,' I said, 'then what *were* they after? Your, uh, house guest tell you that?'

There was a long silence. Eutacticus simply gave me his dead codfish stare and kept it going. I began to sweat again in earnest.

'Listen, Corvinus,' he said finally. 'I've got a lot of time for you. You may not think it, but I have. You're a clever bugger. Plus, anyone who can come to me off their own bat and tell me to my face in my own house that they think I've been suckered into a dodgy half million sesterce deal has guts, and I admire guts.' Uh-huh; I just hoped he was being metaphorical here, although with Eutacticus you could never be sure. 'Even when it turns out he's been talking through his backside and put me to a lot of trouble for nothing.' I winced. 'So I'm going to give you a piece of advice, and if you've any sense you'll take it. Go home, forget this whole thing. I'll even throw in Damon for free: when I find him, and I will, if he has the necklace and gives it back to me the bugger's off the hook, just like we agreed if he turned himself in to you first. You understand?'

Shit; what was going on here? This was *Eutacticus*, for Jupiter's sake! 'Ah, yeah, sure, I understand,' I said. 'But–'

'There are no buts. None. I'm telling you straight and for your own good: drop it. It's none of your business, and it's sure as hell none of mine. My involvement stops here. That's all I'm going to say.' He picked up the pen again and reached for a tablet. 'Now push off, and take your slave with you.'

There was no point in arguing, not with him in this mood. I nodded to Bathyllus, and we left.

I was sorely puzzled, to say the least of it. There was a litter rank just down the hill from Eutacticus's place, and despite his protests I put Bathyllus into one – the little guy was dead-beat and worn ragged – and told the litter-men to take him back to the Caelian. Me, despite the fact I'd had more than enough exercise for the day, I'd walk.

I needed the time to think.

# 13

When I got home Bathyllus had the door open for me before I'd reached the top step. He'd spruced himself up in the interim, and although he was still looking tired and somewhat lacking in his usual bounce and zip there didn't appear to be any lasting damage. He took my cloak and handed me the customary cup of wine.

'Good to have you back, pal,' I said.

'Yes, sir. Thank you. I mean, *really* thank you.'

'None of my doing. If you want to be grateful to anyone be grateful to Eutacticus.'

'I am, sir. Very much so, believe me.'

'The mistress in?'

'In the atrium, sir.'

I went through.

Perilla was on her couch, beaming. 'Marcus, isn't it *marvellous*?' she said. 'I couldn't believe it when Bathyllus came in. He's told me all about it, of course. He was incredibly lucky to escape with no harm done.'

'Yeah.' I stretched out on the couch opposite. 'Yes. He was.'

'Those men. The ones who kidnapped him. Have you any idea who they were, or what they wanted?'

I shook my head. 'Uh-uh. Not so much as their names. Eutacticus must know, but he's not telling. Seriously not telling, which is curious as hell.'

'Yes.' She frowned. 'Bathyllus told me that as well. What do you think it means?'

I shrugged. 'Search me,' I said. 'But it's not good news, that's for sure. Not good at all. The guy was...*scared* is completely the wrong word, but then I very much doubt that Eutacticus does scared to begin with. All the same, I suspect if it'd been anyone else then scared might've fitted. The long and the short of it is that I don't know; I can't think. But it wasn't just that he thought whatever it was was none of his business, it went way beyond that: he didn't want so much as to touch it with a very long pole and gloves. He didn't want me to touch it, either.'

'And will you?'

'Come on, Perilla! I'm hardly likely to give up now, am I?'

'No, I suppose not. But just be careful, please. Particularly since we don't know what's involved.'

'Oh, I will, I will!'

'So what happens now?'

Yeah, I'd been mulling that over on the walk home. Not that I'd got very far.

'Okay,' I said. 'What've we got? Scrub the necklace, but we're still left with the fact that our two kidnappers were looking for something valuable, that Oplonius had in his possession. Some *thing*, right, so it's an object, something small enough to be hidden, carried or passed on. Any ideas?'

'I'm afraid not, dear. How could I have?'

'Right. Me neither.' Bugger, we were wading through mud here! 'Fine. Take it from the other direction, then. Oplonius himself. He's a small-time crook, a professional con-man, an opportunist rather than a big forward planner: he's close to the breadline, obviously used to living hand to mouth and operating on a shoestring. Give him a big heist, like Eutacticus's necklace, and he's way out of his depth and knows it. Me, I think that's what's happened here, at least it's the likeliest explanation. It's the necklace all over again, but not the necklace. He's acquired – stolen – something or other that he didn't know the value of originally, and now he's up the creek without a paddle because whoever he took it from wants it back.'

'Hold on, Marcus. Aren't you assuming far too much of a coincidence here?'

'How do you mean?'

'Well, as you say, or rather as Eutacticus said, Oplonius was only a small-time crook. His operational method was to look for a likely traveller – an *ordinary* likely traveller – and rob him of whatever of value he was carrying. The necklace was an accident that for him should have been a once-in-a-lifetime one. What you're suggesting is that lightning has struck in the same place twice, as it were, and in a ridiculously short period of time. Surely that would be much too coincidental for comfort?'

'Coincidences happen. You have a better suggestion, Aristotle?'

She ducked her head and smiled. 'No, dear, of course I don't. But I'd like the comment to be noted, please.'

'Duly noted and logged. Even so, if it's okay with you, we'll work along these lines for the present until another theory springs to mind. Agreed?'

'Certainly.'

'Fair enough. Fine.' I took a slightly-miffed swallow from my wine cup: the lady could be seriously annoying at times. 'The rest's pretty straightforward, and much the same scenario as we had before. Judging from what Lydia told me, the likelihood is that Oplonius had got in touch with the thing's original owner and done a deal for its return; at least that was what the owner had led him to believe. In actual fact he'd no intention of paying up in the first place; he sends his minions to kill Oplonius and get it that way. Only the minions discover that the whatever-it-is has already been had away by the guy's slave and partner Damon, and the owner's in deep schtook. That all hang together?'

'Yes, of course it does. Except that I'd add the caveat, as we did with the necklace, that your 'original owner' could be another interested party altogether whom Oplonius approached with an idea of selling the thing.' She tugged at a curl of hair. 'None of this takes us very far, though, does it? All we've really done is add another unknown. We assumed that what Oplonius's murderers, whoever they were, were looking for was the necklace. Now we know that wasn't the case, but that's all we know.'

'It's not as black as all that, lady. There's another avenue to explore now.'

'Yes? And what's that?'

'Eutacticus may not be willing to help any more, but he did tell me that Bathyllus was being held in the cellar of a wineshop out by the Latin Gate. A *wineshop*. Tenements are anonymous places; if the kidnappers had been holding him in the room of a tenement they could've stayed anonymous, easy, taken the let special for the job and given false names. But a wineshop's different, that's personal. So we've our own alternative source of information, haven't we?' I raised myself on the couch and shouted, 'Bathyllus!'

He must've been hovering just outside, because he was straight in with even less of a pause than usual.

'Yes, sir.'

'The wineshop where they were keeping you. You remember where it was, exactly?'

'Of course, sir. On Latin Road, just outside the gate on the left.'

'Uh-huh. Thanks, pal,' I said. 'That's all. Unless you'd like to top up my wine cup for me.' I handed it over.

'Certainly, sir.' He hesitated. 'One thing that has been puzzling me, by the way. The men made no attempt to hide where we were going. And if by any chance you had produced Damon at the rendezvous and they'd subsequently released me then I'd have been able to tell you where they were, wouldn't I? It seems a bit odd, doesn't it?' I just looked at him and said nothing. 'Ah.' He swallowed, and paled. 'Ah, I see. Rather a...disquieting thought. I'll go and get your wine, sir.' He tottered out.

'I'll take a trip out there tomorrow,' I said to Perilla. 'The guys themselves are dead, both of them, but someone's sure to know who they were and quite a bit about them: if you're a stranger you don't get the use of a wineshop cellar just for the asking, particularly if you're keeping someone prisoner down there. And like I say if they'd wanted to stay anonymous they'd've booked in to a tenement or found an out-of-the-way disused shack somewhere.'

'Marcus, be careful,' Perilla said. 'The wineshop business goes both ways. If they weren't strangers, which I agree they can't have been, then it's very unlikely that whoever is still there was unaware of what was going on.'

'Yeah, I know,' I said. 'But we'll just have to cross that bridge when we come to it. With any luck–' Bathyllus came back in. 'That was quick, sunshine.'

'No, sir. It's Alexis. He wants to talk to you.'

I frowned: Alexis was our volunteer gardener, and the sharpest of the household bunch. 'What about? No, never mind, just wheel him in.'

He did. The guy was carrying a small kid-skin bag.

'I found this in a rose bed, sir,' he said. 'By the back wall.'

I got up, took it from him, untied the draw-strings and emptied the contents onto the table. They poured out in a single stream of red and sparkling liquid fire.

We all stared.

'Oh, Marcus, it's beautiful!' Perilla breathed.

I held the thing up by both of its ends. It was the necklace, of course: it couldn't've been anything else. And if Eutacticus had paid only half a million sesterces for it he'd got a real bargain: there were at least a dozen fair-sized rubies in it, plus twice that in smaller stones, all set in a delicate lacework of gold filigree. Queen Philistis had been a lucky lady. Occusia certainly was.

'You any idea how long it's been there, pal?' I said to Alexis.

'It wasn't there yesterday, sir. That I'm sure of, because I hoed the bed almost last thing. But I was working in a different part of the garden today, so I wouldn't have seen it straight off.'

Yeah, right. That made sense. Damon – it had to be Damon – had slung it over the wall under cover of darkness. A trade-off or a peace offering, whatever you liked to call it, through me to Eutacticus. At least the slippery bugger was finally showing some sense: he couldn't have offloaded something like this himself, not in a million years. Nor, in all probability now I'd seen the thing with my own eyes, could a low-grade shyster like Oplonius, free man and Roman citizen or not; the pair of them had been on a hiding to nothing in that direction from the start.

And that Damon hadn't delivered it personally didn't surprise me either. Bathyllus had been right: the guy's natural instinct, if he had any doubts about his own safety, was to run and hide, and to stay hidden until he was absolutely, hundred-per-cent, cast-iron sure that the coast was clear. He'd trusted Bathyllus, sure – they were brothers and fellow-slaves, after all, and as a stranger on the run in Rome he'd needed someone's help – but once I was involved all that had stopped. The fact that he clearly still had serious beans to spill and I'd be doing my best to get him to spill them made certain of it.

Ah, well, at least when I took the necklace over to the Pincian, which I would do first thing the next morning, he'd be off the hook where Eutacticus was concerned, I was sure of that: for all his faults Eutacticus was a man of his word and I'd no doubts that he'd keep to his side of the bargain. The other bastards who were looking for him, though, whoever they were, they were another matter entirely. We'd just have to keep keeping our fingers crossed that they wouldn't find him before we cleared this thing up. If we ever did.

'You think I could try it on, dear?' Perilla said. 'Just the once. Just to say I'd done it.'

I grinned: as a general rule she's not one for fancy jewellery, Perilla, but I had to admit this was a special case, and I doubted she'd taken her eyes off it since it had come out of its bag. 'Go ahead, lady,' I said. 'Enjoy. Up you get and I'll put it on you.'

She did, and I fastened it round her neck from behind.

'Mirror, please, Bathyllus,' she said. He went upstairs to fetch it. 'Who did Eutacticus say it belonged to originally?'

'Philistis. Hiero of Syracuse's wife,' I said. I went round the front to look. 'Two hundred years old plus. Not bad. Suits you.'

She dimpled, which is not something you see very often where Perilla's concerned. 'Nearer to the two hundred and fifty, then,' she said. 'Depending when exactly it was made in Hiero's reign. Oh, my!' She ran her hands over it.

'Tell you what,' I said. 'It's not going anywhere until tomorrow, and I'd only be putting it in the strongbox. Wear it for the rest of the day.'

'You think I could?'

'Sure. Why not? As long as you don't decide to sleep in it. Ruby necklaces in bed are a real bummer, worse than cake crumbs. Now lie back down and look regal.'

She did. Bathyllus came back with the mirror and she inspected herself critically and at length.

'Marcus,' she said finally. 'Would it be too late to get Phryne to do my hair, do you think?'

Phryne was her maid. Oh, shit; what had we unleashed here?

'Yeah,' I said. 'Yeah, definitely.'

She glanced sideways at me, smiled, and put the mirror down. 'All right,' she said. 'Point taken, I was only joking anyway. But it is rather beautiful.'

'To change the subject completely,' I said. 'Bathyllus? What time's dinner?'

'Not for an hour or so yet, sir, but I could always ask Meton if it could be a little earlier.'

'You do that, sunshine,' I said. 'I haven't had a bite all day, and I'm starving.'

'Yes, sir.' He exited.

'If you've finished with me, sir, I'll go as well,' Alexis said. 'There's an hour of sunlight left and I've still things that need doing.'

'No problem,' I said. 'Thanks, Alexis.'

'You're welcome, sir. And madam – very impressive!'

I grinned: I've always thought our shy-and-retiring Alexis has a soft spot for Perilla. 'Bugger off, pal,' I said. 'And thanks again.'

He left.

Well, that was that little problem cleared up finally. We'd just have to see what new joys the visit to the Latin Gate wineshop brought. For the present, though, I reckoned we were due some quality time involving a cup of wine, a good dinner, and a complete lack of thought about the case. I stretched out on the couch and reached for my wine-cup...

At which point Bathyllus re-buttled in.

'You, ah, have a visitor, sir,' he said cautiously.

Oh, hell, I didn't believe this: we *never* had visitors, especially this close to dinner. Besides, Bathyllus's face was straight and expressionless as a poker, which was a bad, bad sign. I set the wine-cup down and sat up straight on the couch.

'Yeah? Who's that, then, little guy?' I said.

'Your mother, sir. The Lady Vipsania.'

Oh, fuck. Perilla and I exchanged glances. Bloody hell's teeth, with everything else going on I hadn't even *thought* about Priscus; I'd put the affair completely out of my mind, or at any rate when I had felt a twinge of guilt about doing nothing about it shoved the feeling firmly to one side. It'd been five days now since Mother and I had had our little chat and I'd promised to tail him, four since I'd seen him snogging the brunette in the curio shop, and Mother had never been one to allow the grass to grow under anyone's feet, particularly mine. Now Nemesis had finally arrived, and as a consequence, barring some minor miracle, the shit was about to hit the fan in no uncertain terms.

Ah, well, it couldn't be helped, but all the same I was buggered if I knew what I was going to say to her. I steeled myself.

'Okay, Bathyllus,' I said. 'Show the lady–'

Too late; she was already in, and heading for me like a warship under full sail plus oars closing in for the kill.

'Marcus,' she said. 'I am *totally* disappointed in you! You promised me faithfully that you would–'

–at which point her eyes went to what Perilla was wearing, and she stopped dead.

'Oh, my goodness,' she said. 'Perilla, dear, where on *earth* did you get that?'

'The necklace?' Perilla said. 'Alexis found it in the garden,'

'In the *garden?*'

'Yes, indeed. In one of the rose beds.' She gave Mother her most brilliant smile. 'It's a long story. It isn't mine to keep, unfortunately. We're just looking after it until tomorrow.'

'But it's beautiful! May I see?' She reached out a trembling hand.

'Certainly.' Perilla reached behind her neck, undid the clasp, and passed the thing over. Thank the gods for a woman's priorities. Not even a possibly-erring husband could trump a half-million-sesterce ruby necklace, at least in the short term, and Mother was well and truly sidetracked. I breathed again.

'It used to belong to Queen Philistis. Hiero of Syracuse's wife,' Perilla said. 'Marcus has just recovered it for the real owner. That's why he's been so busy lately. He hasn't had a moment for anything else.'

I grinned; no mention of the fact that the real owner was the biggest crook in Rome and unlikely to figure in Mother's list of socially-acceptable dinner guests. When the lady fudged things she did it in style.

'Well, Marcus, I suppose as an excuse it's more valid than most of the ones you usually come up with, so I'll have to accept it.' Mother sniffed and handed the necklace back with obvious reluctance. 'Even so, I really did expect better of you. Haven't you done *anything* about Titus?'

'Uh, yeah. Yeah, I have, actually,' I said. 'I followed him, like I said I would. On the one occasion, at least.'

'Marvellous! And?'

'Zilch.' I kept my face straight and did a Damon, sticking as closely to the truth as possible. 'All he did was visit a curio shop on the Sacred Way.'

'There was no...hanky-panky?'

Jupiter! I didn't think even Mother used euphemisms like that any more! 'Come on!' I said. 'It was a shop, right? A public place. What could he have got up to in there?' I crossed my fingers. 'Besides, I told you: that's what Priscus does, he goes round the antique and curio shops to check their current stock. It was probably just one of the ones on his list.'

'Hmm.' She was watching me closely. 'Very well, dear. You'll simply have to try a little harder next time. But if you're hiding something from me–'

'Look, I'm on it, right?' Sod it, I didn't deserve this; I had enough to worry me at present without playing piggy-in-the-middle between a tomcatting stepfather and a hell-hath-no-fury mother. 'Like Perilla said, I've been pretty busy lately.' Jupiter! Talk about understatement! 'Just give me more time, okay?'

'All right, dear. Three days. And that is being generous.'

'Three *days?*'

'Three should be quite sufficient. After that I shall broach the matter with Titus myself, and damn the consequences.' Gods! 'Besides, if as Perilla says you've brought your present commitments to a satisfactory conclusion then you'll have plenty of free time on your hands.' Another sniff, and a pointed look at the wine-cup. 'This way I can be sure that it is spent more profitably than usual.' She leaned down and kissed me on the forehead. 'Goodbye for the present, dear. We'll keep in touch. Enjoy your dinner.'

And she was gone.

Fuck.

# 14

I went back over to the Pincian early next morning, hopefully for the last time barring the unlikely possibility of Eutacticus suffering a bout of remorseful guilt and blowing the lid off of the case for me after all, as he undoubtedly could have done. He was in his garden again, feeding the eels; I just hoped the meatball ingredients weren't my Asinian Gardens pal's late associate.

I held up the kid-skin bag. If I'd expected the guy to clutch his forehead and reel back in stunned and joyful amazement it didn't happen; instead, he gave me what amounted to a disinterested glance, picked up another meatball and tossed it into the pool.

'You've brought it, then,' he said. Pleased, sure, but not a smidgeon of surprise.

'Yeah.' I undid the laces and took the necklace out. 'All yours.'

He handed the plate of meatballs to one of the waiting slaves, dipped his fingers in the proffered bowl of water another of them was holding, and dried them on a towel.

'So the slave finally saw sense,' he said. He took the necklace from me and held it up to inspect it. In bright sunlight, the effect was even more impressive.

'Ah...not altogether. He's still missing. He must've come round last night and pitched it over our wall at the back of the house.'

'Yes, he did.' He returned the necklace to the bag and re-tied the drawstrings. 'An hour before midnight, or thereabouts'

'*What?*' I gaped at him. 'You knew?'

'Of course I fucking knew! What would you expect? I told you, I had men watching all the time, front and back. Not even a cat could've come within twenty yards of your place without me knowing.'

'But you didn't take him yourself? Damon, I mean.'

'No. No, I didn't. The lads had their instructions – fresh instructions, in the light of our new deal.'

'That was good of you.'

He scowled. 'Listen, Corvinus. When I make a bargain I play fair. They were told to watch but not interfere if there was no need, which in the event there wasn't. When they saw your pal Damon toss a package over the wall they left him alone.'

'They didn't follow him back to wherever he'd come from, by any chance? Just in case it wasn't the necklace?'

That got me a long and very cold stare: evidently not a good question.

'I'd say that was none of your business,' Eutacticus said quietly.

Uh-oh. 'Right. Right,' I said.

'I told you: so long as I get what's owing the slave's safe from me. He wasn't harmed and he won't be, but that's as far as the bargain goes.'

'Yeah, well, it's just that I'd, uh, really, *really* have liked a word with Damon myself. I don't suppose there's any chance of–?'

'No.' That came out flat. 'I told you. No help, none. Not in this, and that's final.'

Bugger! Still, it'd been worth a try. And at least now I knew that someone knew where Damon was holed up, even if he wasn't telling.

'Fair enough,' I said. 'I'll be on my way, then.'

'You do that. And thanks.' I turned to go. 'Oh, Corvinus?'

I turned back. 'Yeah?'

'I meant to ask, last time you were here. That business in the gardens yesterday.Anyone see you? On your way to the Grotto, that is?'

'Yeah, as a matter of fact they did. I asked an old guy for directions. One of the public slaves.'

'Messy.' Eutacticus frowned. 'You want me to tidy him up for you? It shouldn't be a problem. I could send Satrius back over.'

Gods! My blood went cold. 'Uh, no, no, that's okay, pal,' I said, as easily as I could manage. 'He was blind as a bat in any case and practically gaga.'

'Well, so long as you're sure.' He snapped his fingers at the slave with the plate of meatballs. 'I'll see you around. And don't forget the advice I gave you, about dropping this thing down a very deep hole.'

'I won't.'

Taking the advice, mind, was another matter. I left him to his feeding programme and headed back down the hill towards the First District and the Latin Gate.

The wineshop was where Bathyllus had said it was, just the other side of the Gate and on the left: not a very prepossessing place, from the outside, anyway, but then on this occasion I wasn't looking either for ambience or a good wine list. I pushed open the door and went in.

There was a middle-aged man behind the bar: nothing special, just like the place itself, if anything on the weedy side, with prominent teeth and a receding hairline. No other punters, which didn't argue very well for the quality of the wines on offer.

'Good morning, sir,' he said. 'What can I get you this fine morning?'

At least if he was a wrong-'un he was cheerful with it. I glanced at the board behind him. 'How's the Clusian?' I said.

'New batch just in, sir. Cup, was it, or a small jug?'

'Just the cup, pal.' While he unslung the jar from its place in the rack and poured I leaned on the counter and took out a few coins from my belt-pouch. 'You the owner?'

'Nah,' he said, replacing the jar and taking a couple of the coins. 'That's my sister and her husband. They're both away at present. I'm just minding the shop.'

'That so, now?' I put the rest of the coppers back into the pouch and took a sip. Uh-huh; no wonder the place was empty mid-morning. 'Family trip, is it?'

'For Matia it is. That's the sister. Our other sister was took ill ten days ago – she lives over in Fidenae – and Matia's gone through to nurse her. Won't be back for half a month yet, if past experience is anything to go by.'

'What about her husband? You say he's gone away too?'

'Caprius?' The barman frowned. 'Now that was a very strange thing, sir. Beats me completely. Mind you, he's never been the conscientious sort, my brother-in-law, it's Matia runs things. Far rather drink the wine than sell it, that's Caprius, always has been, and it's me his kin that's saying it as shouldn't.'

'Shame.' I took another sip of the wine; a small one. 'So how was it strange? Him going away, I mean? It wasn't planned?'

'Nah, happened right out of the blue. He just up and left, no warning, nothing. Plain vanished. He was here sure enough two days ago, that I do know because I came round with a bowl of bean stew the wife had set aside for him, Matia being away – we only live up the road, see, 'tother side of the gate, and she's been sending down something cooked regular. When I talked to him not a word about going anywhere did he speak. Only when I call in yesterday morning to pick up the dish he's gone. Door wide open, anyone could've walked in off the street and helped themselves. Anyway, I couldn't just close the place up until he decided to come back; business isn't good at the best of times, and if I didn't owe it to him I owed it to my sister. We've a vegetable stall next the house, me and the wife, but she can manage that well enough on her own, so here I am for the duration.'

'He, uh, wouldn't be a big guy, this Caprius, would he? Thick black curly hair, nose broken and badly reset?'

'Nah, he's about my size, and he'll be bald as a coot in another five years, like I will myself.' He looked at me suspiciously. 'Here, sir, did you come in here just for a cup of wine, or was there another reason?'

Well, I'd have to tell him sooner or later, if only for his sister's peace of mind. 'I'm sorry, pal,' I said gently. 'But I don't think your brother-in-law is coming back at all.'

He stared at me.

'Is that so, now?' he said. 'And how would you know?'

'Because if I'm right – and I think I am – he's dead.'

He went pale. 'Oh, shit!' he said. 'Oh, holy Mothers!'

I passed him the wine cup, and he gulped the rest of it down. Well, better him than me.

Then he said: 'How?'

But that was one thing I wasn't going to tell him, not the fine details, anyway: there would have to be some fudging here. 'My name's Valerius Corvinus,' I said. 'Caprius and a friend of his kidnapped my chief slave two days back, and they were holding him in the cellar. A friend of mine got him out early yesterday morning, probably just before you came by, and took your brother-in-law away with him. There was, uh, an accident later, as a result of which your brother-in-law died.'

'Good sweet Jupiter!' He was obviously in shock. He took the wine cup over to the flask-rack and filled it, pouring with an unsteady hand: the cup overfilled, and wine splashed onto the floor. He replaced the flask and drank the whole cupful in a oner, then wiped his mouth with the back of his free hand and turned back to me. 'You're not telling me the whole truth, are you?' he said.

'No,' I said. 'I'm not. But what I've told you is true as far as the basics go. You've my word on it.'

'Why would Caprius want to kidnap your slave?'

'I don't know. Not altogether. But that's what happened. Now. You feel well enough to talk?'

'Kidnapping? *Caprius?* It doesn't make any sense.'

'You're sure about that?'

He looked at me for a long time. Then he shook his head. 'No. No, you're right. I'm not sure. Caprius was a...well, let's just say that I was sorry when he married Matia, and she's come round since to feeling that way herself. He was never straight, I'll grant you that, but kidnapping's something else altogether, that's well beyond him. Or I'd've thought so, at least.'

'It would've been worse, believe me, if my friend hadn't stepped in.'

'Holy gods!' He shook his head again numbly.

'The other guy I described. The big guy with the curly hair and broken nose. He sound familiar?'

This time he nodded. 'Ligurinus,' he said. 'One of Caprius's cronies. His bosom crony, you might say.' He shot me a sideways look. 'He's a real bad one, that. I'd've believed it of him straight off; I'd've believed anything. He's a blacksmith, got a forge and shop not all that far from here, on Mars Incline, if you're looking for him.'

'Uh-uh,' I said. 'No point. He's dead too.' That got me a sharp glance, but he didn't say anything. 'You know anything more about him?'

'Not much, and never wanted to. He's a freedman, full name Publius Suillius Ligurinus. Been in trouble a few times, violence mostly. Leads Caprius by the nose.' He must've noticed my expression. 'Mean something to you?'

'Publius Suillius?' I said. 'Those are his first two names? You're sure?'

'Of course I'm sure.'

'You know anything about his patron? Who he is, exactly?'

'No. I told you, I keep well away from that bastard. I'd've told Caprius to do the same, if he'd've listened, and so would Matia. She probably did. He was mixed up in this thing too, was he?'

'Yeah. Very much so.'

'Then good riddance to him. It explains a lot. He'd've been the ringleader; Caprius would've just followed on, done what he was told.'

Uh-huh; that was how I'd thought it would be. All the same, the name had rocked me.

Publius Suillius Ligurinus, eh? Jupiter and all the gods!

A newly-made freedman tacks his own, given name on to the first two names of his former owner, who then becomes his patron. And the only Publius Suillius I knew of was Publius Suillius Rufus, Perilla's very-much-ex husband.

The plot was definitely thickening. It was starting to smell, as well.

'Thanks, pal,' I said, getting ready to leave. 'And I'm sorry about your brother-in-law, if you are. Give your sister my condolences.'

'I will. But to tell you the truth after the first shock it'll come as a relief. The good gods forgive me for saying so, but that's the long and the short of it.' He hesitated. 'I should ask you about the body, sir.'

Oh, shit; I'd forgotten about that aspect of things. I fudged again; there was nothing else I could do.

‘Ah...I think that’s been taken care of,’ I said. The harsh probability was that Eutacticus had already made his own arrangements. I just hoped, like I said re the meatballs, that they didn’t involve his piscine pets.

He gave me another long look, then took his eyes away.

‘Fair enough,’ he said. ‘I’ll tell her. Thank you at least for coming, sir.’

A ‘you’re welcome’ wouldn’t’ve been appropriate in the circumstances. I left in silence.

# 15

I headed up Latin Road for the Caelian, thinking hard all the way.

Rufus's path and mine had only crossed directly once in the twenty-odd years Perilla and I had been married. That had been right at the start, in fact the following year, when we'd been in Antioch looking into the death of Germanicus at the behest of the old empress Livia, and he'd commanded one of the Syrian legions. Five years later and back in Rome he'd been nailed for judicial corruption and exiled by Tiberius. Gaius had recalled him, and since then he'd oiled his way back into society and politics, even to the extent of making suffect consul three years before, in Claudius's first year as emperor: I'd've thought the smart old buffer would've had more sense than to make an appointment like that, but there you went, we all have our blind spots.

That, in sum, was pretty well all I knew about Publius Suillius Rufus, except that, from what Perilla had told me about him coupled with my own experience, he was a five-star, gold-plated wrong-'un and a total, fully-paid-up bastard. A perfect match for Ligurinus, in other words. If Ligurinus – forget Caprius, the also-ran – was working for him, which given the usual patron-client relationship was practically a cert, then no great surprises there.

Where, how and why Oplonius came into things, now, that was the real puzzle, and something I had to talk over with Perilla. I'd got a couple of ideas, sure, but they were only that: unsupported theorising. Again, what we really needed was Damon; and Damon, thanks to bloody Eutacticus, we were unlikely to get.

Bugger.

Perilla was having her hair done when I got home – obviously, wearing Queen Philistis's necklace had put her in mind of it – so I lay on the atrium couch and twiddled my thumbs until her maid Phryne had finished and taken all her bibs and bobs back out.

Women's attitude to hair and hair-styling has always been a mystery to me. Oh, sure, I enjoy going down to Market Square for a haircut as much as the next man: barbers are the best, not to say the best-informed, conversationalists in Rome. Go where you will and you can be certain that together with the trim itself a few coppers will buy you a decent, intelligent conversation, as long as you keep off subjects like pre-Socratic metaphysics and pastoral poetry and stick to Green's chances in the next racing meet or how so-and-so's team of gladiators is shaping up. Me, I'm not a big racing or fights fan, so most of the time I tend just to close my eyes and relax throughout the process. Which is fine with them as well, because Roman barbers know when to shut up and get on with it.

The point is, with men a haircut is a haircut is a haircut: you sit down in the chair, the lad gets busy with the shears and razor, and you leave fifteen minutes later looking neater and tidier than when you came, possibly with a hot tip for the up-and-coming Games. End of story. With women the cutting part of things, when it happens at all, is incidental and subordinate to the primping and curling and general to-and-fro of what-does-it-look-like-now, and it can take hours of infinitesimal tweaking and constant interplay between stylist and stylee before they're finally satisfied.

I mean, why the hell do they *bother?* Life is just too fucking short.

So, anyway, there I was, twiddling my thumbs in imposed virtual silence right up to the last tweak.

'Satisfied, lady?' I said when Phryne had finally exited.

'Yes, perfectly, thank you, Marcus,' Perilla moved from the chair to the couch and lay down. 'Now. How was your day?'

I told her. When I got to the part about Rufus she frowned.

‘You’re sure?’ she said. ‘That he’s involved, I mean?’

‘No, of course I’m not,’ I said. ‘But it’s the likeliest explanation, isn’t it? He was this Ligurinus’s patron, after all; he had to be, unless you know of another Publius Suillius Something who’d fit the bill.’

Her hand strayed up to one of the curls and she twisted at it gently. Yeah, well, that’s one good thing about Perilla: when you get down to it she’s no absolute perfectionist. Not where the preservation of recent hair-styling goes, anyway. ‘In that case, why?’ she said. ‘What possible interest could Rufus have in someone like Oplonius?’

I shrugged. ‘Search me. Even so, there has to be some connection.’

‘But they’re from completely different backgrounds, and they move in completely different worlds! Oplonius was a small-time provincial thief and swindler, and Rufus, for all his faults, is a society figure. Not from one of the top families, I grant you’ – the barest sniff; well, they hadn’t got on, even when they were married. Which is putting it mildly – ‘but he is an ex-consul, after all.’

‘There’s the original scenario,’ I said. ‘The necklace one. Oplonius had stolen something belonging to Rufus, and Rufus wants it back.’

‘I’m sorry, but you know what I think of that one, dear. It’s far too much of a coincidence for comfort.’

‘Yeah, fair enough. I agree.’ I hesitated. ‘There is another possibility that occurred to me on the way from the Latin Gate. That Oplonius isn’t Oplonius.’

‘Marcus, please do try to make sense. I haven’t the patience.’

‘Look. We only know him as Oplonius because that’s what he called himself, and it was the name Damon gave us, right?’

‘Of course. But why should–?’

'Perilla, I can't answer the whys. If I could we'd be a hell of a lot closer to solving this thing. Just bear with me, okay?'

'Very well. Go on.'

'According to Damon – and the guy himself, when he was alive – he's Gaius Oplonius, a small-time provincial merchant from Padua, in Rome to scare up some business. Fine, we know now that that last part is phoney, at least in an honest sense, but we've been assuming the first bit, his actual name, isn't. Only that's all it is: an assumption. We've no objective proof.'

'Eutacticus knew him by that name as well; it's how he tracked him down, presumably, because otherwise he would have said. And their involvement predated Oplonius's arrival in Rome.'

'The alias doesn't have to be a recent one. For all we know he might've been using it for years. All I'm saying – or suggesting, rather – is that alias it is; that his real name was something different.'

'Marcus, are you basing this on *anything* concrete, or is it pure guesswork? Because if so–'

'Hang on, give me a chance here. Just think. It would clear up a good few of the problems and puzzles, wouldn't it?'

'Would it?'

'First off: when I talked to Lydia she said Oplonius spoke with an upper-class accent. "A touch of the lah-de-dah" was how she described it. Not what you'd expect from a provincial merchant, which was what he told her he was. She thought he might be from a good family originally and down on his luck. What's to say she was wrong?'

Perilla sighed. 'I'm sorry, dear,' she said, 'but this is pure speculation. The line of work your Lydia is in she probably hadn't ever heard an upper-class accent in her life to compare it with.'

'Cut out the snobbishness, lady. Lydia is no fool, and you sound like Bathyllus.'

At least that got me a grin and a duck of the head. 'All right. Point taken. What other problems and puzzles does it solve?'

'The question of the ring, for starters. Where it came from, and what happened to it. Let's say Lydia was right in her guess again: that it was an heirloom, a recognisable one, and that it was Oplonius's own property to begin with. He didn't sell it, which is what she assumed; he couldn't've done because there was no sign of the money later. So where did it go? My guess is that he used it to prove his bona fides; that he sent it to the prospective buyer, who for sake of argument we'll call Suillius Rufus, to confirm who he was and that he had whatever he had for sale. That'd be another problem solved: he and Rufus weren't from different sides of the tracks at all, they were social equals. Where family was concerned, for all we know our pseudo-Oplonius might even have had the edge.'

'Hmm.' She was twisting the lock of hair. 'I must admit it does sound convincing. As a possible theory, at least.'

'Come on, Perilla! It fits the facts all the way down the line!'

'He was still a crook. The business of the necklace proves that.'

'No one's claiming otherwise. Since when has being one of a family from high on the social register been a guarantee of honesty and moral rectitude? Quite the reverse: half the fucking senate are morally suspect, to say the least; the only things distinguishing them from your low-class thieves, muggers and con-men are that they operate on a bigger scale and the purple stripe and old boys' network means they get away with it. And even with the honest ones you don't need to go too far back into their family histories to turn up some bastard who could run a swindle or milk a province as easy as breathing.'

‘True. But that doesn’t mean you have to swear.’

‘Yeah. Right. Even so. You get black sheep in any family. Chances are, Oplonius had either been slung out on his ear and disinherited or he’d walked out on them off his own bat. That’d explain his lack of funds, certainly: no rich daddy to pick up the tab or keep his wayward son in the lush manner he’d been accustomed to. He’d be completely on his own, living hand to mouth, and the upper classes aren’t trained for that. Not where plying an honest trade’s concerned.’

‘So if he wasn’t Gaius Oplonius then who was he? And what was he selling?’

‘I’ve no idea. Not yet. But obviously Rufus – if our chief perp is Rufus – knows the answers damn well, and whatever the thing is he’s desperate to get his hands on it. So we start from the Rufus end. Me, I’d reckon this is another one for Caelius Crispus.’

‘Oh, Marcus! You think he’d help?’

‘Of course he would; he always does. Not a bad lad, Crispus, if he’s handled in the right way.’ Which involved basically, going by past experience, a sheer unadulterated brazenness of approach, followed up as appropriate by brow-beating and/or blackmail. Mind you, to give him his due, Crispus was also a professional to his metaphorically-grubby fingertips; enough of a professional, certainly, to enjoy his work even when he was squealing about being forced over a barrel to tell you what you wanted to know. So yes, I was pretty certain that he’d help, eventually. ‘I’ll go and see him tomorrow.’

Which is what I did.

# 16

Crispus and I went way back, in fact to pre-Perilla days, when he'd been a ragged-arsed plain mantle of doubtful parentage and even more doubtful morals. The acquaintance – you couldn't call it friendship, not by a long chalk – started when I saved him from a fate worse than death at the hands of an outraged daddy who was after him with a very sharp knife, and it had gone steadily downhill from then, even as Crispus rose. All by his own considerable efforts, I had to admit: what the little rat didn't know, through a lifetime's constant and assiduous gleaning, about the cupboarded skeletons and dirty laundry of Rome's top five hundred wasn't worth bothering about. Which was why, at present, he held down a very responsible and respectable desk in the Foreign Judges' office and the last time I'd seen him had been sporting a newly-acquired purple stripe on his mantle. Usually, to get on in the Roman political or administrative hierarchy, what matters is either who you are or who you know, preferably both. In Crispus's case, you replaced the 'who' in the latter clause by 'what'. Quietly making your boss aware that you know what *really* happened to that stray two million from the accounts, or whose wife, daughter, son or domestic pet he is currently screwing, and being able to prove it, is a pretty effective way of moving up the ladder.

So there I was, not too bright and early – responsible and respectable judicial admin officers need their beauty sleep of a morning – knocking on Crispus's office door.

'Come.'

Nicely brusque and authoritative; he was really picking up the mannerisms appropriate to his new elevated status, was Crispus. I grinned and pushed the door open.

The lad was sitting at his desk with a pile of paperwork either side of him. He looked up at me like I was the grisly spirit of murdered Agamemnon come back to demand vengeance on his slayers.

'Oh, shit,' he said.

'Morning, sunshine.' I went over to the desk, pulled up a stool, and sat. 'How are things in the judging business?'

'I'd hoped you were dead, Corvinus.'

'Nah, not me,' I said. 'Hale, hearty and thriving as ever. Full of the joys of spring. Perilla sends her regards.'

'Bugger off.'

'Come on, pal, we haven't seen each other for ages! How long has it been, now?'

'Three years. And shortly afterwards an emperor was assassinated. You think that was a coincidence? Because I don't.'

'Nothing to do with me, Crispus,' I said. Well, almost true: to be fair, for all Gaius's faults I'd've stopped it if I could. 'But since you ask, yes, you can help me with something. Thank you.'

'I didn't fucking ask, I've no intention of asking, and I've got work to do. Now I told you: bugger off.' He reached for the flimsy on the top of the pile to his right.

'Publius Suillius Rufus,' I said.

His hand paused. 'Who?'

'You heard. Know him?'

'Of course I know him!'

'Good. Let's start there. Tell me about him; the recent stuff.'

'I'll tell you again: bugger off! And stay buggered off!'

I sighed. 'Look, do we really, really need to do this the hard way?' He glanced at me suspiciously but said nothing. 'Okay, if that's how you want to play it. You still got the country villa in the Alban Hills? The one near my adopted daughter and son-in-law's place in Castrimoenium, that you bought to entertain broad-striper bigwigs you want to impress?'

'Corvinus...'

'Only we'll be going down there shortly, Perilla and me, to visit the family and see how the grand-sprog is getting on. If you happen to have a party staying we could drop by some evening, say hello. Nothing formal, no prior warning, and I'm sure your senatorial friends would be delighted if we – Perilla and I, that is – indulged over the nibbles in a few personal reminiscences. You remember that club on the Pincian you belonged to, for example? The one that was closed down suddenly? What was it called, now?'

'Corvinus, you bastard. You promised me faithfully last time that you wouldn't go near the place, particularly when I have guests.'

'Uh-uh.' I shook my head. 'Wrong. If you remember correctly I said that that particular deal was a one-off. I was very careful to stress it, too. So. Publius Suillius Rufus.'

He sagged. 'Okay. Let's get it over with. What do you want to know?'

'I told you: the recent stuff. Anything you think is relevant.'

'Relevant to what?'

'If I knew that I wouldn't be asking. Anyway, you know what I mean.'

That got me a very cagey look. 'Nothing to tell,' he said. 'At least, nothing you couldn't've found out elsewhere.'

'I'll be the judge of that, pal. Just give, okay?'

'He's into the forensic side of things in a big way. Prosecuting.'

'Namely?'

'If you want recently, it'd have to be last year's two big trials.'

'Which big trials?'

He looked at me in amazement. 'You mean you don't already know? Jupiter, boy, where–?'

'I don't keep up with the courts news, Crispus, not as a general rule. Anyway, last year I was abroad for a fair chunk of the time, so I probably missed them. Who were the defendants?'

'Julia Livia and Catonius Justus.'

I whistled softly. Julia Livia I knew, or knew of, rather. Of course I did. She was an imperial, the emperor Tiberius's granddaughter and widow of Claudius Nero, the eldest son of Germanicus and Agrippina who'd been exiled and imprisoned by Aelius Sejanus's doing and put to death thirteen years before.

'Who's Justus?' I said.

Crispus grinned. 'Corvinus, if I knew as little about the great and good of this city as you do I'd still be pushing a pen in the secretaries' room downstairs. Catonius Justus was one of the praetorian prefects.'

I sat back. Gods! We were certainly moving in top-notch circles here. And things were definitely beginning to smell fishy. 'How come Rufus got the job?' I said. 'Of prosecutor, I mean.'

The grin faded. 'I couldn't say.'

'Come on, Crispus! It's a simple question and you know the answer to it well enough. Give!'

'You're not being fair. Politics isn't my main area of expertise. You know that.'

'Crispus, you prevaricating bastard...'

'All right. All *right!*' He hesitated. 'The word is that the emperor chose him personally.'

'Claudius did? *Claudius?*'

Crispus shrugged. 'You asked. I'm answering. And word goes on to say that he wouldn't listen to anything Julia Livia or her friends could offer in her defence, before, during or after the trial.'

'So where did he send her?'

'She wasn't exiled, she was executed. Immediately after her conviction. So was Justus.'

'*What?*' Jupiter, this I just couldn't believe! 'Livia was Claudius's own kin! His cousin's wife! What the hell had she been charged with?'

'Immorality.'

'Screwing around? Is that all? And she gets the chop for it?'

Another shrug. 'Don't blame me, Corvinus. I'm simply telling you like it was. The emperor passed the sentences himself.'

'So what was Justus's crime?'

'Treason, plus immorality with Julia Livia. The two were lovers, seemingly.'

'Convenient.' My brain was racing. We'd been this way before, many times: immorality was a catch-all charge, used to cover a range of crimes or none, when for one reason or another, legitimate or otherwise, the accuser – usually the emperor – either didn't want to be specific for security's sake or was manufacturing a lie from whole cloth. So which was the case here? Julia Livia I didn't know enough about to make a guess; for Justus, given his post as co-commander of the Praetorian Guard, treason was at least within the bounds of credibility; certainly it was a lead to be followed up. Immediate execution, though, now that was definitely weird. For a member of the imperial family like Livia was it didn't make sense, even for treason: females were exiled, sent somewhere they couldn't do any harm, usually to a fly-speck island like Pandateria off the Campanian coast. Even the males were disappeared to be killed off quietly later when they'd effectively been forgotten about.

This needed serious thought.

'Corvinus?' Crispus was staring at me. 'You okay?'

'Hmm?' I blinked. 'Oh. Yeah, I'm fine. So what else can you tell me?'

'That's it. That's all I know.' He held up a hand before I could object. 'Genuinely! I told you, politics isn't my field. You want more, you'll have to ask someone else.'

'Such as who?'

He hesitated again, then glanced over his shoulder – the gods knew why, because we were alone in the room and there was a wall behind him, but this was Crispus; it was probably ingrained, like a tic – leaned forward and lowered his voice. 'Me, I'd have a word with a lady by the name of Pomponia Graecina.'

'Who's Graecina?'

'A friend of Livia's. Her best friend, in fact. Just don't mention my name, okay? In fact leave me out of everything altogether. That's all you're getting. Now push off.'

I stood up. 'You happen to know where I can find her?'

'Big house on the Quirinal, up Long Street just before the junction with High Path.' He reached again for the flimsy on top of the pile. 'Remember, if shoving your nose into this kills you, and I hope to Jupiter that it does, I'll dance on your grave. Now go and lose yourself. Properly, this time.'

I grinned. 'Right. Thanks, Crispus, I'll see you around.' I paused, my hand on the doorknob. 'Oh, by the way, you happen to know anything about a Gaius Oplonius? Posed as a wool merchant from Padua but probably wasn't?'

'No.'

Well, that single syllable had the definite ring of finality and truth to it: if he had known anything about our pseudo-Oplonius the shifty bugger would've wrapped the denial up in fancier language. And it didn't surprise me, really. I was coming round to the belief that whoever *in propria persona* the dead man was he'd been out of circulation for quite some time.

'It doesn't matter,' I said. 'Thanks again, pal.'

He didn't answer, just carried on reading and raised a single finger in salute. I grinned again and turned to leave.

It was still well short of noon; plenty of time, then, to go over to the Quirinal.

The houses there are old-money-rich. Most of them are big and rambling, and they look like they've been there since Scipio Africanus cut his first tooth, which in fact most of them have. The families, too. I asked one of the door-slaves dozing in the spring sunshine for directions and he pointed me to Graecina's place a bit further up the hill.

Crispus's 'big house' was right, and you can add the 'rambling' for good measure: I reckoned, from the length of the outside wall, it took up at least half as much ground again as the houses I'd already passed. I gave my name to the door-slave and waited while he checked whether the lady was At Home.

She was, in the garden, standing chatting to a smallish, thin-branched tree with narrow leaves and sprays of pinkish-white flowers.

Right. Chatting. To a tree.

Uh-huh.

She turned towards me as I came down the path from the house, a youngish woman no older than late thirties, small and dumpy, but not a bad looker. I noticed she was wearing as many amulets draped around her neck as would equip a stall outside one of the more popular temples.

'Valerius Corvinus, welcome!' she said, stretching out both hands to me. There wasn't much I could do, under the circumstances: I took them and gave them a perfunctory shake.

You can add several charm bracelets to the above. The resulting effect was like rattling a couple of tambourines.

'Good of you to see me, Pomponia Graecina,' I said.

She let my hands go. 'Nonsense!' she said. 'Your wife is Rufia Perilla, yes? The poet Ovid's stepdaughter?'

'Ah...yeah. Yes, she is, as it happens.' I was feeling more than a tad disorientated. 'How did you–?'

'My father used to correspond with him regularly. Pomponius Graecinus?' I must've looked blank. 'Never mind, but no doubt your wife would remember. We've met on many occasions, she and I. At poetry readings, mostly. Unlike her, I don't write, but I do take a keen interest. She's very good, isn't she?'

'So I'm told, yes.' I glanced at the tree. 'I hope I wasn't, uh, interrupting anything there, by the way.'

She laughed. 'You mean my talking to the tamarisk? Oh, but you must always talk to your plants. It keeps them healthy and it encourages them to grow. And tamarisks are special, very special. You know that it was embedded in a tamarisk trunk that Mother Isis found the chest containing the Lord Osiris's body? The chest was embedded, that is, not Mother Isis.'

Daft as a brush, this one, I thought. Still, at least she seemed relatively harmless. 'No,' I said. 'No, I didn't know that.'

'Perfectly true. So you must be extra-specially polite to them. But I always make a tour of the garden round about now and have a quick word with everything, especially the ones that are looking a bit peaky. Early afternoon is the best time; they're all fully awake by then. Aulus tells me I'm silly – you know Aulus? My husband Aulus Plautius? – but we have the largest and healthiest plants in the neighbourhood, so I tell him that I don't care.'

Plautius, right? Currently the emperor's commander-in-chief of the British expedition, and so the proto-province's first designated governor. Well, for the sake of our future British prospects I was glad to hear that he, at least, wouldn't be worrying his subordinates by fraternising with the local flora.

'Now.' Graecina signalled to a hovering slave. 'There's a very pleasant little arbour over there in the corner by the lemon tree. Sextus here will bring you a cup of wine – a barley water for me, please, Sextus – and you can sit and tell me why you've come.'

That sounded pretty good to me, especially since I'd done a fair bit of walking that morning and my throat was dry as a camel's armpit. Or whatever. I followed her over to the arbour and we sat down on the Gallic wicker chairs.

'So,' she said. 'The floor – or at least this patch of gravel – is yours.'

I was beginning to like Pomponia Graecina; even if she did talk to the trees and clank like a foundry when she moved there was a definite brain there, and a pretty considerable one, at that. Besides, for all I knew she was spot on about the plants: as I remembered it, our gardener Alexis had had a theory that you could improve the size and yield of pea-plants with the aid of a rabbit-tail brush inserted into the flowers, and Alexis was no fool. I'd have to mention her idea to him and see what he thought of it.

'It's about Julia Livia,' I said. 'I understand she was a friend of yours.'

‘Oh.’ She was suddenly serious. ‘Oh, yes, of course she was, poor girl. What happened to her was dreadful, simply dreadful. And I shall never forgive Claudius, not if I live to be ninety. Mind you, he’ll be long dead himself by then, and good riddance.’

Uh-huh. Well, hardly a tactful opening statement. But I suspected that the lady didn’t do tact to any great degree.

‘She was, uh, accused of misconduct,’ I said.

‘The word is immorality, Valerius Corvinus.’ Her mouth had set in a hard line; no sign of silliness now. ‘Sexual immorality. Complete and utter nonsense. Livia was the most virtuous soul alive, a totally devoted wife and mother. She wouldn’t have looked twice at any man, least of all poor Justus, who was sixty if he was a day and a model of honour.’

‘So why the charge?’

‘I’ve no idea. I said: there was no sense to it, none at all. Mind you, although Claudius behaved quite despicably throughout and must bear ultimate responsibility for her death I very much doubt if he was the moving force. He always was weak-willed and malleable, quite the wrong things for an emperor to be. It was that young hussy of a wife of his who persuaded him.’

My guts went cold. ‘Messalina?’

‘She’s a relative of yours, of course, so I’m sorry if I’m giving offence, and I’ve no objective proof whatsoever, but I am completely convinced of it. Poor Livia was, too; it was practically the last thing she said to me. “Tell Blandus” – that was her husband Rubellius Blandus, Bland by name and bland by nature, unfortunately, but we’ll let that pass – “that this was Messalina’s doing.”’

Oh, shit, this I could *really* do without!

The slave brought the tray and handed me my cup of wine. I swallowed half of it at a gulp, then wished I hadn't: it was Massic, and top-grade Massic at that, which is really saying something. I took another sip; a careful one this time.

Graecina was watching me closely.

'Forgive me,' she said, 'but you haven't actually explained your interest. I mean, Livia was my closest friend, and her death is very fresh in my mind and always will be, so to me the circumstances surrounding it are of considerable weight and independent of time. But the trial and execution were all over and done with almost nine months ago. They really shouldn't be any concern to anyone by now, let alone a complete stranger.'

Politely and indirectly phrased, sure, but the gist was unmistakable: 'What the hell are you doing here, and why are you asking me these questions?' An intelligent brain right enough, and she deserved an answer, even though it couldn't be a full one.

'Actually, my main interest is in Suillius Rufus,' I said. 'For other reasons not directly connected with your friend.' If Messalina was involved then I was hoping desperately that such was the case. However, judging by my past dealings with the little viper I suspected the hope was in the flying pigs bracket.

'Rufus?' She frowned. '*That*' – her lips closed on the next word – 'gentleman. Well, Valerius Corvinus, if you're attempting to bring some other instance of his villainy home to Suillius Rufus then you have my complete support. The man is scum, pure and simple. The world would be a far cleaner place without him.'

Yeah, I'd agree with her there. And it was yet another proof, if I needed one, that the lady didn't mince her words.

'He have any personal reasons for wanting to bring down Julia Livia and Justus that you know of? Any at all?' I asked. It was worth checking, at least; always best to dot the i's and cross the t's.

'Absolutely none. I'm sure of that, in Livia's case, and very probably not in Justus's. Besides, they weren't his first by any means.'

'How's that again?'

'There was Livia's cousin, for a start. Gaius's sister, Livilla.' She sniffed. 'I'd no time for Livilla myself; she was vain and vicious, a spoilt brat from birth and a thoroughly bad lot. If her prosecutor hadn't been Rufus I wouldn't have any sympathy for her whatsoever, she deserved all she got a dozen times over, but as it is I do feel a little sorry for the woman.'

Yeah, come to think of it Livilla was one I had known about. As well as being Gaius's youngest sister she'd been married to Marcus Vinicius, a friend of Perilla's through the lady's poetry klatch. I'd met her a couple of times, most memorably at that hellish dinner party just before Gaius got chopped. And again I agreed with Graecina: although I had a lot of time for Vinicius despite him being solidly on the imperial side of the fence, his wife had been a horror. As I remembered it, like Julia Livia she'd been tried for immorality (although in her case the cap fitted perfectly nem. con.), exiled, and quietly got rid of. That would've been, what, three years back.

I hadn't known that the prosecutor had been Rufus, mind. That was news.

'So who else?' I said.

'Well, let's see.' She frowned. 'There was Junius Silanus. He came shortly afterwards.'

That name rang a very large bell, too. '*Gaius* Junius Silanus?' I said. 'Consul about fifteen years back?'

'Yes, that's him.'

'Accused of?'

'Attempting to assassinate the emperor.'

'*What?*'

'Indeed. If it weren't so tragic it would be funny. There was no actual attempt at all, as far as I'm aware. The evidence came from a dream, or rather two dreams, which Messalina and the emperor's secretary Narcissus had simultaneously – or rather said they had, of course; each is as bad as the other – of Silanus with a dagger in his hand standing over Claudius while he was asleep in his room. That, seemingly, provided sufficient grounds for the emperor to have the man tried and condemn him to death.' Another sniff. 'For such a clever man – and Claudius certainly is that – he can be a complete, gullible fool at times.'

Junius Silanus and attempted assassination of the emperor by dagger, eh? History repeating itself, or rather going one step further this time round. And she was right: it was ludicrous. It had been ludicrous the previous time, too.

'Then, let me think, oh, yes, Annius Vinicianus, a few months later. He was the last one before Livia.'

The hairs on the back of my neck prickled. Oh, shit; this was becoming far too relevant for comfort. I knew Vinicianus as well, and from the same context as Livilla: he'd been Marcus Vinicius's nephew, definitely a wrong-'un if there ever was, and a crony – at the least – of Messalina's herself. I must've missed Vinicianus's trial, though, for some reason, because that little snippet of information came as a surprise.

‘What was he charged with? You happen to know?’ I said. Not that I suspected it mattered, because it wouldn’t’ve been the real reason, whatever that might be, but still...

‘Treason, I think. I’m not sure. Anyway, he killed himself before the trial was convened. No great loss there, either.

Sweet immortal gods, we’d really been getting names out of my past here, and no mistake. Vinicianus’s made the set. And I was feeling more than a touch of chill on my spine: when you added all that up and took a cold, hard look at it it didn’t leave all that much room for doubt. While if Suillius Rufus was the common factor, then it didn’t leave any room at all...

We were in it up to the eyeballs yet again. Fuck. Double fuck. Perilla would be delighted.

I swallowed the last of the Massic and stood up.

‘You’re going?’ Graecina said.

‘Yeah, unless there’s anything else you think I should know.’ I set the empty cup down on the ground. ‘Thanks for your help, Pomponia Graecina, *really* thanks: you’ve given me a lot to think about.’ That was putting it mildly: my head was buzzing with it all, and what I really needed now was the walk back to the Caelian to put it into some sort of logical order.

‘Do give my best regards to your wife, then.’ She was regarding me critically, head tilted to one side. ‘You know, you do have the most extraordinarily bright aura. I noticed it straight away when you were coming from the house, even with the sunlight, but in this partial shade it’s very clear indeed. Perhaps I shouldn’t mention it, because no doubt you’ll think I’m silly at best or cracked at worst, but I couldn’t let you leave without saying something.’

'Ah...right. Right.' I backed away hastily. 'Thanks again, lady.'

'You're welcome. And I do hope you'll manage to hand Suillius Rufus his deserts, whatever he's involved in. A shame you can't do something about Valeria Messalina directly, but I'm afraid that will be impossible until that idiot Claudius wakes up to what she really is.'

True. That was partly what was worrying me. Still, we'd cross that particular bridge when we came to it.

I set off back home.

# 17

Perilla, too, was in the garden. I nodded in passing to the miniature palm beside the portico exit – we weren't on speaking terms yet; I'd work up to that – and went over to where she was sitting with an open book-roll on her lap.

She smiled at me. 'You're looking rather grim, dear,' she said. 'Anything wrong? How did your meeting with Crispus go?'

'We're in deep trouble, lady,' I said, putting Bathyllus's welcome-home wine cup on the garden table and pulling up the other chair. 'The case has just turned political. And whatever is going on six gets you ten that Messalina's at the bottom of it.'

The smile disappeared. 'Oh, Marcus!'

'Right. Joy in the morning.' I fortified myself with a hefty swig of wine and took her through the whole horrific boiling.

'It could be a coincidence,' she said after I'd finished. 'I mean, the only common factor linking our Oplonius business with the trials is Rufus himself. And bringing Messalina into the equation was only Graecina's idea, got from Julia Livia herself at a time when she might well not have been thinking very rationally.'

'Fine. You want to bet on all that, or should I just take your money now?'

She grinned and ducked her head. 'No, I'm sure we'll find you're perfectly correct. Unfortunately. What did you think of Pomponia Graecina, by the way? As a person?'

I hesitated. 'I'm not sure,' I said. 'Oh, in some ways she's six tiles short of a watertight roof, but she doesn't miss much, and she struck me as a smart, smart cookie.'

'Smart she certainly is. She's an excellent mathematician and an expert on Aristotle: I believe she has the whole of his *Physics* by heart. It's a pity about her other side, mind you, all this mystic nonsense, and quite surprising, too, considering the juxtaposition, but then that's Graecina. And if she believes that Messalina is behind Rufus her opinion is worth taking seriously.'

'Yeah, that's what I thought.' I frowned. 'Okay, in that case let's lay what we've got out on the table and have a look at it.'

'Fair enough.' She put the book-roll aside. 'Where do you want to begin?'

'Take it in the same order Graecina did, starting with Julia Livia herself. You ever meet her, by any chance?'

'I knew her slightly, through Marcus Vinicius. He and she were always very close, even given the rather tenuous family connection, practically uncle and favourite niece. And from what I could tell Graecina is quite right: Livia wasn't the philandering type. Her marriage to Nero was an arranged one, of course. She could only have been about fifteen at the time, and they weren't really suited; I'm not surprised there were no children, and when he was exiled and put to death I suspect that if anything she was rather relieved. She married again a few years later; her own choice, I think, because although he wasn't very prominent either politically or socially the man was much more her type.'

'Yeah, Graecina mentioned him. Rubellius Blandus, right? She was a bit dismissive.'

'Ah.' She smiled. 'That's typical Graecina again, I'm afraid. She doesn't do things, or judge people, by halves, and she has very strong likes and dislikes which aren't always logical. Livia wasn't an intellectual of her standard, nowhere near, but she did take a keen and intelligent interest in books, history especially, and Graecina felt that she was rather wasted on Blandus. I don't think, whatever she says to the contrary, that she really understood that all the woman wanted was a steady family man for a husband. Which is what Blandus was. They had a son quite quickly, I believe. He'll be about eight or nine years old now.'

'So why should Rufus – Messalina – target her?'

'I honestly don't know, Marcus. Oh, she was one of the imperial family, yes, but on its own that would be no reason at all as far as I can see. I mean, she wasn't ambitious or interfering, quite the reverse; all she wanted was a quiet life. She wasn't a danger, and she couldn't have had anything at all that Messalina wanted.'

'What about Blandus himself?'

'You mean as a lover?' She shot me a look, smiled again, and shook her head. 'No, dear. Definitely not. I've met him as well; he's in his late fifties, fat and balding, and dull as ditch-water. Hardly a *femme fatale*'s daydream, particularly not one as choosy as Messalina.'

'Okay,' I said. 'Leave Livia for now and move on. Catonius Justus. Praetorian prefect, condemned and executed for treason and immorality with Livia. Any ideas there?'

'Given his position the treason side of things is certainly a possibility.'

'Yeah, I thought that myself.' I took a swallow of the wine. 'We don't know anything about Justus. Still, Graecina seemed to think pretty highly of him, and linking the treason aspect of things with the obviously trumped-up immorality charge makes it suspect to say the least. Anyway, it's something else to follow up. Maybe Gaius Secundus could help.' Secundus was a long-standing friend of mine, currently in military admin. 'Let him go for the present. Now we come to the biggies. Julia Livilla.'

'Ah.'

'Ah is right. As far as the charges are concerned, she had all-round form in spades.'

'In Livilla's case *big* and *all-round* are quite appropriate, aren't they?'

'Come again?'

'Well, she was fairly large, wasn't she? You remember her at that dreadful dinner party? She practically needed a whole couch to herself.'

'Don't be catty, lady. This is serious.'

She stifled a smile. 'I'm sorry, dear. You're quite right, and it isn't relevant. So. What about Livilla?'

'If we're being honest we have to admit she was prime accuser bait to begin with. On the immorality front she must've screwed half the eligible studs in Rome in her time, including that tick Annaeus Seneca. Not to mention Brother Gaius himself.'

'There's no need to be crude, Marcus. Mind you, I agree with you about Seneca; he is a complete tick. And a terrible poet, what's more.'

I ignored her. 'She had form where the treason aspect of things is concerned, too,' I said. 'We know that from the Gaetulicus business. Okay, she was a complete bubblehead suckered into the plot by Lepidus and her sister, but still.'

'It doesn't explain why Messalina should engineer her trial and death, though, does it? If you're assuming that she did, of course. She's no more an obvious victim than Livia was. Or Justus, for that matter.'

'No, it doesn't.' I frowned; bugger! 'We're not doing too well here, are we?'

'I'm afraid not, dear.'

'Then we're missing something. If Rufus instigated the prosecutions, and Rufus was Messalina's man, then there has to be a reason common to all of them that's in her interest.'

'Unless you and Graecina are completely wrong and she wasn't involved to begin with. Perhaps Rufus was acting for himself after all.'

'Why should he do that? What's in it for him? Look, two out of the three were Claudius's relatives. A comparative nobody like Rufus wouldn't risk going against four-star imperials unless he had some powerful backing of his own, and from someone who had serious clout with the emperor himself, at that. It had to be Messalina.' A thought struck me. 'Rufus's suffect consulship. When was it exactly?'

'Three years ago. November and December, right at the end of the consular term.'

'The same year as the prosecutions. The bastard was squeezed in at the last minute, given his consular status as a reward for services rendered. Come on, Perilla! It fits all the way down the line, and you know it does.'

'Marcus,' she said gently, 'suffect consuls are chosen by the emperor. If you were claiming that Rufus's employer, as it were, was Claudius himself then unlikely as that would be, knowing the man, I might be more sympathetic to the idea. But–'

'Lady, show some sense! Messalina has led that guy around by the nose like a performing bear ever since the wedding, especially since–' I stopped. Oh, shit! Shit, I'd got it! Or maybe I had. 'Wait a minute. Okay. So what else happened that year? Involving Messalina herself, personally?'

'Well, of course, that was the year she had–' I saw it hit her too. She stared at me wide-eyed. 'Oh, my!'

'Right. She had Britannicus. Their first male child. It's about the succession again, protecting the line. Justus, okay, fine, we don't know where he fits in. But both Livia and Livilla were female imperials of child-bearing age; in fact, Livia had a son already. Once she'd provided Claudius with an heir Messalina couldn't take the risk of there being any other front runners in the future. And even if Rubellius Junior had been a likely contender his mother's disgrace, plus the fact that his father was a virtual nobody, would've put the kibosh on his chances pretty effectively.'

'But Livilla didn't have any children.'

'True. All the same, we don't know why that was. She could've been barren, sure, but given her predilections it could equally have been out of choice: having a child would've cramped her style pretty effectively in that department, at least on a temporary basis.'

'Marcus...'

'Yeah, well, it would. Admitted, after all this time it wasn't at all likely she and Vinicius would start a family, and it was pretty plain they weren't on sleeping-together terms to begin with, but Messalina wouldn't've wanted to chance it. Accidents happen. Plus what if the lady had suddenly got ambitious and set her cap at Claudius herself?'

'Oh, now you really are fantasising!'

I shook my head. 'Uh-uh. It was at least a viable possibility, or I bet it would've struck Messalina as such. Livilla might've been a bit on the well-padded side, but she was young, from the same class, virtually estranged from her husband, and a past and practised mistress where seduction was concerned. You know Claudius yourself. If she'd really set out in earnest to land the poor boob he would've been a pushover.'

'That is pure gutter-reasoning!'

'Even so. For that matter, what about Livia? For totally different reasons, granted, but still. Oh, sure, from what you tell me she was happy enough with the husband she'd got, but when all's said and done he was a nobody, and a pretty dull one at that. You said she was a reader, interested in history; so's Claudius, the guy's a history nut, and what's more he knows his stuff inside out. They'd have common ground in spades. On the other hand, I doubt if Messalina's read a book all the way through in her life, and she sure as hell couldn't keep up a conversation about the Etruscan League over the breakfast porridge. He was the emperor, for the gods' sake! If he'd decided that he wanted Livia all he'd've had to do was order Blandus to divorce her and that would've been it, end of story. It's happened before, after all. Look at Augustus and the old empress before she *was* the old empress.'

'I'm sorry, Marcus, but this is getting silly. Stop it.'

I shrugged. 'Fair enough. But remember, we're thinking like Messalina would here. She may not be all that clever, but she's thorough, and when it's a case of self-protection she doesn't take prisoners.'

'Hmm.' She reached up and pulled at a curl. 'Well, you may be right. Not that I'd agree that any of it goes beyond the purely theoretical, mind. If that. In fact, I'd say "fanciful" would suit better.'

Definitely sniffy. I grinned.

'Have it your own way,' I said. 'The thing's academic now in any case. Both the ladies are long dead.'

'What about Graecina's other two victims? Silanus and Vinicianus? They can't fit the same pattern, can they?'

'Uh-uh, they can't. Or at least there's no obvious connection that I can see.'

She was twisting at the curl. 'Silanus was married to Domitia Lepida, wasn't he?' she said. 'Messalina's mother.'

I gave her a sharp look. 'Yeah. Yes, he was. So? There's the connection with Messalina, sure, but–'

'Then perhaps I might indulge in a little gutter-reasoning of my own. From a female perspective.'

‘Ah...sure. Sure, no problem.’ Jupiter! I wondered if I really wanted to hear this! ‘Feel free, lady.’

‘It’s the daughter/father thing. Oh, yes, of course, I know Silanus wasn’t Messalina’s biological father, of course he wasn’t, that’s just the point: he was no blood relation, and yet he was in an obvious sexual relationship with her mother. Perhaps she was just a little jealous, and being a mature woman with her lack of inhibitions she–’

I held up my hand. ‘Fine. Fine.’ Jupiter Best and Greatest! ‘Got you. You don’t need to spell it out.’

Perilla grinned. ‘You’re blushing, dear,’ she said. ‘You really are quite a prude underneath it all, aren’t you?’

‘So what you’re saying is that Messalina tried it on with her stepfather, he turned her down flat and she decided to pay him back.’ Gods!

‘That would more or less cover it, yes. Just a suggestion, no more, but I think you’d find that in the absence of a more obvious reason it’s a perfectly tenable theory. The circumstances of the charge are a bit odd, though, aren’t they? I mean, a dream, for goodness’ sake! I honestly wouldn’t have believed it of Claudius; he’s usually such a sensible man.’

‘Yeah, well, if you’re an emperor you’re bound to get a bit jumpy in the context of guys with knives. Particularly when your predecessor got himself chopped. Besides, Silanus had tried the same thing before, years ago with Tiberius, hadn’t he? Or would’ve done, rather, if I hadn’t queered Servaeus’s pitch for him by explaining to the gullible bugger how he’d been suckered.’ I took another sip of the wine. ‘But Claudius would know the story, and of course so would Messalina and Narcissus. Which is probably what put the idea into their heads.’

‘It’s interesting that Narcissus backed her up, though, isn’t it?’ Perilla said. ‘I mean, yes, we know from past experience that the two of them are hand-in-glove, or at least they were over putting Claudius where he is, but it was always a clandestine arrangement on both sides. And I would've expected that the business of two coincidental dreams might have raised Claudius's suspicions rather than otherwise, even if he was afraid of assassination.'

'Yeah. I thought that was a bit odd, myself. Particularly if, as you say, the quarrel with Silanus was Messalina's alone and Narcissus had no personal axe to grind. Certainly, given that Claudius is no intellectual slouch, it brought its own added risks. Still, no doubt the scheming bastard had his reasons for coming out of the woodwork, whatever they might have been.' I shook my head. 'Hell. Leave it and move on. Last one, Annius Vinicianus.'

'Yes.' Perilla frowned. 'Marcus, Vinicianus makes no sense at all. Again we know that, like Narcissus, he was involved in the final conspiracy against Gaius, the real conspiracy, and he was one of the inner circle, very much so. Why should Messalina want to destroy him?'

'Could be he'd decided to change sides for some reason, blow the whistle on what she and Narcissus were up to, or at least she was, over the succession, and Messalina had caught him out.'

'No, dear. Oh, it's an obvious solution, yes, but it won't work.'

'Is that so? Why not?'

'First of all, because there *aren't* any sides any more, not practically speaking: Messalina has won, she has everything she wants, all the power she needs, and Claudius trusts her absolutely, even to the extent of blindness, that much is only too clear. Vinicianus would be a fool to risk going against her; he'd never be believed, not for a moment, and he'd be well aware of the fact. Secondly, why would he betray her at that late date? He had nothing to gain personally, quite the reverse: he was definitely persona grata where Messalina was concerned, and that meant through her with the emperor. Thirdly, where was his proof? If he had gone to Claudius and told him Messalina had been central to the plot which killed Gaius for the emperor to believe him he would have to have revealed his own part in it. No, I'm sorry, but the whole thing would simply be too dangerous and completely pointless.'

Bugger. She was right, sure she was, all the way down the line. 'Even so,' I said, 'Vinicianus was chopped. And by Messalina; he had to be. We can't get round that.'

'No.' Perilla sighed. 'No, we can't. So. What now?'

'There's Secundus to see re Catonius Justus, of course. We need to check that angle. But I was wondering whether it might be an idea to have a word with Marcus Vinicius.'

She stared at me. '*Vinicius?* Why him?'

'You have a better idea, lady?' I finished off the wine and put the empty cup down. 'Look. We know already that Vinicius had close personal connections with at least three out of our five victims: Livilla was his wife, Vinicianus was his nephew, and you told me he thought of Livia practically as a niece. Plus the fact that barring Claudius himself for obvious reasons he's the nearest we've got to a friendly imperial, and I reckon that's going to be important. Oh, sure, he might not be able or willing to help, in fact he might well throw me out on my ear, but it's worth a shot.'

'Very well, Marcus.' She smiled. 'You can be sure he won't throw you out, anyway; Vinicius is far too polite to do any such thing, even if he didn't have a genuine regard for you, which he does.'

'Fair enough,' I said. 'I'll go round tomorrow.'

Well, at least things were moving.

# 18

Like I say, I had a lot of time for Marcus Vinicius. Five-star imperial he undoubtedly was – his marriage to Livilla had been at Tiberius's own suggestion – and he'd been one of Claudius's closest friends long before he became emperor. Perilla had known him for years, of course, through her poetry klatsch and various reading parties, but I'd only met him twice, the first time during the Macro business and the second at that dinner party just before Gaius's assassination. On both occasions he'd struck me as a pretty okay guy, upper-class Rome at its best, which believe me you don't get all that often; certainly someone I could talk to in the knowledge that he'd be as straight with me as he could manage. How far that would extend, mind you, was a different matter entirely. We'd just have to see.

Vinicius's house, as befitted one of the inner circle, was on the Palatine not far from the imperial complex itself: big, but not flashy, in the old Augustan style. I gave my name to the door-slave and kicked my heels in the vestibule until Vinicius's chief slave came through from the house proper.

'Valerius Corvinus,' he said. 'A pleasure to see you again, sir.'

'Uh...' I searched my memory. 'Tynnias, isn't it?'

'That's right, sir.' The major-domo smiled. He was an oldish guy, sixty at least, so he had ten years on Vinicius himself. Still, he had the same solid, dapper feel to him as his master. 'And if you don't mind my saying so you look a good deal better than you did the last time you were here.'

I grinned; yeah, that I'd believe. On my last, and only, visit to the place six years before, for one of the lady's poetry parties, I'd come fresh – if that wasn't exactly the word – from an almost-fatal encounter with a runaway mason's cart on the Staurian Stairs.

'Is Vinicius at home?' I said.

'Unfortunately not, sir. The senate's in session today, and I doubt if he'll be back much before late afternoon. Was there something urgent, or can I take a message?'

Damn. 'No, that's okay,' I said. 'It's not urgent, exactly, but I did want to speak to him personally, and it isn't about anything I can put into a message. You think it'd be all right if I go down to the senate house and try to catch him as he leaves?'

'I'm sure it would, sir, if you prefer to do that. Although naturally I can't guarantee the timing. It depends completely on the business being transacted, and that may prolong things until sundown.'

Damn again. Still, it was no big deal: being on the Palatine already, I was just round the corner from where Gaius Secundus was based in army admin headquarters. I could go round there first, talk to Secundus if he was available about Justus, and then head down the hill to the senate house in plenty of time to hang around until the meeting broke up. I just hoped that wouldn't be too late, certainly not as late as sundown: Meton had very definite views on the subject of people not turning up for dinner on time without having given due warning, and I had enough troubles at present without adding a seriously-miffed chef to the mix.

'Thanks, pal,' I said. 'Oh...just in case I do miss him, could you tell him I called, maybe ask him to send someone over to the Caelian with a time when he'll be free? He knows where I am.'

'Certainly, sir. I'll be sure to do that.'

I left. Next stop Secundus.

I climbed the steps of the military admin building tacked onto the edge of Augustus House, nodded to the two squaddies on guard duty at the door, and went up to the reception desk.

'The boss around this morning?' I said to the clerk behind it. 'Vibullius Secundus?'

'Yes, sir, he's just come in.' The clerk signalled to a hovering slave. 'Your name, please?' I gave him it. 'You have an appointment?'

'No,' I said. 'Just dropping in. On a personal matter.'

'Then I'll have to check if he's free, sir. If you'd care to wait?'

Fair enough. The gopher disappeared on his assigned errand, while I moved over to one of the benches and sat down.

Gaius Secundus was the oldest friend I had. We'd hung out a lot together in our late, wild teens, gone to parties, even shared a girlfriend at one point, but then we went our very different ways. I'd opted out of the usual political rat-race, much to my father's disgust, before I even got started; Secundus had stuck it, and thrived. Like most well-born youngsters, barring oddball drop-outs like me, he'd begun things with a posting as tribune to one of the legions, whereupon the silly fool had fallen badly from his horse, shattered most of the bones in his right leg, and had to be invalided home. End of military career, which was a pity, because if anyone had been cut out for the army it was Secundus. Since then we'd seen each other off and on as he moved up the ladder – he'd been a city judge ten or so years back – and he was currently sitting behind the top desk in the department of military administration, where as far as I knew he was happy to stay for the foreseeable future.

A nice guy, Secundus, and political life hadn't spoiled him a bit.

The slave arrived back and I was taken in to the august presence. Secundus was at his desk, talking to another of the freedmen-clerks.

'Marcus!' he said. 'How's the boy?' Then, to the clerk, 'That's fine, Acastus. We'll finish up later.' The man went out. 'So. How's it going? It's been, what, two years?'

'More. Over three. I'm sorry, Gaius. I should've kept in touch.'

Secundus shrugged. 'It's as much my fault as yours,' he said. 'I knew where you were. How's Perilla?'

'Fine. She sends her regards.' I pulled up a stool and sat. 'You, uh, got anything going yourself in that direction these days?' The last time I'd seen him he'd been two years divorced from Furia Gemella and playing the field again, which before his injury and Gemella's subsequent appearance on the scene as nursemaid had been Secundus's natural state. Still, he wasn't young any more, no more than I was, and it wasn't unreasonable to suppose he was settling down.

He grinned. 'Yeah. I married again, a couple of years back last December. One of Gemella's pals, actually, but Helena's a different thing altogether. You'd like her.' Well, in that case it'd make a change from said Gemella: even on the shortest of acquaintances we'd never got on.

'Look, pal, you have time to split a jug?' I said. 'We could go down to Tasso's.' His local, at the foot of the Palatine on the Market Square side. If I remembered, they did a good Massic; pricey, but that went with the place's broad-striper clientele.

'Sorry, Marcus. Not today.' He indicated the pile of flimsies and tablets on the desk. 'I'm snowed under. And I've an important meeting this afternoon that I have to get ready for.'

Bugger. Well, he wasn't a man of leisure, like me; he'd a proper job to do. I made to get up.

'If you're busy,' I said, 'I can–'

'No, no, you're fine for half an hour or so,' he said quickly. 'Call it an early break. It's just we have to go over to Tibur in four days, Helena and I – family wedding – and there're things I need to clear up before then.'

'Okay,' I said. 'In that case, dinner before you go, nothing fancy, just a family meal, us, you, and this new wife of yours. Can you manage that?'

'Sure. Dinner's no problem.'

'Call it the day after tomorrow, then? Sunset do you?' That'd give Meton sufficient time to reconcile himself to cooking for four, and if it didn't then tough luck: the recalcitrant bugger could go and fry himself.

'Perfect.' He settled back in his chair. 'Now. What did you want to see me about?'

'Ah...'

He laughed. 'Come on, Marcus! I may be cabbage-looking, but I'm not as green as all that. It's connected with the sleuthing, isn't it?'

'Uh, yeah. Actually it is.' Hell; I felt rotten, and more than a little guilty. Two and a half years' silence, and then when I did get back in touch it was because I needed his help with a case. It'd been that way last time as well, for that matter, even though the meeting in Tasso's wineshop had been accidental.

'Then go ahead. As long as you don't want me to spill any military secrets this time around. I enjoy my job and I want to keep it.'

'No. No, there isn't anything undercover involved, at least I don't think so. Just straightforward information. Catonius Justus.'

Secundus's eyebrows rose. 'The Praetorian commander? He's dead. Tried and executed last year for treason.'

'Yeah, I know,' I said. 'But that's all I know at present. That's why I'm asking. You have any more details for me?'

‘Not a lot. The trial was held behind closed doors, with the emperor himself presiding.’

‘So what form did the treason take?’

‘Pass again. Presumably, given who he was and the fact that Claudius took a personal interest, it had something to do with a planned assassination attempt. That’s a guess, of course, but it’s a logical one. The Praetorians are the emperor’s private guard, they’re the only guys allowed to come anywhere near him armed on a regular basis, and naturally since Gaius was murdered he’s been a bit wary of that arrangement. What else could it have been?’

‘So what’s the likelihood of the charge being true, do you think? He a likely candidate for treason? Justus in himself, I mean?’

Secundus gave me a long, considering look: not Rome’s deepest or fastest thinker, Gaius Secundus, sure, but like he’d said green he certainly wasn’t.

‘That what this is about?’ he said finally.

‘Yeah. That is what this is about. But I’d appreciate your opinion.’

He cleared his throat and steepled his fingers. ‘In that case, no,’ he said. ‘Not your obvious one, anyway. He’d a good record of loyalty, to begin with, which was naturally why he got the prefect’s job in the first place. Claudius chose him himself.’

‘*Claudius?* Claudius made the appointment?’

‘Sure he did. As soon as he was made emperor. Justus had served as a centurion with his cousin, Tiberius’s son Drusus, in Pannonia, the time of the revolt just after Augustus passed on. Served with distinction, too: in fact, Drusus chose him to send back to Tiberius as his and the squaddies’ rep. When the mutiny spread to the Rhine legions he did well enough to be promoted into the senior officer class, and after that he never looked back.’

Uh-huh. And Drusus, eh? Drusus had been Julia Livia's father. Things were definitely shaping up here. 'You ever meet him?' I said.

'Sure I did. I knew him quite well, actually. And respected him, totally.' He hesitated. 'The simple truth is, Marcus, Catonius Justus was old-style legion to his fingertips. He hadn't a treasonous bone in his body, that I'd swear to.'

Shit. I sat back. 'He was also accused of being Julia Livia's lover,' I said.

That got me another look. 'That's pure garbage. Wineshop filth, and not even barely believable wineshop filth at that. Justus was in his sixties, happily married with grandkids, and like I said he was one of the straightest, most honourable men alive. He wouldn't have looked at Livia that way, never, not in a million years. I'd sooner believe the treason charge, and I wouldn't believe that at all.'

Well, that was pretty categorical, and more or less what I'd been expecting. The direct connection with Livia's father Drusus was new, though, and news. And, like I say, it went with the theory like fish sauce on beets. I stood up.

'Thanks, pal,' I said. 'I'll get going, let you get on.' One last thought struck me. 'Oh, incidentally. Justus's replacement as prefect. Who would that be, now?'

'A guy called Rufrius Crispinus.' Secundus frowned. 'I've met him as well. A complete no-accounter. He's from Egypt originally, and rumour has it he started out selling fish down the market. None too fresh fish, either, which having met the slimy bastard I'd believe. After Justus he's a disgrace.'

'So how did he get one of the top jobs in Rome?'

‘Search me. The gods know he’s not up to it, not nearly, that’s for sure. I’ve a lot of respect for the emperor’s judgment normally, but this time he had his head up his rectum.’

I grunted non-committally. Me, I very much doubted if the idea for Crispinus’s appointment had originated with Claudius himself at all; where Messalina was concerned, a weak, venal ally in one of Rome’s key political and military posts might prove useful. Still, that was by the way.

‘Well, at any rate,’ I said, ‘thanks again, Gaius. You’ve been a great help.’

‘No problem.’ Secundus stood up too. ‘Any time. Good luck with the case, whatever it is. And thanks for the invite. We’ll see you in two days, Helena and I.’

‘Looking forward to it,’ I said, and left.

So. What now?

The answer to that, unfortunately, was obvious. I’d a couple of hours to kill, at least, before the senate meeting was likely to end, and the walk between Priscus’s curio shop on the Sacred Way and the senate house was no any distance at all. As a consequence, I’d no excuse *not* to go and have my little chat with Priscus’s bit on the side. Besides, although I’d half-forgotten about it – or maybe just subconsciously shoved it to one side in my memory – today was the day that Mother’s three-day ultimatum was due to expire.

It was time to grit my teeth, take the bull by the horns, grasp the nettle, and get the finger out. Or whatever.

Fuck; I was going to *hate* this!

I knew I'd struck the first snag as soon as I came through the door. No curvy brunette proprietrix this time: a burly, dark-skinned guy who looked more like a wrestler than a shopkeeper.

'Yes, sir,' he said. 'Can I help you?'

'That's okay, pal,' I said. 'I'm just looking.' Damn! Although to be fair I felt a small prickle of relief: embarrassing encounter postponed, and not by my doing either.

He smiled. 'Look all you like, sir. No hurry; take your time.'

I wandered round the shelves. I'd misjudged the place: there was some pretty nice stuff here, even as a non-expert I could see that. Small, sure, and not-all-that-old Greek, mostly, but in very good nick, and when I checked the tags the prices seemed better than fair. If I hadn't seen Priscus playing the elderly satyr with my own eyes I wouldn't have had the least suspicion about his coming here: as I'd said to Mother, that was what he did, keep a lookout for likely places, particularly newly-opened ones, and add them to his browsing list.

There was a small pottery exercise-oil flask in the shape of a goose on one of the shelves. Perfect. I picked it up and checked the tag: fifteen silver pieces. Slightly more than I'd expected, but it wouldn't break the bank. And it would give me the conversational in that I needed. Okay; so here we went. I took it to the guy behind the counter.

'Found something you like, sir?' he said. I handed the thing over. 'Oh, yes, the oil flask. Nice little thing, isn't it? Corinthian, not very old, perhaps a century or so. Would you like me to wrap it as a gift for you?'

'Sure, if you wouldn't mind.' I reached into my belt-pouch for the coins while he took a scrap piece of thin paper and made it up into a small parcel. 'You Greek yourself, pal?'

'I am. Athenian born and bred.' He put the money into a box on the counter. 'We only moved here from Athens three months ago.'

'"We"?'

'Me and the wife.' He handed the parcel over.

Uh-huh. 'Right,' I said. 'Dark-haired lady, quite short, yes? She was in charge the last time I was here.'

'You've been in before, sir?' I said nothing; if he assumed I'd actually come inside rather than hung about in the street watching Priscus snog his wife, then fine. 'Well, that's encouraging. We're trying to build up a regular clientele, but it's quite difficult in Rome, what with all the competition and the antiques business being such a specialised market. Yes, that was my Polyxene.'

'She look after the shop on a regular basis?'

'Oh, yes, indeed. Her family's been in the antiques business for generations, and she knows more about the trade and the stock than I do. In fact, if anyone looks after the shop in a temporary sense it's me, not her. She's only popped out for half an hour to get the stuff for dinner.'

Hell; so the relationship was definitely adulterous on both sides. And the husband seemed a nice enough man, fond of his wife. I felt really, really bad about this.

Still, it had to be done.

'By the way,' I said. 'I think you have a regular customer by the name of Helvius Priscus. Elderly man, looks a bit like a mildewed sheep buried in dry sand for a decade or so? Bleats a lot?'

The change was remarkable. The guy stiffened, and the friendliness left his face.

'Just exactly who are you?' he said. 'A relative?'

Bugger; well, there went the ball game. I'd far rather have gone to this stage with the lady herself, gradually and in private, but it seemed confidentiality wasn't an issue after all. Whatever was going on between her and Priscus, he was obviously aware of it already. This was *not* looking good.

'Yeah, actually, I am,' I said. 'My name's Valerius Corvinus. Priscus is my stepfather.'

'Is that so, now? Then you can bloody well–' He stopped. The shop door had opened and the woman herself came in. Her husband hadn't actually taken me by the throat, but it would've been obvious to anyone who wasn't completely insensitive to atmosphere that a situation was developing and now was definitely not the time to intrude. She paused on the threshold and her eyes went from him to me and back again.

'What's the matter, dear?' she said.

'This man's your g–' The husband hesitated. 'He's Helvius Priscus's stepson.'

Her hand went to her mouth. 'Oh, no!' she said, and switched to Greek. 'Euthias, you haven't told him about us, have you?'

'Of course I bloody haven't!' Greek as well. 'I only just found out myself.'

'Only–' She glanced through the open door behind her.

Uh-oh; I knew what was going to happen next; I just *knew* it.

I wasn't wrong, either. Priscus sidled in, holding a string bag of vegetables.

'*Mmaah,*' he said. 'Hello, Marcus, my boy. Now this *is* unfortunate.'

Oh, shit. 'Unfortunate' wasn't the word I'd've used. 'Fucking embarrassing' came close, but even that wasn't half strong enough. The mind boggled: what the hell had we got here? Some sort of weird *ménage à trois* with a complaisant husband?

'Ah...hi, Stepfather,' I said. 'Look, I didn't mean to–'

'Did Vipsania put you up to this?' he said. Then, when I didn't answer, 'Ah, well, it had to come out sooner or later, I suppose.' He closed the door carefully behind him and set the bag down. 'In you go, darling.' This to Polyxene, who was staring at me like I was some sort of nine-headed monster. 'It'll be all right, but we have to talk things over.'

Perfectly true. And it was time for a little tact, on my side. Gods! I *really* didn't need this!

'Hang on, Priscus,' I said. 'No hassle, okay? Not as far as I'm concerned. We're both men of the world.' I thought for a moment. 'At least, I am. So if you've, uh, decided you need some sort of an outlet for your feelings apart from Mother then it's–'

I stopped; Priscus was chuckling. Or snuffling, rather, which was as close to it as the old bugger had ever been able to manage all the time I'd known him.

'No, no!' he said. 'You have it all wrong, Marcus. *Mmaah!* Polyxene isn't my mistress. She's my granddaughter.'

I blinked. 'She's your *what?*'

'My granddaughter. One I never knew I had until about a month ago.' Oh, Jupiter! First Bathyllus, now Priscus. Maybe there was something in the air that was spontaneously creating long-lost relatives. 'She's my daughter's child. I never even knew I had one of those, either, up to then, but there you are. Her name's Melite, seemingly; my daughter, I mean. Lovely name. Lives in Athens.'

I couldn't get my head round this. 'You have a daughter in Athens?' I said. 'How the hell did you manage that?'

Another prolonged snuffle. 'Dear, dear, boy! How do you *think* I managed it? In the usual way, of course.' He turned to the husband. 'Bring us out a couple of stools, will you, Euthias? I'm ready to drop, I'm afraid, and Marcus here could probably do with sitting down as well. A cup of wine, too, if you've got it. Not for me, for him. He looks like he needs one.'

Too bloody right I did! The man disappeared into the rear of the shop.

'You want to explain?' I said.

Priscus shrugged. 'There isn't much to tell,' he said. 'And it was seventy-odd years ago, after all. I was seventeen. My father had sent me to Athens to finish me off.' Yeah, right; par for the course. It still happened; once they've finished their schooling boys from upper class families are sent abroad for a year, usually east to one of the Greek cities like Athens or Pergamum, to give them a bit of culture. Unofficial liaisons aren't too uncommon, either, although Greeks tend to be even more careful about what their womenfolk get up to than we are. Things were beginning to make some kind of sense. 'The girl's name was Polyxene, too. Her father had an antique shop in the Collytus district near Roman Market Square, and she helped out there sometimes. We – *mmaah!* – became friendly, and that was that.' He glanced at the current Polyxene, who was standing stiff as a statue. 'After I came home she never tried to get in touch, or if she did my father destroyed the letters. I forgot about her eventually. Heady days, my boy. Heady days. Anyway, she's long dead now, poor girl.'

Gods! You think you know someone and... Mind you, like he'd said, it was a lifetime ago, practically two lifetimes. Although *that* version of Priscus I just couldn't get to grips with; even seeing him as a raw seventeen-year-old with an eye for the girls was pushing the bounds of imagination to their limits.

Euthias came back with the stools, and we sat. I took the cup of wine he gave me and swallowed half of it at a gulp.

'So how did you know that this lady' – I nodded towards Polyxene – 'was your grandchild?'

'Oh, my dear boy, she's the spitting image of her grandmother!' Priscus said. 'Slightly older than when I knew her, of course, but it was quite eerie. I knew who she was as soon as I came into the shop, and when I asked her her name and where she came from... Well, it just confirmed things. In any case, there you are.'

'So what happens now?'

For the first time Priscus looked his usual sheepish self. 'I suppose now that you're here – *mmaah!* – I'll have to tell Vipsania. She'd have had to know eventually anyway. All the same, it isn't something I'm particularly looking forward to.'

Right. Right; and I didn't blame the poor sap. I doubted whether the crime of retrospective adultery existed on the statute books, but that would make no difference to Mother: whether she'd reasonable cause to or not, when her husband owned up to having a daughter in Athens and a spurious grandchild who ran a second-rate antique shop on the Sacred Way she would hit the sodding roof.

'Unless, of course–' Priscus paused meaningfully and looked at me.

I stood up quickly. Some things need nipping in the bud before they even *think* about getting started, and the gleam in the old bugger's eye was definitely one of them.

'Uh-uh,' I said. 'No way. *Absolutely* no way. I am *not* breaking the happy news to Mother. Your problem, pal, you solve it.'

He sighed. 'Very well, Marcus, if you're going to be unreasonable about it.' Jupiter! 'I suppose you're right. In any case, the affair was long dead and buried before I even met Vipsania, and finding Polyxene was a complete accident, so she can't really complain, can she?' I said nothing; pigs might fly. 'All right, perhaps she can, at that. But worse things happen at sea, and at least I have a granddaughter I never knew existed.'

Bathyllus again.Yeah, well: *unexpected depths* was right, although maybe not quite in the way that Mother had meant the phrase. Like I say, you can know someone for years and at a pinch they can still surprise you.

'You're sure you're up to it?' I said. 'Telling Mother, I mean?'

'Oh, yes, I'll think of something.' A quick, sharp look that I would've said until ten minutes ago was completely unPriscan. 'You can't be married to someone like Vipsania for twenty-odd years without developing some talent for invention. Off you go, my boy. Don't worry; I'll take care of things.'

'Fair enough, Stepfather,' I said. 'Good luck.'

I nodded to Polyxene and her husband, and left.

Gods!

After that little revelation all I wanted to do was go home, or maybe find a wineshop somewhere, but I still had the case to consider and Marcus Vinicius to see, if I could catch him. The flag was flying above the senate house, showing that they were still in session; all the same, I hadn't been kicking my heels outside for long before the doors opened and the august city fathers streamed forth, their deliberations ended, bound for a well-earned truffled quail or two and a pint of Falernian.

Vinicius was one of the last to leave. I peeled myself away from the wall that I'd been propping up and went over to him. He paused, and turned towards me.

'Valerius Corvinus, isn't it?' he said.

'Yeah, that's right.' I held out my hand, and we shook.

'My dear chap!' he said. 'How very nice to see you again!'

Definitely cheerful and brimming with positive bonhomie. Good sign.

'You too, sir,' I said.

'You're well? And Rufia Perilla?'

'Yeah, we're both fine.'

'Good. Good. We don't see you very often in this neck of the woods. Slumming it, are we?'

'Uh, no.' I hesitated; here we went. 'Actually, sir, I was waiting for you to come out. If you're not in a hurry I'd appreciate a word or two. In confidence.'

'Oh, my, that does sound ominous!' He smiled. 'What about?'

'I'd rather lead up to that gradually, sir. If you don't mind.'

'Is that so, now?' He gave me a very sharp look indeed, and the smile disappeared. 'Well, as it happens, no, I'm in no real hurry. But if the matter is sensitive, which I assume it is, perhaps we should go somewhere more private. In fact, somewhere very private. I could take you home with me, of course, but then again–' He stopped and looked around. 'Ah, yes. The King's Palace might be the best plan.'

'Sure,' I said. 'Anywhere you like.' The King's Palace was the official residence of the Chief Priest, and almost literally round the corner. 'If you think it'd be suitable.'

The smile was back. 'My dear fellow, that is one good thing about Tiberius Claudius, and not the only good thing by any means. He's very hands-on where religion is concerned, and although naturally he is ex officio Chief Priest himself he hasn't appointed a deputy. Consequently, while the Palace is staffed it's not in actual use at present. I think it would be eminently suitable.'

'Fair enough,' I said.

We set off in silence, but I could almost hear his brain ticking. For all his bluff all-pals-together manner Marcus Vinicius was a very smart cookie indeed, with one of the sharpest minds in Rome; in fact, when Gaius had been shoved off his perch there had been a very fair chance, if he'd wanted the job, which he hadn't, of his being chosen to succeed. *Chosen*, mark you, not emperor by self-selection, which to my mind was another big point in the guy's favour. Vinicus was not someone to be taken lightly, not by any means.

There was a door-slave on duty outside the Palace, but Vinicius simply nodded to him and he opened up straight off, tugging his forelock in the process. Yeah, well; we were moving in very high circles now, weren't we?

I'd been inside the King's Palace before, quite some time ago, when Furius Camillus had been in residence and deputising for the Wart, but it hadn't changed all that much: it was still grand, old and seedy, with a faint underlying smell of must and mouse droppings. The major-domo who greeted us wasn't familiar, which was fair enough: it had been ten years, at least, since the affair of the dead Vestal, and in any case the one I'd known would've been Camillus's own slave to begin with.

'Ah, Castor,' Vinicius said to him. 'This is my friend Valerius Corvinus. I wonder if we might use the study for a while, if you don't mind.'

'Yes, of course, sir.' The man smiled. 'For as long as you like. You know the way?'

'Of course I do. Corvinus?'

I followed him along the corridor and into the study. That was familiar, too, even down to the book-rolls in the wall-cubby. All that was missing was the big table where Camillus had been staging his re-fight of Zama. In its place was the usual desk and, between it and the door, a reading couch. Vinicius closed the door behind us, went over behind the desk, and sat.

'Well, now, Marcus Valerius Corvinus,' he said. 'Make yourself comfortable on the couch there and let's have it. Straight to the point, please, because I dine early and this morning's meeting was bloody.'

I sat on the couch. 'Very well, sir,' I said. 'Straight to the point it is. The trials three years back. Of Junius Silanus and your nephew Annius Vinicianus.'

'What about them?' Bland as hell.

'I just wondered why. Why they were charged and condemned.'

He raised an eyebrow. 'Would this have anything to do with your sleuthing activities, by any chance?' he said. I didn't answer, and he grunted; the eyebrow was lowered. 'Never mind; I won't press you, and there are no secrets involved. The reasons were simple enough. Silanus was charged with planning to assassinate the emperor. My nephew was charged with treason. Whether the first charge was sustainable I don't know.' He gave me a straight look. '*Genuinely* don't know; the man was a complete fool, and he was capable of any degree of foolishness. The second I know for a fact was fully justified. Lucius was a traitor, and he did well to kill himself before the trial could take place.'

'A traitor in what way?' I said.

'You remember Arruntius Scribonianus?'

'Uh...the name rings a faint bell, yeah. He got himself into a bit of trouble three years back, didn't he? Just after Claudius became emperor.'

Vinicius's lips twisted in a half-smile.

'"A bit of trouble"?' he said. 'Oh, my dear fellow, for a supposedly intelligent man you really don't follow events all that closely, do you?'

'Ah...'

'No, don't apologise. In the company I keep, am forced to keep, that's a rare and quite endearing quality. Refreshing, too.' He took a deep breath. 'Well, to educate you. Scribonianus was military governor of Dalmatia, appointed by that tick Gaius, and for his sins that rare beast all but extinct a dedicated Republican. Meaning he thought that instead of faffing around with emperors we should go back to the good old days when the senate was in charge of messing things up.'

'Uh-huh.' I was beginning to get the picture here. 'So with Gaius dead – assassinated – Vinicianus writes to Scribonianus suggesting that he might like to stage a revolt?'

'That's more or less the strength of it, yes. Of course the escapade was a complete no-hoper from the start, and when that anachronistic idiot Scribonianus told his troops his intention was to restore the Republic that put the lid on it: they mutinied and his goose was cooked. The whole thing was over and done with inside of a month. And when it came out, as it was bound to do, that the original suggestion had come from Lucius his goose was cooked as well. Brought it on himself, the silly bugger.'

'So why did he do it in the first place?' I said. 'Encourage Scribonianus to rebel?'

'Pique against the emperor. And a desire to do him down.' He frowned. 'No; forget that, Corvinus, it's not by any means the whole story, and it isn't fair on Lucius at all. Oh, I wasn't blind to his faults, don't think so for a moment: nephew or not, in many ways, which we won't go into but which having had dealings with him before you can guess at, Lucius was a complete stinker. He did, though, have one virtue, the old Roman loyalty to friends. "Friends" in the technical sense, I mean: those he'd worked alongside, been associated with, in the past. Silanus was one of them.

Lucius took it very badly when he was charged and put to death. Very badly indeed.'

'Badly enough to make him commit treason? Or at least incite someone else to it?'

'Presumably. What other explanation for his actions is there? And he certainly performed them, there's no doubt of that.'

Yeah; right. My brain was buzzing; this was something I had to talk over with Perilla. I shelved it for the present.

'Uh...one thing more, sir,' I said. We were treading on really sensitive ground here, but it was the only chance I'd get. 'The other trials round about that time and later. Your wife's and Julia Livia's. You think they were justified?'

'Ah.' His face...shut; there was no other way of putting it. Then he said: 'Valerius Corvinus. Now listen to me, please, because I am being very serious. Very serious indeed. There are certain topics on which I don't wish to speculate. Livilla's crime, and poor Julia Livia's, if crimes they were, fall very firmly into that category. I suggest most strongly that you follow my lead. You understand me?'

'Uh...yeah,' I said. 'I do, sir. Perfectly.'

'Good.' He smiled, but it was not an amused smile; quite the opposite. 'Don't forget it. That way we might both survive into old age.' He stood up. 'Now I really do think I should be going. It was a pleasure to see you again, my dear fellow, and of course do give my warmest regards to Rufia Perilla.'

I stood up as well. 'I'll do that, sir. And thank you.'

'Oh, no need to hurry off in your case. Castor is extremely accommodating; in fact, there might be a cup of wine on offer if you ask him nicely. Good wine, too: they keep a very respectable cellar here, for all the place has been left empty these past few years. Anyway.' He held out his hand, and I shook it. 'As I say, a pleasure. Do look after yourself, won't you? And don't overdo the sleuthing; it's not good for your health.'

He left.

Uh-huh. So I'd been warned. In the nicest possible way, sure, but the warning was unmistakable.

I passed up on the wine and went straight home.

# 19

I was just in time for dinner, which was a blessing: ten minutes later and the sun would've been well below the yardarm and my stock with our touchy chef seriously depleted. I handed Bathyllus my cloak, collected the welcome-home cup of wine and went straight through to the dining-room where Perilla was already ensconced on her couch.

'You've cut it fine, dear,' she said, holding up her cheek for the kiss in passing. 'Successful day?'

'More or less.' I settled down on my couch, opposite hers. 'I've got to the bottom of the Priscus mystery.'

'Oh, my.' She frowned. 'You mean you went to the curio shop and talked to the woman?'

'Yeah. At least, yes to the first, anyway. Things aren't as black as we thought they were, albeit a tad weirder. It turns out she isn't his mistress after all. She's his grandchild.'

Perilla sat up sharply. '*What?* Marcus, that is *impossible!*'

'Uh-uh. True. And it's all perfectly credible. If you can manage to put the current version of Priscus completely out of your mind, that is. Backtrack seventy years, think in terms of teenaged sharp dude-about-town with an eye for the local talent, the town being Athens, and you've got it.'

'Hold on. We're talking about *Priscus? Our* Priscus? The man who throws sauce on my best mantle and has a thing for recherché points of grammar in dead languages?'

'As ever is, lady. Listen and marvel.' I explained, while the skivvies laid out the plates of starters. By the time I'd finished, we were both at the giggling stage. Well, it did have its funny side, when you thought about it.

'Vipsania will go absolutely spare,' Perilla said. 'When is he going to tell her? *Is* he going to tell her?'

'He said he would.' I reached for a stuffed olive. 'Or at least that he'd tell her something. But it's their problem to sort out between them. Me, I'm keeping well clear.'

'So what's she like?' Perilla dipped a celery stalk into the fish sauce. 'This Polyxene?'

'She seems okay. I didn't really have a chance to talk to her.'

'That's a pity. She is a relative of yours in a way, you know; a distant one, granted, very much collateral, and I'm not sure what the exact term is. But even so you will have certain commitments where she's concerned.'

I set the olive down. I hadn't really thought of it that way; what with Bathyllus and Priscus both turning up long-lost relatives out of the blue it would seem that family commitments in general were figuring pretty strongly this time round. 'Fair enough,' I said. 'We'll keep a watching brief, see how things develop. That satisfy you?'

'Yes, of course it does, dear, certainly until Priscus manages to fix things up with Vipsania and the dust settles. If he does manage.' She chewed on the celery, and I picked up one of Meton's cheese pastries. 'So how did the rest of your day go?'

'Yeah, well, that side of things was a bit more problematical.' I told her the details of my chat with Vinicius, and what he'd said about Annius Vinicianus and his connection with the Dalmatian revolt. 'Me, I don't think Vinicianus did it at all. Wrote the letter to Scribonianus, I mean.'

'That's hardly logical, Marcus.' Perilla was carefully peeling a quail's egg. 'After all, Vinicius believes it, and he was the man's uncle, so he would know if anyone would. Besides, Vinicius is a very intelligent man.'

'Sure he is. He's also careful as hell; he has to be, in his position. You think it was coincidence he suggested the Palace for our talk rather than taking me back home with him? Or that he engineered things so we left separately when we'd finished? Personally I wouldn't bet on the fact that he'd swallowed the official version of events for one minute, whether he told me so or not. And when I asked about the other trials – his wife's and Graecina's pal Livia's – he clammed up completely and more or less advised me to drop everything down a very deep hole.'

'Hmm.' Perilla dipped the egg into the fish sauce. 'So what are your reasons? For believing that Vinicianus *didn't* write the letter?'

'Come on, Perilla!' I set the pastry down on my plate. 'Why should he? Vinicius's claim that he did it because he was so upset at Silanus's death and wanted to get back at Claudius is pure hogwash. We're not talking Harmodius and Aristogeiton here, anything to avenge a pal.'

She smiled. 'Oh, well done, Marcus! A historical allusion, or at least close to one. You are improving.'

I ignored her. 'Look. We've been through all this. The guy was smart, he was streetwise politically speaking, he was all out for Number One, and as Messalina's accomplice he was already sitting pretty with both her and the emperor. He wasn't going to risk rocking the boat, and even if he had been fool enough to want to he certainly wouldn't've chosen such a damn stupid way of going about it. He'd know perfectly well that Scribonianus wouldn't have a hope in hell of staging a successful revolt; he was a political nobody, he was half the world away from Rome with only a couple of legions to play with, and he had no military support pledged anywhere else, or any other kind of support, for that matter. Even if he had got the length of marching on Italy he'd've been mopped up before he crossed the fucking Alps.'

'Don't swear.'

'Yeah, well. Besides, Vinicianus would've known he had a bee in his bonnet about restoring the Republic. I mean, how far is that idea going to get you in this day and age? Promise your men a good cash bonus when they set your or whoever's backside on the throne, fine, you're in with a shout at least. But tell them you're out to restore a system that went down the tubes before their grandfathers were born and you're on a hiding to nothing. No wonder they gave him the finger and the whole thing collapsed.'

'All right.' She pushed her plate away. 'So if Vinicianus didn't write the letter then where *did* it come from?'

'That's obvious. Messalina forged it and sent it in Vinicianus's name. Or she and Narcissus did, working together. To set him up.'

'Why on earth should she want to do that?'

'I don't know. But it makes sense.' I pushed my own plate away. 'Look. You'd agree that Vinicianus had no valid reason to send it himself, yes? That in fact he'd've been a bloody fool to?'

'Yes, I suppose so,' she said cautiously. 'For the sake of argument, at least.'

'Good. Okay. Now assuming that Messalina did have her reasons for wanting Vinicianus chopped the Scribonianus ploy is perfect. Like–'

'Hold on, dear. Why not just engineer a charge of treason against him? That would be a much simpler method, wouldn't it?'

'Maybe. But this way is safer and surer.'

'Really?' The barest sniff. 'How so?'

'For a start, there'd be no doubt in Claudius's mind that an act of treason had taken place, because it had, in a form to scare the willies out of him: one of his military governors going rogue at a time when he had four legions committed to the British campaign. And if it subsequently transpires that someone in Rome started it all off by pushing the guy's button then he's unlikely to be all that forgiving and sympathetic. Fair enough?'

'Hmm.'

I grinned. 'I'll take that as a yes. Okay. Back to Vinicianus. As far as he's concerned the whole thing comes like a bolt from the blue, and it's a *fait accompli*: he knows about the revolt, sure, but suddenly he finds that he's being accused of starting it, for the reason that Vinicius gave me, resentment over his pal Silanus's death; that he's supposed to have sent Scribonianus a letter saying the senate is behind him to a man and are all looking forward to a restored republic. The poor bastard's screwed: he can't deny sending the letter because no doubt there it is, or a copy of it, duly signed, in Suillius Rufus's little hot-and-sticky, ready to be flashed around in court as Exhibit One, and he can't claim the whole thing's a stitch-up because who would believe him? Certainly not Claudius, with Messalina whispering sweet nothings in his ear. He can't accuse her of being behind the stitch-up, either, for much the same reasons. So whatever happens he knows he's for the chop, and there isn't a thing he can do about it. His only options are to slit his wrists or wait for the government executioner to do the job for him.'

'It still begs the question of why, Marcus. Even if Messalina did engineer the accusation what possible reason would she have for doing it in the first place?' Perilla retrieved the shelled egg. 'As you said, Vinicianus was firmly on her side and she was completely in the ascendant where influence over Claudius was concerned. Naturally she'd have cause if she suspected that he was a threat, but you're right, he'd have had to be an absolute fool to even think of crossing her at that stage. It makes no sense at all, however you look at it.'

I frowned. 'No,' I said. 'It doesn't, and that's the bugger. Leave it for the present.' I picked up the pastry again. 'Catonius Justus, now, at least from what Secundus told me about him we're on firmer ground there.'

'How so?'

'To begin with, according to Secundus, and he knew the guy personally, the claim that Justus was having an affair with Julia Livia is total garbage; Secundus was absolutely definite about that, and given their characters as we know them and the differences in their ages it doesn't sound even remotely possible. The treason side of things is a non-starter as well; where loyalty was concerned – again according to Secundus – Justus was squeaky-clean, a career soldier up from the ranks with a first-rate military record stretching back all the way to Augustus's time and the Rhine and Danube mutinies. He'd never put a foot wrong loyalty-wise in his life.'

'Neither had Cassius Chaerea, dear, and his background was identical. That didn't stop him being involved in the assassination of Gaius, did it? Quite the opposite.'

I reached for my wine cup. 'Come on, Perilla!' I said irritably. 'You're quibbling and you know you are. Chaerea snapped precisely because he was the man he was, not in spite of it, and he'd good reason to, seeing how Gaius treated him; we saw that for ourselves at the dinner party. Claudius is no Gaius, nowhere near, he appointed Justus to the prefectship himself, and the guy had no grounds for resentment whatsoever. Quite the reverse. Plus there's the family connection: Justus's career began under Claudius's cousin Drusus, when Drusus gave him his big chance to shine the time of the Pannonian revolt. A thing like that is important to a bred-in-the-bone soldier, you know it is, particularly if he'd started life as a humble squaddie like Justus had. It'd have taken a hell of a lot of provocation to cause him to turn against the Claudian family, and as far as we know he had zilch.'

'Hmm.' Perilla re-dunked the egg. 'Yes, well, dear, I suppose you're right. It was a quibble. Even so, as with Vinicianus, we are still left with the question of why.'

'True. Oh, sure, the basic reason's clear enough, association with Julia Livia; genuine association, I mean, not the sexual kind. Livia was Justus's old boss Drusus's daughter, so loyalty to the family would kick in again. Secundus didn't say so, but I'd bet a gold piece to a used corn plaster that the guy took a proprietorial – avuncular, whatever you like to call it – interest in the woman, and he wouldn't've just sat idly by if he'd thought she was being threatened. Which of course she was, and she knew who by.'

'Messalina. Because of the succession issue.'

'Right. And if Livia voiced her suspicions – certainties, rather – to Pomponia Graecina then the chances are she'd also tell Justus, who was in a far better position than Graecina was to get something done about it because he was a guy Claudius knew, respected and trusted. Maybe he even put together some sort of formal dossier which he thought he could use to pull the lady's plug for her. Only they both underestimated Messalina's hold over the poor sap: when they were accused of immorality and treason Claudius wouldn't even go the length of giving them a hearing.'

'It certainly all fits together, doesn't it?'

'Yeah. Yes, it does. The only thing is, even if it's right it doesn't get us an inch further forward. That's the really dispiriting thing about this case; we can theorise until we're blue in the face, but we can't actually *prove* anything. And even if we could, what good would it do? At the end of the day, if Messalina is your grey eminence it'd be suicide to take it further. Literally. However much proof we offered him, however nice a guy he is at base, Claudius would just give a hollow laugh and have us chopped out of hand without a second thought.'

Perilla set the egg down and gave me a sharp look. 'So what exactly *do* you want to do, Marcus?' she said. 'Give up?'

'Uh-uh.' I grinned. 'No way. We'll just have to keep our fingers crossed, that's all.'

Bathyllus came in with the tray-skivvies. He eyed the practically-untouched selection of starters and sniffed.

'You *have* finished, sir, have you?' he said. 'Madam?'

I glanced at Perilla, and she nodded.

'Yeah, little guy,' I said. 'It would seem so. Sorry about that. Things intervened.'

'Indeed.' Another sniff. He signalled to the skivvies, who began to remove the dishes, half-turned to go, then hesitated. 'Incidentally, I was wondering if there had been any further developments. Where my brother is concerned, I mean.'

As a bit of ham acting, it was perfect. Mind you, I didn't blame him for pushing the question. Not at all.

'I'm sorry, pal,' I said gently. 'Everything's much as is in that direction. I want him to get in touch as badly as you do, but that's not looking likely. Not in the near future, at least.'

'No. No, I understand that,' he said. 'Thank you, sir.'

He went out after the skivvies.

'He's very worried, isn't he, Marcus?' Perilla said. 'You're sure there's nothing you can do?'

‘Absolutely zilch,’ I said. ‘Eutacticus knows where Damon is hiding, sure, but he won’t tell. And I can’t force him. I’d be a fool if I even tried.’

‘So what now?’

‘The gods know, lady. The gods know.’

Yeah, well, maybe they did, at that. But if so they weren’t letting on, either.

# 20

It rained the next day, and I had sod all to do as far as the case was concerned anyway, so I gritted my teeth, took an abacus up to my study, and gave some badly-needed attention to the month's accounts. I hate that side of things, but it has to be done on a regular basis at some stage, and with Perilla out in the litter on a shopping binge to the Saepta I'd no valid excuse.

So the accounts it was, gritted teeth or not.

I'd messed up the totals for the third time and was giving the balls on their wires one last chance to get it right before I reduced the little bastards to their common denominator when there was a tap on the door and Bathyllus edged in.

'This had better be important, sunshine,' I snarled, 'because if it isn't–'

'You have a visitor, sir,' he said.

Uh-oh. This didn't sound good: Bathyllus knew very well that interrupting me on an accounts day was a bad, bad idea, and he wouldn't do it lightly. Besides, he had his Courier of Doom expression on again, and his tone had serious overtones added.

'Yeah?' I said. 'And who would that be, now?'

'Suillius Rufus.'

'*What?*'

'He's downstairs, sir. In the atrium. Shall I bring him up?'

'No. No, that's all right, Bathyllus.' My brain had gone numb. 'Tell him I'll be right there.'

Gods.

I straightened the piles of tablets and flimsies on the table, more for something to do with my hands while I got my mental act together. There wasn't any question of the subject of Rufus's visit in general terms, sure, but for the bastard to come out into the open like this wasn't a good sign. Not good at all.

Well, there was no point in guessing, or in putting things off. I took a deep breath and went downstairs.

Like I say, I hadn't seen Rufus since that one time in Syria, over twenty years back, when he'd been in charge of the Third Legion under the province's governor, Aelius Lamia. He'd lost a fair amount of his hair since then, and a lot of the muscle had turned to flab, but he was still a big guy, built like a gladiatorial Chaser and with the same don't-mess-with-me air about him. Plus he had a certain fat-cat smoothness in the way he was dressed and barbered; "upwardly mobile" was right, except that when you thought of what he'd been moving through to get him looking like that, and how he'd been doing it, the phrase lost its positive connotations.

When I came in he was stretched out on my usual couch like he owned it. Bathyllus was hovering in the background like a messenger in a Greek tragedy who'd strayed into the wrong play.

'That's okay, little guy,' I said to him. 'You scoot. I'll take it from here.'

Bathyllus scooted.

'No offer of a cup of wine for an old acquaintance, Corvinus?' Rufus said. 'What happened to your duties as a host?'

'Bugger them. You're not welcome here.' I sat down on Perilla's couch facing him. 'What do you want? Just tell me straight and then fuck off out of my house.'

Rufus smiled.

'Hardly being friendly, are we?' he said. I didn't answer. 'And don't mistake me, this is a friendly visit.'

'Is that so, now?'

'Oh, yes. Mind you, to be fair it is the only friendly visit I'm going to make. Don't mistake me on that account, either.'

'So what's the reason for it? A warning? Lay off or else?'

The smile widened. 'Something like that, yes. Personally, I'd be delighted if you ignored it, but that's up to you. Of course, if we could reach an agreement whereby you carried on your search for the missing slave and promised to hand him over to me when you found him that would be almost as good. Disappointing, true, but we can't have everything we want, and I'm not absolutely sure you'd stick to your side of the bargain.'

'Why do you want him in the first place?'

'He has something we need very badly. You know that.'

'"We"? You mean you and Valeria Messalina?'

'We,' Rufus said blandly. 'Let's leave it at that. Your assumptions are your own concern.'

'Okay. So what is it, this "something"? At least you can tell me that.'

'Oh, I don't think it's really necessary. It's not a necklace, at any rate. I'll give you that much for free.' I felt my right hand bunching into a fist and had to make a conscious effort to unclench it. 'Naturally we'll find your friend Damon ourselves eventually, but it really would be in your interests to co-operate in a positive way. Show a little goodwill. Because, Valerius Corvinus, and read my lips here, you are going to need a great deal of it in return.'

'Yeah? and how's that, then?'

'Just to give an example, the most obvious one. I had a freedman, a blacksmith by the name of Ligurinus who ran a business down by the Latin

Gate. You met him briefly, I think? Four days ago, in the Asinian Gardens?'

'Yeah. So?'

'So the poor man was stabbed to death, wasn't he? Murdered, in fact.' I said nothing, but my guts went cold. 'Now, whether or not you were directly responsible for that I don't know, and I don't particularly care because whoever actually wielded the knife isn't important to me. What is important is that prior to his murder you asked one of the public slaves for directions to the Shrine of the Nymphs, where the murder took place. We have the slave, and the slave's description of the man he talked to, which believe me is surprisingly detailed for someone of his age and condition. As Ligurinus's patron it would be my duty to bring his killer to justice in open court. Which, again believe me, I would be very happy indeed to do, if you'll just say the word.'

'You bastard,' I said quietly.

Rufus shrugged. 'Ligurinus was only a freedman,' he said, 'and you're a purple-striper, so under normal circumstances you'd probably get off with a hefty fine. Unfortunately, as it is...well, in the event I don't think the emperor would be inclined to take a very lenient view of the matter. It would mean exile at best, and to somewhere a great deal more unpleasant than, say, Athens or Massilia. But I'm afraid it's much more likely that Claudius would decide to make a proper example of you.' He drew his finger across his throat. '*Chkkkk!* Get my meaning? So please, Corvinus, *don't* agree to give up your investigations or to co-operate with us. It'd be such a shame if you did.'

Oh, gods. The cold feeling in my stomach had solidified into a block of ice. He could do it, sure – in fact, he was right: bringing a charge against his client's murderer, if the perp was known, was a patron's duty – and with Messalina on the team if he wanted to get me chopped he could do that as well, easy as spitting.

I was well and truly screwed.

Rufus had been watching me closely. He must've seen what he was looking for, because he grunted in satisfaction, eased himself off the couch, and stood up.

'I see I've given you some food for thought,' he said. 'I'll leave you to digest it. Don't bother to see me out, I can find my own way. Oh, and do give my regards to Perilla. It was the best thing I ever did, divorcing that vinegary bitch. You're welcome to her.'

He left, chuckling.

Shit; what the hell was I supposed to do now?

I was half way down the jug and still stone-cold sober three hours later when Perilla got back, accompanied by the litter lads carrying a fair proportion of the Saepta's erstwhile stock.

'That's all right,' she said to them. 'Just put the packages down and I'll deal with them later.' Then, when they'd done so and trooped out, 'Hello, Marcus. Did you have a nice quiet morning?' She eyed the wine jug and sniffed. 'Yes, well, I can see you did. Marcus, dear, I really do think you should–'

'Suillius Rufus dropped by,' I said.

She stared at me. '*What?*'

'Your ex husband. Publius Suillius Rufus.'

She sat down on the other couch like someone had cut her strings. 'Rufus?' she said. 'What did he want?'

‘To warn me off the case, naturally. Oh, and to threaten me with a murder rap followed by a quick trial and a short stay in the Mamertine if I didn’t feel like being warned.’

The stare had turned to a look of horror. ‘Rufus is going to prosecute you for murder? Whose, for heaven’s sake?’

‘His freedman Ligurinus’s. You remember the guy in the Asinian Gardens that Eutacticus’s tame gorilla killed?’

‘But you had nothing to do with that! And in any case the man was a criminal and a murderer himself.’

‘You think that’ll make a blind bit of difference?’ I poured myself another cup of wine and sank half of it. ‘I was there, I was seen, they have the slave I asked directions from and he’s given them my description. Any court in Rome would convict me on that evidence alone, and quite rightly so because I wouldn’t have a fucking leg to stand on. Then with the emperor in their pocket Rufus and Messalina could peg me out for the crows without breaking sweat. I’d be dead in a month.’

She was quiet for a long time. Then she reached over, picked up the wine cup and drained it.

‘So what are you going to do?’ she asked finally.

‘Give up the case.’ I took the cup back and refilled it. ‘What else can I do?’

‘Claudius knows you. And me. You’ve had dealings with him before. He’s a fair man, he wouldn’t even consider–’

‘Come on, Perilla, show some sense! The guy’s already sat back and watched his own kin chopped on that pair of beauties’ say-so, on even flimsier evidence than Rufus can bring forward. Justus, too, that he’d known and respected for years. He’s even signed the fucking execution orders with his own hand. What chance do you think I have?’

'Oh, Marcus!'

'Right. So that's the ball game. We can't carry on, not under these circumstances. The bastard's got me cold, and he knows it.' I emptied the cup and slammed it down on the table. '*Fuck!*'

'Gently, dear.' She sat back, frowning. 'Now listen to me. It's not the end of the world, far from it. You said yourself, Rufus will only bring the charge if you *don't* give it up. And even if you did carry on, what would be the point? You've gone as far as you can go in any case, you know who was ultimately responsible for the man Oplonius's death, and you also know there's no possibility of bringing the perpetrators to justice. What more is there?'

I poured out more wine; the jug was looking pretty empty now, but the wine still didn't seem to be having any effect.

'I still don't know the who, the what, and the why, okay?' I said. 'Who Oplonius really was, what he had that Rufus and Messalina wanted, and why they wanted it. And I've never, ever given up on a case before I was satisfied that I'd gone as far as I possibly could. That answer your question?'

'Yes, it does. Still–'

'Still, there's a first time for everything, and this is it. Agreed; no arguments, no fucking arguments whatsoever.' I sank most of the wine. 'I'm not happy about it, not happy at all, but this stops now. It has to.'

She took a deep breath. 'Thank you, Marcus. For being sensible for once.'

'You're welcome.'

'So.' She smiled; a forced and brittle smile, mind, but even in my current mood I could appreciate the effort she was making. 'If you like we could go down to Castrimoenium tomorrow, spend a month or so with Marilla and Clarus. See how young Marcus is doing. A spring break, yes?'

'Yeah.' I took a morose swallow of the wine. 'Yeah, good idea. That'd be great. Not tomorrow, though, we've got Secundus and his new wife coming round for dinner. Make it the day after.'

'Fair enough. That'll give us time to send word we're coming in advance. Marilla and Clarus wouldn't mind us dropping in on them unexpectedly, I'm sure, but it's just as well to give them a bit of notice. Also' – she indicated the packages she'd brought back from her shopping binge – 'I bought a few things to give them that I was going to put away for the next time we went through, or they came to us. A trip to the Alban Hills would fit in quite well.'

'Okay. We'll do it.' I raised my voice. 'Bathyllus!'

He was straight in. He'd been listening, of course, probably from the moment I'd originally sent him out while I talked to Rufus, but I didn't blame the little guy for that. He had a vested interest, after all.

'Yes, sir,' he said.

'Send someone through to Castrimoenium to say we'll be down in a couple of days, will you?' It wasn't too late in the day, and on horseback the trip wouldn't take all that long. 'And tell Lysias to have the coach ready. He'll need a bit of notice as well.'

'Certainly, sir.' He hesitated. 'I'm terribly sorry. There isn't anything I can do, naturally, but–'

'Thanks, pal. It can't be helped, these things happen.' I waved him away.

Perilla was watching me anxiously.

'You'll be all right really, won't you dear?' she said. 'I mean–'

'Yeah, I'll be fine, honestly.' I poured the last half cup from the jug. 'I just need a bit of time to adjust, that's all.'

I felt drained, and sick. Drained, sick, and hopeless.

Fuck.

# 21

It's amazing what a good night's sleep will do. I woke up next morning not exactly full of the joys of spring, but at least reconciled to throwing in the towel. Like Perilla had said, it was the only sensible thing to do by a long chalk: I was beat fair and square, and although I might not like it considering the alternative it was no big deal. Rufus, I knew, would keep to his part of the bargain; personalities aside, he'd no reason to do otherwise, particularly since if he did go through with the trial whatever the outcome was he'd be publicly opening a can of worms that both he and Messalina would be far happier to keep closed.

Besides, I was looking forward to the family break in Castrimoenium: the grand-sprog, young Marcus, was rising five-and-a-half now, just getting to the interesting stage. Oh, sure, we were back and forward two or three times a year, or Marilla and Clarus came to us if Clarus could find a locum for his medical practice, but even so it was good to keep up. And if all that rustic bosk didn't exactly suit a confirmed townie like me at least the place had a decent wineshop.

So I spent a very pleasant day bumming around while Perilla supervised the packing. Where dinner with Secundus and his wife was concerned, Meton had risen to the occasion: evil-minded, anarchic, antisocial bugger he may be, but the guy is a true professional, and one of the best chefs in Rome. So we were having a full range of starters followed by poached mullet in a honey-mint sauce, then pork in a cumin-lovage sauce with vegetables for main, and various tarts, candied dates and fresh fruit to finish. All served with a very nice Velletrian white that I'd picked up on our last Alban trip and set aside for a special occasion, plus whatever fruit juice abomination Perilla currently favoured for her and Helena, unless the lady showed a bit of sense and went for the wine instead.

Yeah, well, life wasn't too bad, after all.

They arrived just short of sunset; perfect timing. From what Secundus had said, and knowing the guy's tastes, I'd expected Helena to be another Furia Gemella, especially since he'd told me the two women had been friends: good looking and knows it, sassy and brassy, with a penchant for over-jewellerying themselves and a brain the size of a pickled walnut. Good looking Helena certainly was, but although I couldn't make any judgment re the brainpower yet she didn't fit the rest of the description at all: mid- to late thirties, slim, fairish hair, medium height, simply and tastefully dressed, and with a quiet, confident air about her that was still a long way from mousey. Large clashing earrings were something that definitely didn't feature.

'Valerius Corvinus,' she said, putting out her hand for me to shake. 'I'm delighted to meet you at last. Gaius has told me a lot about you.' A fleeting smile that lit up her face. 'Most of it good, you'll be glad to know. And...Perilla, yes?'

'That's right.' Perilla smiled too. 'Pleased to meet you, Helena.'

Her eyes widened. 'Did Gaius call me that?' She laughed and half-turned to Secundus, who shrugged. 'Actually, Helena's just a family nickname. Gaius uses it, of course, but practically no one else does now except my brothers. Brother, rather. I'm really Sentia.' Bathyllus, busy with the cloaks, paused and gave me a startled glance over her shoulder. I nodded briefly to him to show that I'd made the connection as well. 'And no, it doesn't matter a bit. Call me Helena, by all means.'

'Sorry, Marcus.' Secundus was grinning. 'My fault.'

‘Always is, pal, always is.’ My brain was itching; oh, sure, the purple-striper world was a small one, it could easily be a coincidence and probably wasn’t important in any case, but still... Leave it for now, certainly. ‘Dinner’s on its way, but we’ve time for a quick drink first. Atrium or dining room, Bathyllus?’

‘Dining room, I think, sir. Meton is almost ready to serve.’

‘Fine.’

I led the way through and we parked ourselves on the couches, Perilla and me versus Secundus and Helena. Bathyllus did the rounds with the wine and fruit juice. Helena stuck to juice; well, no one’s perfect.

‘So,’ I said to Helena, ‘how did you happen to get landed with this guy?’

‘*Marcus!*’ Perilla snapped.

Helena laughed. ‘Oh, that’s perfectly all right, Perilla. And Gaius did warn me.’ She turned to me. ‘We’ve been married for over two years now. Both divorced: mine didn’t work out either, and I went first. We met through Gemella.’

‘Ah,’ I said. ‘Right. Right.’ Shit; straight in with both feet.

Secundus chuckled. ‘No cause for embarrassment, Marcus,’ he said. ‘Our divorce – Gemella’s and mine – was perfectly amicable on both sides. And although we’d known each other for two or three years by then Helena was definitely an after, not a before. Let alone a because, if that was what you were wondering.’

‘Perish the thought.’

‘Mind you, we’d always been attracted. We’d’ve married sooner after my divorce came through if–’ He hesitated, and I felt, rather than saw, Helena stiffen. ‘If we’d been able to.’

Interesting: that hadn't been what he was going to say originally. Still, it was none of my business, not even to the length of speculating.

In came the skivvies bearing loaded trays, plus a hand-washing bowl and napkin. Meton had done us proud: as well as the usual quails' eggs, fish sauce, olives, and crunchy raw vegetables there was an assortment of small pastries, grilled chicken livers, and a dish each of snails in oil and thyme.

'This is amazing,' Helena said, holding out her hands for the skivvy to pour water over. 'I thought this was supposed to be an informal family meal.'

I grinned. 'Yeah, well, we don't do much in the way of entertaining,' I said. 'And Meton – that's our chef – likes to do things properly. Besides, like I told Gaius here it's a guilt-offering for being out of touch for so long.'

The trays emptied and the skivvies left us to it, leaving Bathyllus on drinks duty. Time for a little gentle fishing.

'By the way, Helena.' I reached for a snail. 'You happen to be any relation to the Sentius Saturninus who used to govern Syria?'

Beside me, Perilla froze and then shot me a sharp look over her shoulder. Probably just suspicious on principle, because I hadn't mentioned to her that Saturninus had been Damon's first owner, but the lady wasn't stupid. No doubt I'd pay for this later, but at present I gave her a bland smile in return.

'That was my father.' Helena was shelling an egg. 'Or maybe my grandfather, depending what time you mean. They were both out there as governors. Why do you ask?'

'It's just that Bathyllus here's just got back in touch with a long-lost brother he hadn't seen since they were kids.' Perilla made a small, exasperated hissing noise through her teeth and dug me hard in the ribs. I winced, and covered the movement by digging the snail from its shell with the spiked end of my snail-spoon. 'They were both sold at the same time, in Pergamum. His brother was bought by the governor, Saturninus.'

'Grandfather, then. How interesting.' She turned to look at Bathyllus. 'What's his name? Your brother?'

'Damon, madam,' Bathyllus said.

'Damon.' She frowned. 'No, sorry, no bells. Mind you, Grandfather died before I was born, and of course he had hundreds of slaves. Was he part of the actual household, do you know?'

'I'm not sure, madam. When the governor's tour of duty finished he was brought back to the family's Paduan estate.'

'We certainly had property near Padua, yes. We still have, in fact.' She turned round fully on the couch. 'How absolutely fascinating! And quite a coincidence. Is he there now?'

'No, madam. I understand that when your grandfather died he was sold on to a local merchant by the name of Oplonius.'

'Really; what a pity. Ah, well.' She rolled over to face the table again. 'But it is a coincidence, isn't it, Gaius?'

'Yes. Yes, it is.' Secundus was eyeing me speculatively. 'This, uh, wouldn't have anything to do with why you came round to see me at the office, would it, Marcus?'

*Not so green* was right.

'Absolutely nothing whatsoever,' I lied. 'In fact, that side of things is in abeyance, probably permanently.' I surreptitiously massaged my bruised rib; the lady could be downright vicious when she put her mind to it. 'You mind if we leave that alone? It's delicate ground at present.'

He shrugged and helped himself to a stuffed olive. 'Sure. No problem.'

‘I think, perhaps, dear, we’ll change the subject altogether.’ Perilla gave me her best dazzling smile, and I winced again, internally this time; shit, that *really* boded. Well, if there was going to be trouble later when she got me alone – as there undoubtedly was, in spades – at least I’d got something out of it: whatever had happened to him subsequently I was pretty sure now that Damon had told the truth about his connections with the Sentius family, which left open the possibility that...

Yeah, yeah; I know. Call it the ingrained habit of half a lifetime, sure, but with the best will in the world – and I was serious about closing the lid on the case completely, deadly serious – I couldn’t stop myself thinking. So long as it went no further than that, and I promised myself that it wouldn’t, whatever the temptation, we were okay.

Not that Perilla would’ve agreed, mind.

It was a very enjoyable dinner, and Secundus had been right: I did like Helena, I liked her a lot. But as far as any more furthering of the case went, even in the academic sense, the sum total was zilch; which, I supposed, was reasonable under the circumstances. We had the dessert, and then the ladies went off to powder their noses. Or whatever the hell women do together for half an hour when they leave the crude men behind to neck a few more cups of wine and swap all the dirty jokes they’ve been holding in all evening.

We could manage the wine part, at least, because with only the two of us drinking it there was plenty of the Velletrian left. And if not a descent to the dirty jokes level a certain degree of loosening up.

‘So, Marcus.’ Secundus held out his cup for Bathyllus to refill. None too steadily, mind: plenty of the stuff left or not, we were both of us well on the way to being stewed. 'You sure this case of yours is permanently on ice, or were you just saying that for Perilla's sake?'

I grinned. Yeah, he was no fool, Gaius Secundus. Mind you, we'd known each other practically all our lives, and if anyone could read between the lines as far as I was concerned then Secundus was the boy.

'Uh-huh,' I said. 'I'm afraid so.'

'Want to tell me why?'

'Yes. But I won't.'

'Political again, right?' I didn't answer, which I suppose was an answer in itself. He grunted and swallowed some of the wine. 'Fair enough. But don't forget, if I can help in any way you only have to ask. Okay?'

Well, you couldn't say fairer than that, and something had definitely been niggling, in fact banging on the door to get in, as it were. You couldn't really dignify it by calling it an idea, but still...

*Brothers. Brother, rather...*

Shit; go for it. After all, it was likely to be the only chance I'd get.

'Uh...listen, pal,' I said. 'This might sound strange, but–' I hesitated and started again. 'You married Helena just over two years ago, yes?'

'Sure. I told you. Or Helena did. Actually, two years and five months, if you're counting. We married a few days before the Winter Festival.'

'And you said you'd've got married before then if you'd been able to.'

'That's right.'

'You care to tell me why you couldn't?'

He frowned. 'Marcus, what is this about, exactly?'

'Maybe nothing,' I said. 'Just an itch. But believe me, I've learned to trust itches.'

'She was in mourning. For her brother.'

*Yes!* 'Ah...which brother would that be?'

'She had two. Three at one time, if you want to be picky. This was the youngest one, the baby of the family, four years younger than her. Gaius.'

'So how did he die?'

'He was executed. For treason.'

'*What?*'

Secundus made a face. 'Yeah. Right. Simple fact is, she's never quite got over the shock. They were always really close, far closer than she's ever been to Gnaeus; that's the surviving one, the ex-consul. Not that that should come as much of a surprise. I don't like to say anything against a brother-in-law of mine, but–' He waved his hand, luckily not the one holding the wine cup. 'Well, there you go.'

'So what did Gaius do?' I prompted. 'To deserve execution?'

'Not a lot, if you believe Helena, which I do. But he was Scribonianus's aide. You heard of Scribonianus, Marcus? Arruntius Scribonianus? The Dalmatian governor who staged a revolt three years back? Scribonianus committed suicide, sure, but Gaius got himself chopped a month or so later. Agents sent out from Rome specially for the purpose.'

Oh, shit. The ice was forming in my stomach. 'Sent out by who?'

'Claudius, of course. The emperor himself. The two legions, the Seventh and the Eleventh, that had refused to back Scribonianus, they had "Dutiful Claudian" tacked on to their titles, and the officers were given a pat on the back for being such good boys, all forgiven and forgotten. But Gaius, he was chopped. He'd been too close, you see, or that's what was claimed.'

'Look, pal, how do you know all this? Or how does Helena, rather?'

'One of Gaius's fellow officers came back and told her. We were due to get married a month later, but as it was we had to wait half a year.'

Oh, Jupiter! Good sweet Jupiter! My head was buzzing, and not altogether because of the wine.

'Hang on, pal,' I said. 'One more thing. You said Helena had three brothers. Gaius and the consular, that makes two. Who was the third? Did he die or what?'

'Uh-uh. That was Sextus. He was the second eldest, between Gnaeus and Helena.'

'You know anything about him?'

'Only what Helena told me, which wasn't much. He was wild and bad both, seemingly, and there was a scandal of some kind. A big one. Helena doesn't know the details, but the upshot was that her father managed to hush the matter up for the sake of the family and then threw the guy out on his ear. Disinherited, never wanted to see him again, the whole works.'

*Yes!* The back of my neck was prickling. 'When was this?' I said.

'About twenty years back. Helena was sixteen, seventeen when it happened. She wasn't too fussed – she never did take to Sextus, he was too clearly a bad lot – but young Gaius was gutted. As far as he was concerned the sun shone out of Sextus's backside.'

'And that was the last time Helena saw him?'

'More or less. He came mooching back when her father died – that'd be ten or so years ago – but Brother Gnaeus sent him packing. He hasn't shown his face or tried to get in touch since. Dropped completely off the map.'

Dear holy gods, I'd cracked it! It couldn't be a coincidence, no *way* could it be a coincidence! We'd got our Oplonius!

'Uh...look, pal,' I said. 'This was just between us, right? Not a word even to Helena.'

'Forgotten already.' He grinned. 'Missing piece of a puzzle, was it?'

'Yeah, something like that. Mind you, if I hadn't asked–' I froze as the implication registered. Oh, shit! Oh, holy ever-loving Jupiter God Almighty!

Secundus was staring at me. 'You okay?'

'Yeah. Yeah, just a thought. Nothing to do with you, Gaius.' The hell it wasn't; it had everything to do with him, and possibly with Helena as well...

Oh, gods!

At which point the girls came back, and all I could do was lie there and worry.

'What on *earth* made you do it?' Perilla snapped when we'd waved Secundus and Helena off in their coach and were back in the atrium. 'I thought we were past all that!'

Here it went. I took a deep breath.

'I can't drop the case,' I said.

The anger disappeared from her face, and she simply looked at me for a long time. Then she said, very quietly, 'Marcus, you bloody, *bloody* fool.'

I held up a hand. 'Just hear me out. It's not what you think. And it isn't as bad as you think, either.'

She sat down on the couch; I was still standing.

'Very well, I'm listening,' she said. Just that, and in the same quiet, expressionless voice. 'Carry on.'

'When I asked Secundus and his wife round for a meal I hadn't the slightest idea who she was, right?'

'If you say so, dear. Knowing you, however, I wouldn't be surprised if–'

'Jupiter, Perilla, come off it! It's the simple, honest truth! How the fuck was I to know she'd turn out to be our Oplonius's sister?'

Her chin came up. '*What?*' she said sharply.

Yeah, well, at least I wasn't getting the ice-maiden treatment any longer. And I'd certainly got the lady's full attention. 'Fact. I had an interesting talk with Secundus while you and Helena were out of the room using the facilities. It transpires that up until twenty years back she had a ne'er-do-well brother by the name of Sextus who was disinherited by their father and who she hasn't had news of since. Her younger brother–'

'Hold on, Marcus. Why should this man be Oplonius?'

'That's Damon again, keeping as close to the truth as he can. He told me his first master was the Syrian governor, Sentius Saturninus; oh, sure, he didn't have any alternative, because Bathyllus already knew that from the enquiries he'd made, but still. The next step was his smoke-screen. According to Damon, when the old man died he was sold on to the Oplonius family and passed down to the son. My guess – my bet, and it's a good one – is that there was no sale at all; that he carried on being a slave of the Sentii, and when young Master Sextus got his marching orders he went along with him.'

'Very well.' I noticed that her left hand had strayed to the curl of hair above her ear. Good sign; we might live through this after all. 'You were going to say. Her younger brother...?'

'Right. Turns out that he was Scribonianus's aide in Dalmatia, the time of the abortive revolt. And that after Scribonianus killed himself he was executed for treason on Claudius's orders. Only him, no one else.'

'In Rome or Dalmatia?'

‘I didn’t ask, but from the way Secundus told it I’d imagine Dalmatia. Agents were sent out from Rome to see that he was chopped, and one of his officer pals brought the news home to Helena.’

‘Hmm.’ She pulled on the curl. ‘So your assumption is what?’

‘Perilla, I don’t know, okay? All I’ve got at present are unconnected facts.’ I sat down on the couch. ‘Two more for you. Gaius – that was the younger brother’s name – hero-worshipped Sextus, or that’s how I see it reading between the lines. And Sextus and his elder brother Gnaeus were pretty much at daggers drawn; certainly Gnaeus had no time for him, however it went the other way. That’s it, unless you want the theory.’

‘If you’ve got one, yes, we may as well have it.’

I hid a grin; offhand as hell, a sure sign that the lady was hooked and trying to pretend she wasn’t. We were home and dry. ‘I’d say Gaius posed a threat to Messalina in some way, had something in his possession that could harm her, maybe a document linking her to the revolt, and Messalina had him chopped. Only she was too late: he’d already sent the whatever-it-was to his brother Sextus.’

‘How could he know where Sextus was? And even allowing for the fact he wanted to send it to a family member, why him? Why not his elder brother? Or Helena, for that matter?’

‘Helena wouldn’t be an option; whatever the thing was, just having it in her possession would’ve been dangerous, and he was too fond of his sister to do that to her. Gnaeus... I’m guessing, sure, but from the way Secundus talked about him I’d say young Gaius simply didn’t trust him. Sextus, well, he’d always had an idealised view of Sextus. It’s not too illogical a choice. As far as knowing Sextus’s whereabouts goes, there’s no reason to suppose the two of them hadn’t kept in touch after the guy was kicked out. Secretly, granted, but that'd be natural, considering the rest of the family had washed their hands of him.'

'All right. All very interesting and convincing. But you still have to drop the case.'

I shook my head. 'I told you,' I said. 'I can't do that.'

'Marcus, *please* see sense! We've been all through this and you know that it isn't a matter of choice. If you're too pig-headed obstinate to–'

'No. I told you that as well; it's got nothing to do with me. Look. Rufus warned me that if I didn't take my nose out of his and Messalina's business he'd see me nailed, yes?'

'Of course. That's the whole point.'

'So what happens when he finds out – and he will, because one gets you ten he has this place and me staked out round the clock – that a couple of days after I visit Secundus, who's head of military admin, he and his wife, who Rufus knows damn well is Gaius Sentius's sister, drop round for dinner? You think he'll believe it was a coincidence? I wouldn't, myself, not for one fucking minute, and that bastard is not in the business of making allowances.'

She was staring at me in horror. 'Oh, Marcus!'

'Right. It's not just me who's threatened, either. He can only assume that now Helena and Secundus are involved, or at least there's a good chance that they're aware of what's going on. So how long do you think it'll be before they're chopped on a trumped-up charge as well?'

'What can you do?'

'The only thing I can do. Go for Rufus's third option.'

'What third option?'

Yeah, I hadn't told her about that, had I, because it hadn't seemed viable at the time. 'I can play on his and Messalina's side. Find Damon for them and hand him over. If I do that then we're all square again.'

'But, Marcus, you can't! He's Bathyllus's brother! They'll kill him!'

'Why should they? They don't want Damon, any more than they want me. They want whatever Damon has got, courtesy of his master, and as far as I'm concerned now they can have it.'

'You don't know where Damon is!'

'I don't, but Sempronius Eutacticus does.'

She shook her head. 'Eutacticus won't help. He told you so.'

'Yeah, well, that was before, when I didn't have the information he was trying to keep from me, that he'd accidentally beaten out of Ligurinus's sidekick. That the two of them were working for the empress. He's got no reason to cover up now. Besides, it was his man Satrius who knifed Ligurinus, and if I'm being threatened with a murder rap then he's the root cause of it. Eutacticus may be a crook, but he works to his own code. I reckon that would weigh, certainly enough to justify a little arm-twisting.'

'So what are you going to do?'

'Have another talk with Eutacticus, of course. See if he'll act as middle-man between me and Rufus, try to broker a deal.' I yawned; suddenly I felt dead beat. 'Tomorrow. It'll mean putting off the trip to Castrimoenium, sure, but hopefully not for too long. Or you could go ahead and I'll catch you up.'

'You really think I would do that?'

I grinned. 'Yeah, well, maybe not.' I stood up, went over and kissed her. 'Bed?'

'Bed.'

# 22

I went over to Eutacticus's immediately after breakfast. He was in the back garden again, sitting on a bench beneath a cherry tree with an open book roll in his hands. When he saw me coming he set the roll down beside him, but not before I'd glimpsed its title-tag: *The Girl from Halicarnassus*.

Well, well: so he was a clandestine Alexandrian tunic-ripper reader, was he? I was learning a lot about Sempronius Eutacticus this time round.

'Morning, pal,' I said. 'Sorry to disturb.'

He shifted the book so that the tag was hidden. 'Corvinus, are you trying to get seriously up my nose or what?' he snapped. 'I told you the last time you were here that–'

'Oplonius was a guy named Sextus Sentius.' There was a wicker chair to one side of the bench. I pulled it towards me and sat. 'His younger brother Gaius was aide to Arruntius Scribonianus, the Dalmatian governor who tried to stage a revolt three years ago. The brother sent Sextus something, maybe a letter, I don't know exactly, but whatever it was Valeria Messalina and Suillius Rufus wanted it very badly. They used Rufus's freedman Ligurinus and his pal Caprius to get it for them, but they screwed up. To cut a long story short, you put the heat on Caprius thinking he and his pal had something to do with your stolen necklace, only to find you'd accidentally bagged one of the empress's agents who coughed up a lot of things – political things – that you really didn't want to hear. Now tell me I'm wrong.'

That got me the cold fish-eyed stare.

'So?' he said.

'Just making a point. The stable door's wide open and the horse is long gone. I'm grateful that you tried to protect me by keeping me away from Damon, sure, but it isn't appropriate any more. Quite the reverse.'

'Really?'

'Yeah, really. In fact, I need to see him asap.'

'You mind telling me why?'

'Because it might just save his life. And mine. Rufus is threatening to hit me with a murder rap for killing Ligurinus, that your boy Satrius zeroed in the Asinian Gardens.'

'That's your own fault, Corvinus. If you'd just let things be when I advised you to you wouldn't be in this mess. And if you remember I offered to take care of that witness for you before he could cause any trouble.'

'Yeah, well, slitting the throat of a garden slave just because he's been good enough to point a stranger in the right direction is just a tad over the top, for my money.'

Eutacticus grunted. 'Fair enough,' he said. 'I can't see the problem myself, but it was your decision to make. So. You want to know where Damon is holed up?'

I hesitated. 'Actually, I was hoping for bit more than that.'

'Were you, indeed?'

'Yeah.' Here we went. 'Matters have sort of suddenly reached a crisis. Through no fault of mine, at least not a deliberate one. What I need to do is get whatever Gaius Sentius sent to his brother and do a trade-off with Rufus, pretty damn quick. Only I could, like, really use a middle-man to broker the deal and see fair play on both sides.'

'And you think I'll do that for you?'

'Uh...yeah. Yeah, more or less. Or I was hoping you would.'

'Fuck off.'

'Come on, Eutacticus! It's no skin off your nose, and if things go pear-shaped I'm cooked.'

'My heart bleeds.'

'You want me to beg?'

The cold-fish look again. I began to sweat.

Finally, he said, 'Okay, Corvinus, you've got it, just this once. If I let you get chopped I'd probably regret it afterwards.' I sagged in relief, and his lips twisted in a half-smile. 'That's *probably*, note, so don't pat yourself on the back too hard. But don't forget, you owe me again. Seriously.' He stood up. 'Okay. Follow me and we'll get you set up somewhere.'

'What about Damon? I'll need to find him first.'

'Use your brain, boy. If your friends have any sense they'll've been watching you. You lead them to Damon, or Damon comes to you at home, and you're both in the bag before you can say knife. You're my guest for the duration. I'll get my lads to pick the slave up and bring him here.'

'So what's to stop your boys being jumped on too?' I said. That just got me a long, uncomprehending stare. Yeah; right. Well, I supposed Rufus and co would be welcome to try it, but unless they had a squad of Praetorians on call I doubted if they'd get very far.

Eutacticus set out for the house. 'You want me to send someone back to your place?' he said over his shoulder. 'Tell them where you are and not to worry?'

'Yeah, that'd be great.' Mind you, if the skivvy was anyone of the size, shape and physiognomy of Satrius I couldn't see the reassurance working to any degree. Still, I appreciated the thought. Consideration, now, no less. Maybe the bastard was mellowing. 'How long do you think it'll take?'

'To get Damon? No more than an hour, maybe two. He's been working as a trampler in a fuller's shop off Cyprian Street. Where the rest of the business is concerned you tell me.'

So Damon had stuck with the Subura after all. Mind you, he'd be as safe there as anywhere: the Subura is a rabbit warren, particularly where the alleyways off the main streets are concerned, and the locals pride themselves in minding their own business. But a fuller's trampler! That didn't augur well. I just hoped that if I was to be in Damon's company for all that long wherever Eutacticus was putting me up was well ventilated. Not that I had very high hopes in that direction, mind: given the sadistic bastard's twisted sense of humour I might well be spending my next few hours in a broom cupboard. Sharing it with the brooms, what's more. Still, beggars couldn't be choosers, and I'd no illusions about my status, or lack of it, at present.

'You know how to get in touch with Rufus?' I said as we cleared the peristyle and entered the house itself.

'Don't teach your granny to suck eggs, Corvinus.' There was a slave waiting inside. Eutacticus snapped his fingers at him and he obediently fell into line behind us.

Yeah, well, that was me told. I clamped my lips together firmly.

We threaded the labyrinth in silence. Finally, Eutacticus turned down a corridor leading to a closed oak-panelled door. He opened it.

'That's you for the duration,' he said. 'Be grateful.'

I almost whistled. Forget the broom cupboard, despite the guy's surly manner he'd done me proud: the place was clearly one of the upmarket guest suites, with its own pooled atrium complete with assorted bronze statuary, a couple of seriously pricey murals on the walls, and a private courtyard garden from which drifted the tinkling sound of water from an ornamental fountain.

Crime obviously didn't just pay in Eutacticus's case; it factored in a whacking great entertainment allowance as well.

'You'll be fine here,' he said. 'Bedroom's next door' – nodding towards an opening to one side – 'if things take longer than expected. You hungry?'

'Uh-uh. Some wine would be good, though.'

'No problem. Flavillus here'll look after you.' He turned to the slave and raised an eyebrow. The man scuttled off. 'Now, I've a business to run and you're an extra complication that I could do without. I'll see you later.'

He made to go.

'Hang on, pal,' I said. 'What happens now? I just sit here and twiddle my thumbs, do I?'

He paused, then turned back. Slowly. He wasn't smiling.

'Look, Corvinus,' he said. 'Let's get this clear. You ask for my help, you play things my way, completely. No arguments, no back-chat, no clever repartee. When I've fixed things up I'll come and tell you. In the meantime, your part of the deal is to possess yourself with fucking patience. Just that, full stop, end of story. Understand?'

'Uh...yeah.' Jupiter! 'Yeah, right. Got it.'

'Good. Pleasure to have you. Enjoy your stay.'

He left.

The wine came – top of the range Massic, in a silver jug, so I couldn't complain – and I settled down on the couch to wait. I took it easy, though: if dickering with Rufus in the near future was on the cards then I'd need to keep a clear head.

I was looking forward to seeing Damon again, mind. That slippery bastard had questions to answer.

He turned up, accompanied by the slave Flavillus, an hour or so later, edging into the room eyes fixed on me like it was the arena on a games day and I was one of the cats.

‘Morning, Corvinus,’ he said. ‘You all right, are you?’

‘Yeah, well, *all right* is a sort of relative term, isn’t it, pal?’ I said. ‘Finding that through no fault of your own you’re up to your neck in the political shit isn’t exactly conducive to a feeling of general well-being.’ I nodded to Flavillus. ‘That’s okay, sunshine. I can take things from here.’

The slave didn’t move. A big lad, Flavillus. Solid.

‘The boss told me I should stay and keep an eye on him, sir,’ he said. ‘In case he tries for another runner.’

Given where we were the bugger’s chances of making a dash for freedom and the outside world were comfortably within flying pigs territory; besides, where would he go? Still, it wasn’t my shout, and if Eutacticus wanted to play things careful then that was his privilege.

‘Fair enough,’ I said; at which point I got a noseful of the guy’s recently-adopted professional environment. Talk about bringing your work home with you. ‘You mind if we move outside, though?’

‘Not a problem, sir. There’s a bench, and’ – he glanced at Damon and sniffed – ‘I can bring out one of the stools.’

‘Perfect.’ I got up. ‘Right, Damon, let’s finish our interrupted chat, shall we? And we’ll have the truth this time around.’

He shrugged. ‘Suits me.’

Well, I doubted that very much, but there again he didn’t have the option any more. And whatever else he might be, Bathyllus’s wayward brother was your archetypal pragmatist. If there had been even the slightest chance of his getting himself off the hook he’d’ve wriggled like hell, but both he and I knew that this time he was well and truly gaffed.

We trooped outside into the courtyard garden, Flavillus leading the way with the stool. The garden wasn’t big – no more than twenty feet or so either side – but the fountain was more of a water feature let into the far wall, so there was plenty of clear breathing space. I settled onto the promised bench beneath an ornamental pear tree. Flavillus put the stool down for Damon to sit on, leaving a decent distance between us, and stood with his back against one of the portico pillars, arms folded.

'Okay, pal,' I said to Damon. 'Here's how we do this. Just to save any more faffing around I tell you what I know, or think I know, and you take it from there. If at any point I go off beam you bring me back. And don't even *think* about lying or covering up this time round, because if you do I'll hand you over to Rufus myself before you can say "porky" and whistle while he guts you. Agreed?'

He swallowed; the name had registered, and knowing I knew it had hit him hard, as I meant that it should.

'Fair enough,' he said.

'So. Your master was really Sextus Sentius, who was disinherited by his father twenty-odd years back. He took you with him, he became Gaius Oplonius, and the two of you set up a nice little racket as itinerant con men.'

'Forget the "nice", Corvinus. We made ends meet, sure, most of the time, just about, but that was as far as it went. And the old bastard, my master's father, hadn't left him much of an option.'

'You are breaking my heart, friend; a crook is a crook, and Sentius was as bent as they come, probably since he cut his first tooth, from what his sister tells me. Anyway, that side of things isn't relevant. What is, is that a month or so ago – call it that, for the sake of argument – he gets a surprise visit from a pal of his younger brother's, who until he was chopped for treason three years back was aide to Arruntius Scribonianus, the Dalmatian governor. Why the delay, incidentally? You know, yourself?'

'No mystery there. It took the guy that time to track us down. Oh, the master had kept in touch with Gaius, off and on, and he'd told him about the name change, but we didn't have what you might call a permanent address. For obvious reasons. The master was just lucky that young Ventidius – that was the friend's name – was such a persistent bugger. If lucky's the right word.' He winked. 'Mind you, reading between the lines, the two of them, him and Gaius, had been pretty close, if you catch my meaning, so maybe it wasn't so strange after all.'

'And this Ventidius had a something-or-other that Gaius had asked him to hand over, yes?'

'That's right.' We were getting to the nub of things now, and I could tell that Damon wasn't quite as cool, calm and collected as he wanted me to think he was.

'So what was it? A letter?'

'No. Something longer. A dozen or so sheets of writing put together into a package.'

'You have it with you?' I kept my tone even when I asked the question, but I was holding my breath.

'Sure.' He patted the breast of his tunic. 'Keep it strapped to my chest all the time, don't I? You want it now?'

Glory and trumpets!

'In a minute,' I said. 'So long as I know it's there, that's the important thing. Why should Gaius choose Sextus to send it to? Why not the eldest brother, Gnaeus? He'd've been far easier to find, for a start, and he was an ex-consul, so he'd have some clout. Not much, sure, but some.'

'That sycophantic, self-serving bastard?' Damon turned his head round to spit. Flavillus shifted against his pillar and frowned, but said nothing. 'Nah, Gaius wouldn't've trusted him as far as he could throw him, and quite right. The master, now–' He shook his head slowly. 'Look, Corvinus, I can't explain this, right, so don't ask me to. You know what he was like yourself. But for young Gaius he never could do no wrong. Oh, sure, far as I know the lad didn't know nothing definite about the...well, call them our business activities, but he was always a clever kid and he must've had his suspicions. Only they didn't seem to matter to him, see? Odd, but that's human nature for you.' He paused. 'There wouldn't be a cup of wine going spare, would there? My mouth's like a sand-pit.'

'Sure.' I glanced over at Flavillus, who nodded and went inside. 'So. What did Gaius want his brother to do with the package?'

'See it was put in the right hands. That's what Ventidius said, anyway. What he'd been told to say.'

'The right hands? Whose would those be?'

'No idea. Me, I don't think Gaius himself knew, either. But that was the message. All there was.'

Okay, now we were getting to it. 'So what were they, these written sheets? Who were they from, who were they meant for, and what were they about?'

'Pass again.'

'Come on, pal! You expect me to believe that?'

'Your choice there, squire, but it's the gods' own honest truth. Ventidius didn't know, because the lad hadn't been told, and the package was sealed. He didn't even know there was a document inside, as such. The master only found that out when he opened it.'

'At which point you'd know what the contents were too, presumably.'

'Uh-uh.' Flavillus came back with a cup of wine. Damon took it from him, downed it in a oner, and handed it back. 'Holy Mercury, that's good stuff! Any chance of a refill, friend?'

'Bugger off.' Flavillus went back to propping up his pillar.

'So why didn't you?' I persisted. 'Know, I mean.'

'Because the master didn't tell me.'

'Fine,' I said patiently. 'That might've been true enough then. But you've had the thing yourself for over half a month now. You saying you weren't the teensiest bit curious? You never thought to read it?'

'Yeah, well, you've sort of put your finger on the nub of the problem there, haven't you, squire? What you'd call a mistaken basic assumption.'

Oh, shit; the penny dropped. 'You're illiterate,' I said. 'You can't read.'

'Never learned, never wanted to,' Damon said proudly. 'Dad didn't have the time or the money for it when I was a kid back home, and there's never been the need since. Besides, I thought maybe if I did manage to pull off some kind of a deal in my own right being able to put hand on heart and say that to me it was pure gibberish might just save me a lot of grief.'

There was the shadow of a half-question in his voice; no more than that, but it was there. And because the guy was Bathyllus's brother the question needed answering.

'Listen, Damon,' I said gently. 'A deal was never going to happen, not in a million years, not with those people, not at any price. Your master tried to make one and it killed him. If you'd tried to do the same you'd have gone the same way; that is hundred-over-hundred, cast iron certain. You get me?'

He grunted. 'Fair enough,' he said. 'Don't mean I have to like it, though, does it?' His shoulders lifted and fell. 'Well, fuck it. These things happen.'

As gnomic philosophical statements went, I'd heard less cogent examples, and ones far less pithily expressed. Old Zeno would've been proud of him.

‘They do indeed,’ I said. I held out my hand. ‘Okay. Give.’

He put his hand down the neck-hole of his tunic, fumbled around a bit, and brought out a parchment packet stuffed with sheets of paper. He hesitated for a moment, then passed it over.

I unwrapped it. Inside, folded round the sheets themselves, was a letter. I smoothed it out, and read:

*‘Gaius Sentius Saturninus to his brother Sextus. Greetings.*

*The enclosed arrived yesterday from Rome, carried express by secret courier, for Governor Scribonianus, now fled to Issa in an attempt to escape his captors after the failure of the revolt. In his absence I opened it and have read the contents, albeit not in detail. From what I* have *read, however, I know that they are of vital political importance.*

*Sextus, I am at a loss. In all probability, I will never see Rome again myself, and so will be unable to act personally in the matter. Nevertheless, someone must, and accordingly I am forwarding the packet to you by way of my close and trusted friend Marcus Ventidius, in the hope that it will reach you. After that...*

*Well, Sextus, after that I simply do not know. You must do with it as you see fit. I only ask that you ensure that it reaches safe and responsible hands.*

*The gods bless and keep you, brother.*

*Farewell.*

That was it, barring the date, which must’ve been only days before the guy’s arrest and execution. I turned to the sheets themselves.

There were a dozen or so of them altogether, small sheets of flimsy covered with cramped writing, more of a scribble than anything else, as if whoever had written it had been seriously pushed for time and had a lot of ground to cover. I skim-read: a lot of it was names and dates, with blocks of narrative interspersed. I turned to the end. There was a signature at the bottom of the last page, together with the wax impression of a seal...

Oh, shit! Oh, holy gods!

What I had here was a complete account, chapter and verse, of Valeria Messalina's under-the-counter and between-the-sheets doings and adulteries, including details of her involvement in the plot against Gaius and the fomenting of the Scribonianus revolt itself. And the signature was Annius Vinicianus's.

I lowered the last page and found Damon watching me closely.

'Important, is it, squire?' he said.

My brain had gone numb. 'Yeah,' I said. 'Yeah. You could say that.' Shit! No wonder Messalina was desperate to get her hands on the thing! Unless Claudius was a complete, blind, head-banging idiot even he would have to admit, after reading this, that his darling wife had serious questions to answer.

So what did I do now?

The answer to that, unfortunately, was glaringly obvious: apart from what I was doing at present, nothing. Zilch. Zero. If I was fool enough to take it direct to Claudius himself the chances were I'd be dead, one way or another, before the month was out. And for what? I'd no personal axe to grind here, none at all. In any case, I'd known all along, at least subconsciously, that it had to be something like this, albeit nothing quite as detailed or as damning. So the deal with Rufus – and Messalina – it would have to be.

Bugger! I could have wept!

Well, if nothing else at least and if only for my own satisfaction I could dot the i's and cross the t's where the case itself was concerned. I laid the packet down beside me on the bench.

'Okay,' I said. 'So what happened next? After Ventidius called round?'

'We came to Rome, to see what we could make out of it.' Damon gave me a shifty, sideways look. 'Come on, Corvinus! I am what I am, right, no argument, and the master was the same. If young Gaius believed any different then that was his bad judgment. I'm making no excuses, for him or me.'

'I never said you needed to, pal,' I said mildly. 'All I'm interested in are the facts.'

'Fine.' He frowned. 'So. The master, he says he needs to make contact with a guy by the name of Suillius Rufus. You'll know why yourself, now you've read the stuff' – I said nothing – 'but it was just a name to me then. Still is, for that matter, and to tell you straight I'm just as happy to keep it that way. Anyway, he said he reckoned this Rufus would pay through the nose to get his hands on his brother's little package, enough to set us both up for life. So we take the let on a tenement flat and he starts putting out feelers.'

'His signet ring. He sent that to Rufus to show his bona fides. To prove that he was Gaius Sentius's brother.'

'Yeah. Well, you know the next bit, or you can guess it. They had a first-off meeting, all sweetness and light and promises on Rufus's side. Only then he has his men follow the master home, doesn't he, and they do for the poor bugger good and proper.' I noticed that Damon's fist had bunched. 'Why did he do that, Corvinus? You just tell me. The bastard had no call, none. We were asking a lot, sure, but from what the master said about how much the thing was worth we weren't being greedy. A nob like

Rufus, he could've afforded it, easy. And if he'd paid up that would've been it. The pair of us would've gone abroad, to Greece or Asia, maybe, and he'd never have heard from us again.'

'I told you,' I said. 'That just wasn't going to happen.'

'Right. Right.' Bitter-sounding as hell.

'So how did you manage to get hold of the packet, yourself? Sentius give it to you for safe keeping?'

'Nah, I never touched it, hardly ever even saw the thing. I said: it was the master's show from the start, and all I did was tag along. He took up one of the floorboards in the flat and left it there hidden.'

Well, at least Perilla's floorboard guess had been right, anyway. Even so...

'Come on, Damon!' I said. 'I'm not stupid, and I've thought all this through. Rufus's men knew you had it, that's clear enough, or they would've spent more time and effort looking. The only question is how they knew.'

'It's simple enough. The master had sent me down to the cookshop to fetch the dinner, and while I'm away the bastards drop in and start working him over. All just like I told you, right?' I nodded. 'When I get back and shove my head round the door the master's dead like I said he was. Only difference is that he's not alone; the two of them are still in there, searching the place. There isn't nothing I can do, so I make a run for it, with the pair of them after me.' He grinned. 'One thing I'm good at, because believe me I've had plenty of practice, and that's running. That, and not getting caught.'

'So you gave them the slip and doubled back.'

'Had to. That package was our future, see? The only chance for a life I'd ever have, or at least that's what I thought at the time. So I had to check whether it was still there, where the master had put it. Which it was, along with your pal's necklace. I take them both out, but before I can put the board back I hear the lads coming up the stairs again. I've just time to get to the landing and upstairs to the next floor before they get high enough to spot me.' He shrugged. 'That's it. The whole boiling. I hung around until I was sure they'd left then cut and ran.'

Leaving Ligurinus and his partner without the packet but – thanks to the missing floorboard – knowing the chances were that Sentius's slave and sidekick had come back and taken it. Right. Simple, like he'd said, once you knew the answer.

'So why didn't Sentius tell them about the hiding place himself?' I said.

'I told you, squire. That package was our future, his as much as mine. Maybe the poor bugger just stuck it out a bit too long, until it was too late or the bastards lost patience with him. Maybe it was just sheer bloody-mindedness. The master got that way, sometimes, he was an obstinate cove when he chose to be.' Another shrug. 'Who knows? Who'll ever know?'

Yeah, fair enough, and cosmically speaking it didn't matter all that much. Certainly it all hung together now.

'Okay, Damon,' I said. 'That just about wraps it up. The best thing you can do now is–'

Which was as far as I got before Eutacticus came out through the portico entrance. And he had Suillius Rufus with him.

# 23

'Morning, Corvinus.' Rufus smiled. 'I hear you've decided to be sensible. I'm delighted. And disappointed.'

'Yeah, well,' I said. 'Like you said, we can't have everything we want in life. Me, I'd just love to see you gutted for doing Messalina's dirty business by sharking up fake prosecutions, or just for being you, but there you go. A pleasure postponed, I'm afraid.'

'Indeed. This the slave?'

'Yeah. That's Damon.'

Damon was staring at him, expressionless, but I could see a twitch had started above his right cheekbone.

'So where was he hiding?' Rufus said. 'Come on, it doesn't matter now. And I assume you knew all along.'

'Uh-uh. I'd no more of an idea than you had.'

'So he gave himself up after all?' I said nothing; there wasn't any point in bringing Eutacticus further into this than I had already. 'Wise chap. Not that it'll do him any good in the long run, of course.' I saw Damon stiffen. 'He's given us far too much trouble, and I won't take that, not from a slave.'

My blood went cold. 'Hang on,' I said. 'The deal was if I gave you and Messalina what you wanted, and here it is' – I picked up the package beside me; his eyes went to it straight away – 'then we were all square, right? No comeback, no nothing.'

'Absolutely. And we've every intention of keeping to the bargain. But that was for you, Corvinus, as you very well know. This bit of offal is another thing entirely.'

'Now you just wait one fucking minute, pal–!'

'Relax, boy,' Eutacticus said. 'It's not going to happen.'

Rufus turned slowly, with a look on his face like he'd just caught a whiff of Damon's industrial-grade perfume.

'What was that?' he said.

'You heard. You're on my ground, here at my invitation. You play by my rules or you don't play at all, understand?'

Rufus took a step towards him.

'*You–!*'

I'd forgotten about Flavillus, and now I never even saw him move. One moment he was leaning against his pillar, the next he was standing behind Rufus, one hand on his neck, the other pressing flat against the side of his head. Rufus froze.

'Now that's sensible,' Eutacticus said to him. 'You just keep it that way, because if you even breathe wrong Flavillus will break your fucking neck. So let's just go back a bit and take that part again, shall we? Blink if you agree.' Rufus blinked. 'Well done. Okay, Flavillus, you can let him go for now.'

Flavillus backed off. Rufus rubbed his neck and glared at Eutacticus.

'You know who I am?' he said.

'Sure.'

'Well, then, I–'

'You're the bastard I'm giving one last and final chance to keep to the deal you made with Corvinus here. Welsh on him, even think about it, and I'll send you home in a box.'

'Are you threatening me?'

'No, I'm telling you. But the decision's yours. Think carefully, now.'

Their eyes locked. Finally, Rufus looked away and shrugged.

‘Fair enough,’ he said. ‘It’s of no real importance. If you want him as badly as that you can keep the little bugger with my blessing.’ He held out his hand. ‘Right, Corvinus. Let me see.’

I passed the packet over. He read the covering letter, grunted, then laid it aside and leafed through the flimsies. I waited.

‘That all seems in order,’ he said. ‘Well done, Marcus, I’m grateful. And of course the boss’ll want to see you, to thank you in person. In fact, if you’ve nothing better to do we might as well go over to the palace now.’ He tucked the package under his belt.

‘Hang on, pal,’ I said. ‘I’ve had one of those little clandestine chats with Messalina before, and I’ve no particular wish to repeat the experience. You can give her my regards, sure, if you like, but I’d really prefer it if you both just buggered off and left me alone.’

‘Oh, really?’ Rufus smiled. ‘How very graphically put. But what makes you think I’m working for Messalina?’

*What?*

I left Damon with Eutacticus and we made our way down Broad Street towards Market Square and the Palatine. Understandably, it wasn’t a chatty journey; Rufus and I loathed each other’s guts, and neither of us felt particularly obliged to start the conversational ball rolling. Besides, the inside of my head was busy enough without having to worry about how to satisfy the social niceties.

We got to the palace. I’d been expecting that we’d go in the usual way, at the front, but Rufus took me round the far side to what was obviously, from the rubbish piled outside, a servants’ entrance. I paused, eyebrows raised.

‘In you go, Corvinus,’ he said. ‘You’re getting the below-stairs tour.’

So; *clandestine* was right. Not a heart-to-heart with Claudius himself, then, unless he'd taken to laundering his own underthings.

'Just carry on straight.' Rufus followed me in. 'There's a stair to your left. Take it up to the second floor.'

We met a couple of skivvies on the way, but after an initial startled glance at us they looked away and scurried past. Obviously forewarned, which was interesting in itself. The stair, when I came to it, was a service one, running between the outside wall of the building and the palace's inner shell, worn, dirty and poorly-lit. I climbed to the second floor and pushed the door that opened off the small landing.

I'd thought we'd be into frescoed walls and polished bronzes territory, but although we'd clearly gone up a couple of grades as far as decoration and general appearance were concerned the corridor beyond the door was definitely middle-management bracket, if that.

'Nearly there, now,' Rufus said. 'Third door along on your right's the one you want. Just knock and go in.'

I did. I'd been half-expecting an office, but although there was a desk and a set of document-cubbies against the far wall the room had an unused look to it, and I caught the musty smell of mildewed paper and mouse droppings. Sitting behind the desk was a nondescript, late-middle-aged man in a tunic and freedman's cap making notes from a set of wax tablets. He looked up and laid the pen aside.

'Ah, Valerius Corvinus,' he said. 'Delighted to meet you at last. I'm Claudius Narcissus. Do have a seat, please. I apologise for the surroundings, but as you'll understand we're being a trifle cloak-and-dagger here.'

Uh-huh. So our grey eminence – and you didn't get much greyer than this little guy, although 'eminence' didn't really fit him at all – had turned out to be Claudius's top-echelon freedman and advisor Narcissus, had he? Well, it made sense, I supposed, and it came to the same thing in the end: if not Messalina herself then her equally-crooked pal and collaborator on the imperial staff.

'That's okay,' I said. 'I'd rather stand.'

Rufus had come in behind me. He put his hand on my shoulder, hooked a stool over with his foot, and pressed me down into it.

'Don't get smart, you bastard,' he said. 'You're getting off lightly, remember. Just be grateful.'

Narcissus had been watching the exchange, a tolerant smile on his face.

'You have it, Rufus?' he said.

Rufus took the document out of his belt and handed it over. Narcissus flicked through the set of flimsies, grunting and tutting occasionally.

'That's excellent,' he said. 'Better than excellent, in fact. Vinicianus did well. Not a bad piece of writing, either, particularly considering his circumstances at the time.'

'Fine,' I said. 'You've got what you wanted and we're all square. So let me go.'

Narcissus put the pages down and looked at me directly. 'Now that would hardly be fair, would it?' he said. 'Not without an explanation on my side. And, Corvinus, I do owe you that much, at the very least.'

'I'll pass. What you and Messalina have going in your dirty little partnership is no concern of mine.'

Narcissus's lips twitched. 'Ah,' he said. 'You haven't worked that bit out for yourself yet, then. How disappointing. *Definitely* the time for a chat.' He glanced at Rufus, standing behind me. 'You're making him nervous, Publius. Perhaps you'd better leave us alone. Don't worry, I'll be perfectly safe. Valerius Corvinus may be many things, but he isn't a fool.'

'*Nervous* isn't the word I'd use with reference to your stooge, pal,' I said. 'He makes me sick, that's all.'

Rufus chuckled and ruffled my hair. I didn't turn round as his footsteps moved towards the door, which opened and closed behind him.

'Now.' Narcissus leaned forwards, elbows on the desk, and steepled his fingers. 'I am about to destroy your illusions, so listen carefully. I am *not* working with or for Messalina in this. Quite the contrary.'

I stared at him. 'You expect me to believe that?' I said.

'Oh, it's an understandable mistake for you to have made, I know. Particularly when you consider things in the context of past events, although even then everything depends on viewpoint. But trust me, Valeria Messalina knows nothing whatever about any of this.' Again the twitch of the lips. 'At least, I sincerely hope she doesn't, or I'm in real trouble. Probably of the fatal sort.'

'Okay. So you have dirty little plans of your own. Not much difference there that I can see.'

I thought he'd lose his temper, but he just shook his head. 'No. I've no plans, dirty or otherwise,' he said. 'Or at least if I do have any they're of the long-term variety, and I've made them with the safety and well-being of the emperor and the empire in mind.' He was watching me closely. 'I am no traitor. I am Claudius's faithful servant and completely loyal to the state. I always have been, and I always will be.'

'Come on, Narcissus!' I folded my arms. 'I know for a fact you were involved with Messalina in the plot against Gaius, for a start. And that you helped her to stitch up Junius Silanus on that fake assassination charge. Besides, Rufus is Messalina's creature; he wouldn't go against her, not in a million years. So cut the flannel, right? I told you: what she and you get up to is none of my business, and as far as I'm concerned it's wasted.'

'Gaius had to die. You know that; he was destroying Rome. And your own wife wasn't altogether innocent in engineering his death either, if I remember correctly.' I said nothing. 'Silanus...well, I'm genuinely sorry about Silanus, but it was essential at that point that Messalina be convinced that we were allies, open ones. Besides, she would have made sure he was condemned without any help from me. And Rufus' – he smiled – 'Suillius Rufus, as you're well aware, is a completely bad lot, self-serving and venal to the core. I simply convinced him that his long-term interests lay on my side of the fence rather than Messalina's. As indeed they do.'

Yeah, well, if he wasn't telling the truth he was sounding pretty convincing. And if you made the shift and looked at things from his perspective what he said was reasonable enough. Besides, what would he have to gain from lying? As far as I was concerned, the guy was untouchable, completely so; he could tell me what he liked, and whistle while he did it. If I still wasn't wholly convinced at least I was prepared to listen.

'Does the emperor know?' I said. 'About any of this?'

Narcissus laughed. 'Good gods, no! You think my head would still be on my shoulders if he did?'

'So what was the point? I mean, if you can't use this' – I indicated the document on the desk between us – 'then why all the fuss?'

'It's an investment, Corvinus. Short-term or long-term I don't know which, but it's the best I could ever have. It was written by someone in Messalina's complete confidence who was one of her lovers himself, and it's absolutely factual and thorough: names, dates, intimate details, everything. With the added bonus that Messalina doesn't know it exists. Had the person concerned been someone other than her, or the emperor someone other than Claudius, it would be more than sufficient to have them executed for treason a dozen times over. As it is' – he shrugged – 'it will simply have to wait its time.'

'So why did Vinicianus write it?'

'Who knows?' Narcissus said blandly. 'A feeling of guilt, possibly, and a desire to make amends. Annius Vinicianus was no Rufus; he was ambitious and self-seeking, crooked as they come when the need arose, yes, but at heart he was a good Roman.' Yeah; his uncle had said as much when I'd talked to him. For all his many flaws, loyalty to friends had been genuinely important to the guy, and knowing that he'd been set up over the Scribonianus affair and had consequently betrayed a friend to his death might well have triggered it. 'In any case, he did, and I'm grateful to him. Rome will be, too, eventually.'

Even so...

'Bugger all that,' I said. 'It was you who framed him, wasn't it? Not Messalina?'

'Oh, well done!' Narcissus smiled broadly. 'You're thinking at last. Yes, that's right, it was. Although of course I was very careful to see to it that he himself believed otherwise, indeed as you'll readily understand that part of it was completely necessary if I was to persuade him into taking his revenge on her. Nothing too crude or overt, naturally: a small hint dropped into a receptive mind by a carefully-primed casual visitor ostensibly sympathetic to the wronged man can work wonders. And Vinicianus really had been becoming quite a danger, so getting rid of him was of use in itself.'

'You had Gaius Sentius executed too, didn't you?'

'Unfortunately yes. Young Sentius was a necessary casualty. He'd read the document, you see, the only other person who had, and I couldn't risk word of it reaching Messalina. Not even word of its existence.'

Cold and bland as hell. Gods!

'How did you find that out yourself, in the first place?' I said. 'That the document did exist, and that Vinicianus had sent it to Scribonianus?'

'Ah.' The smile again. 'I do have my spies. As indeed has Messalina, only on this occasion mine were the more efficient. Unfortunately they were too late to intercept it on its way to Dalmatia, and then, of course, young Gaius Sentius passed it on and it disappeared completely. I'd quite despaired of finding it again when Rufus reported that he'd been approached by Sentius's brother offering it for sale.'

Right; now we came to it. 'So you had Sextus Sentius – aka Oplonius – tortured and murdered. Why the hell couldn't you just have bought the fucking thing in the first place?'

Narcissus winced. 'A fair comment,' he said. 'You're absolutely right, and for that I've no excuse. All I can say is that I made the mistake of giving Rufus a free hand to take care of the matter as he thought fit. I knew nothing of events until after the man was dead.'

'Convenient.'

For the first time, a splash of colour flooded the grey cheeks. 'Don't you get self-righteous with me, Corvinus!' he snapped. 'Haven't you ever made a decision that you've regretted bitterly later? Besides, as I understand it both the men directly involved in his murder are dead now themselves. Killed by your criminal friend.'

'What about my major-domo? Would you have let Rufus kill him as well?'

'Of course not! He was perfectly safe. We only needed him as a bargaining chip. Rufus would have returned him unharmed whatever the outcome.'

Yeah, well, he may have genuinely believed that, but I didn't. There was a world of difference between idealists like Narcissus and cold-hearted opportunists like Suillius Rufus, let alone between him and the murderous thug that Ligurinus had been. If it hadn't been for Eutacticus Bathyllus would've been dead meat from the moment he was lifted. Still, it was good to know that Narcissus, ruthless bastard at base though he might be, wasn't totally devoid of scruples.

'So what happens now?' I said.

'Absolutely nothing. You walk away and get on with your life as if Gaius Oplonius had never existed. As indeed he didn't. I give you my solemn word that, for my part, everything ends here. The matter is closed. Closed, locked, bolted and buried. I only ask for your own promise that that much holds good on your side as well.'

'What about the slave? Damon?'

'What about him? Oplonius never existed, so I see no reason why his slave should. Certainly he's safe from me and mine, as long as he keeps his mouth shut. But I don't think that'll be an issue, do you? Not if he values his own skin.'

Uh-huh. I'd tend to agree: if there was one thing Damon couldn't be accused of it was the lack of an instinct for self-preservation. 'And that?' I indicated the pile of flimsies.

'That is none of your concern. It'll be kept very safe and very secret, believe me. Eventually – next month, a year, ten years from now, I don't know – it will be used to help bring Messalina down, I guarantee that. After a little doctoring, naturally, to save my own blushes, and possibly my neck into the bargain.' He held out his hand. 'As I said, Valerius, a pleasure to have met you. And my thanks and apologies. You can find your own way out, I hope?'

‘Yeah.’ I stood up, hesitated, then reached over and shook. ‘Goodbye, Narcissus.’

Case, as he’d said, closed.

# 24

Which only left the problem of Damon himself. He might be off the hook now as far as both Eutacticus and Narcissus were concerned, but much though I'd have liked to I couldn't just pat him on the head, turn him loose and forget all about him. No way could I do that: the guy was a slave, after all, technically an escaped one with the threat of a murder rap hanging over him. Plus the fact that if I did wave him off into the sunset I wouldn't be doing him any favours, quite the reverse: wherever he went, whatever he did, sooner or later, probably the former, he'd be caught and passed over to the authorities. And that would be that. Chop.

On the other hand – and it was a real sticking point that I couldn't get round, nothing to do with the legal aspect of things – proved liar, swindler and all-round crook Damon might be, but as Bathyllus's brother he was family, and as Head of Household I had a moral responsibility to look out for him. Not that I could simply and quietly absorb him into the Corvinus ménage, because that would be illegal, too: I'd no rights of ownership, which would mean that technically I was guilty either of theft or of harbouring an escaped slave. I might just get away with it, because after all at present the guy was a loose pebble rattling around the world, but still...

Hell!

I thought about the problem all the way home, only to find when I got in it had already arrived and was waiting there for me. Eutacticus had obviously decided that Damon was my responsibility too, because while I'd been having my little chat with Narcissus he'd had the bugger delivered to the Caelian. As a result, there he was in the garden, where Bathyllus had put him with instructions to help Alexis with the weeding. Smart move on the little guy's part: except for the gate at the back, which was locked, the only way Damon could take off for fresh cons and pastures new was either through the house itself or over our eight-foot wall. And Alexis was on hand to make sure he didn't even try for that option.

When he saw me coming through the portico he straightened and leaned on his hoe.

'So you're back, squire,' he said. 'How did it go?'

'Okay,' I said. 'You're in the clear, as far as Rufus and his boss are concerned, anyway.' I wasn't going to mention Narcissus; the fewer people who knew what had been going on behind the scenes the better.

I saw the flash of relief in his eyes. Yeah, well; he might be a cocky bastard, but I suspected most of that was for show, like the con-man's patter. He'd been worried, seriously worried, and rightly so: like Bathyllus had said, a slave has no comeback, and when it's him against the world the world will screw him every time.

I made my decision.

'Get your bibs and bobs together, sunshine,' I said. 'We're going for a walk.'

He gave me a suspicious look. 'Is that right, sir?' he said. 'And where would that be to, exactly?'

'To a pal of mine's house. Guy by the name of Vibullius Secundus. His wife's your ex-master's sister.'

His face cleared. 'Helena?' he said. 'The Lady Sentia, I should say?'

'That's the one. You knew her?'

'Only to look at, sir, and the last time I saw her was a good while ago. Twenty years ago now, when the old ba–' He stopped. 'When old Gnaeus Sentius threw me and the master out. Master had a lot of time for Helena. Well, well. Married now and in Rome, eh?' He set the hoe against a bean-pole. 'All right, I'll go with you gladly.'

'Fine,' I said. 'I'll wait for you while you get your things.'

'No need for that, squire. There was just an old tunic and a couple of other bits round at the fuller's shop, and when Eutacticus's boys picked me up I'd no chance to collect them. They're no great loss, believe me.'

Oh, shit. The guy was pushing sixty and all he had was what he stood up in. Life on the edge was right. I felt, for no accountable reason, angry.

'No problem, pal,' I said. 'And there's no real hurry. I'll wait like I said while Bathyllus puts something together.'

'That's good of you. You're a gentleman, Corvinus.'

I went back inside, to where Perilla was lying on the atrium couch. I'd already told her about developments on the Narcissus front, and she was deep in conversation with Bathyllus about preparations for our delayed trip to the Alban Hills.

'You gave Damon the good news then, dear,' she said.

'Yeah.' I lay down on the other couch and filled a cup of wine for myself from the jug Bathyllus had left there. 'And I think our best bet would be to take him round to Gaius Secundus's. He's a Sentius family slave, so Helena's the logical person to decide what happens to him.' I looked up at Bathyllus, who was hovering. 'Suit you, pal?'

'Yes, sir. Of course. It would be the ideal arrangement, in fact.'

'Fine. Go and scrounge up a bagful of clothes for him, would you? It appears he's a bit short in that department, and my clothes chest could do with sorting out.'

'Certainly.' He cocked his head. 'I think that might be the front door. If you'd excuse me?'

He went out. I looked at Perilla.

'You expecting any visitors?' I said.

'No, dear. Nothing to do with me.'

Bathyllus reappeared.

‘Your mother, sir,’ he said. ‘And Helvius Priscus.’

Oh, hell! Still, I supposed it had had to happen sometime.

Mother drifted in, with Priscus close on her rouge-tinted heels, wearing an expression like a smug tortoise’s. So when he’d revealed the awful truth about the existence of Polyxene she hadn’t battered him to death after all, then; from the looks of things, quite the contrary.

Which was promising. Very promising. Maybe we’d live through this after all.

‘Good afternoon, Marcus,’ Mother said. ‘Perilla. I’m sorry to barge in on you like this, but we thought you might like to hear our little bit of recent news.’ She turned to Priscus. ‘Didn’t we, Titus?’

‘*Mmaah!* Yes indeed, Vipsania.’

Well, here it came. I steeled myself for what evidently was intended to be a surprise revelation, and I noticed that Perilla was doing the same.

‘It appears that a month or so ago Titus discovered, completely by accident, that the granddaughter of a very old and dear friend from his time in Athens had opened a small antique shop on the Sacred Way.’ Mother fixed me with her eye, daring me to comment. I said nothing. ‘He has been visiting her and her husband regularly ever since. Clandestinely, since the silly man had got it into his head that I might suspect him of, well...’ She hesitated.

‘Hanky-panky,’ I said, keeping my face straight. I glanced at Perilla. There were bright spots of red on her cheeks, and her lips were firmly pressed together and trembling.

‘Indeed.’ Mother sniffed. ‘Complete nonsense, of course. As you well know, it would never even *occur* to me to suspect Titus of that sort of behaviour, not for one second.’ Another gimlet stare at me. ‘Anyway, he took me round to the shop to meet the girl. Polyxene, her name is. She really is quite charming, although hopelessly rustic for an Athenian. Breeding, probably: Titus didn't go into details concerning the old friend, but reading between the lines I suspect he was in trade.' I shot a look at Priscus; he had his head down, and he was communing with his knees. 'Nevertheless, once I take her in hand I believe I might be able to make something of her socially. Time will tell.'

'That's splendid, Vipsania.' Perilla had herself under control now, although she was still looking a bit frizzed at the edges with the effort. 'Bring her and her husband round here for dinner some evening. We'd love to meet them.'

'Actually, dear, you'll see them before that. I've invited them to dine with us tomorrow, so you can come along then. Phormio has promised to cook something extra-special for the occasion.'

I winced. Fuck. Double fuck. Well, we'd just have to batten down the hatches, reconcile ourselves to a seriously-disturbed post-dinner night, and lay in a decent supply of our family doctor Sarpedon's patent indigestion mixture, that was all.

'Oh, what a shame!' Perilla gave her a dazzling smile. 'We're planning to leave for Castrimoenium tomorrow, and Clarus and Marilla will be expecting us.'

Beautifully done, and I couldn't've lied more convincingly myself. I breathed again.

'Now that is disappointing.' Mother frowned. 'Never mind, it can't be helped. You'll simply, as you say, have to meet them when they come here.' She glanced at Titus. 'And now we've taken up quite enough of your time. Have a lovely holiday, won't you, and do give our love to the family.'

They left.

'The crafty old devil!' I said admiringly. 'He's weaselled out of it!'

'I wouldn't be too sure about that, dear,' Perilla said. 'I never *am* completely sure where your mother's concerned. She's a very intelligent woman, and I suspect she might well just be playing along for the sake of peace.'

'You think so?' I shrugged. 'Yeah, well, maybe. In any case, Priscus's by-blow has got her feet under the table pretty nicely.'

'Literally, too.' Perilla smiled. 'Although I don't envy her the dinner invitation, particularly if Phormio is going to be especially creative over the menu.'

'She'll survive, lady.' I reached for the wine jug and topped up my cup. 'Besides, it's a cheap price to pay for acceptance, even if she and her husband do spend the next twelve hours throwing up and dumping down as a result.'

'Don't be crude, Marcus.' She got up. 'And now I really must finish talking to Bathyllus about the Castrimoenium trip. I had actually planned on the day after tomorrow, but under the circumstances we'd better leave when I told Vipsania we would. Just in case she checks.'

'Fair enough. Tell him to let me have that bagful of stuff as soon as he likes and me and Damon will get off.'

She went upstairs, and I stretched out on the couch with the cup of wine. Yeah, well; things hadn't gone too badly this time around. If I hadn't scored an outright win I reckoned I could at least claim an honourable draw. And Vinicianus's document was in the best of hands, of that I was sure: it'd do the job it was intended to do in the end, whenever that might be, or at least when the time came it would serve as one hell of a contributing factor to back up whatever ammunition Narcissus had to put the skids under Messalina. On the family side, Bathyllus was up one brother, warts and all, and Priscus had sneaked a surprise granddaughter under the fence. Even Damon, if everything panned out well with Secundus and Helena, was back in the Sentius family fold, and in a position that was a lot more secure than he'd been used to for the past twenty-odd years. So not a bad result there, either. And to put the cap on it, last but by no means least, we'd successfully evaded one of Mother's dinner invitations. All in all, I'd say that where family commitments were concerned all of us had done okay.

Life might not be absolutely perfect, but me...well, I wasn't complaining too hard.

---

## AUTHOR'S NOTE

The story is set in May AD44.

As with all the 'political' Corvinus books, I've tried to integrate my purely fictional plot with actual historical events. It's only fair, then, to distinguish fact from fiction here, and also to give a brief rundown of what happened subsequently to a few of the historical characters.

The treason trials are all factual, as are the charges involved. It may come as a surprise that Claudius, who was of course a very intelligent man, would countenance for one moment the 'dream' evidence put forward jointly by Messalina and Narcissus to convict Junius Silanus, but he did, and Silanus was duly chopped. It's also true that Suillius Rufus served as Messalina's tame prosecutor, at least in the prosecution of Julia Livia, although I must admit I've extended this function unilaterally to the trials of Messalina's other victims. My only excuse is that in their case no prosecutors are named, and for Rufus to reprise the role – at least, as far as my plot was concerned – would make perfect sense. On the other hand, laying the deaths unequivocably at Messalina's door in the first place and citing as her motive a wish to secure the succession of her son Britannicus are purely devices of my own invention. They do, however, fit very well with the historical facts and dates involved, so I don't feel too guilty.

Factual, too, are the background circumstances of the Scribonianus revolt; but except for the fact that the historian Cassius Dio says that Scribonianus was encouraged to rebel by Vinicianus, citing as the latter's motive disgust at the execution of Silanus, this part of the plot is cut from whole cloth: Gaius Sentius is an invented character, and neither Vinicianus's document detailing Messalina's crimes nor Narcissus's framing of him as *agent provocateur* have any historical justification whatsoever.

Now for the characters. Just three of them will do.

**Pomponia Graecina**

A close friend of the executed Julia Livilla, she never forgave Claudius for condemning her, and mourned her for the whole of her long life (she died in AD83, in the reign of Domitian). Tradition makes Graecina one of the earliest Christians, and although this side of things would be too late to figure in my story I have tried to foreshadow it by giving her an interest in the occult and mystery religions in general, with which early Christianity had strong links

**Narcissus**

He was instrumental in the destruction of Messalina in AD48, but lost a large part of his influence with Claudius because of his opposition to the latter's proposed marriage to Agrippina. It's interesting, from the point of view of my story, that another reason given for his decline in significance was that, at this point, he supported Britannicus's claim to the succession; but since the looming alternative was Agrippina's own son Nero perhaps this isn't quite the anomaly it might appear. Besides, his quarrel had been with the mother, not the child, and Britannicus was as much Claudius's as hers. Predictably, following Claudius's assassination in AD54 he was forced into suicide.

•

**Publius Suillius Rufus**

Rufus went from strength to strength under Claudius, but eventually (AD58) fell from grace. A head-to-head quarrel with the emperor Nero's advisor, the philosopher and playwright Annaeus Seneca, resulted in his prosecution on a variety of grounds including maladministration of his province when governor of Asia, the embezzlement of public funds, and involvement in Messalina's crimes. Half his estate was confiscated, and he spent the rest of his life in self-indulgent exile.

---

22779485R00155

Printed in Great Britain
by Amazon